Dancer's Paradise

An Erotic Journey

By Debrena Allen as told to Terry B.

NHouse Publishing, L.L.C.
P.O. Box 1038
Newark, New Jersey
973-223-9135
www.nhousepublishing.com

Dancer's Paradise: An Erotic Journey
ISBN 0-9726242-1-X
Library of Congress Catalog Number 2004100018
1.   Women, Hip-Hop, African-American, Multicultural, Gay & Lesbian--Fiction

Cover design and layout by Asen James
Interior layout and design by Nancey Flowers
Edited by Chandra Sparks Taylor

Printed in Canada

INTRODUCTION

Life is life. Regardless of race, gender, class, political affiliation, religion or orientation, there are common denominators that relate us to one another if allowed. When it comes to race and sexual orientation, however, it seems empathy and understanding are tossed out the window. Though we've struggled with the race issue for hundreds of years, the topic of homosexuality and bisexuality is the new subject for heated debate, met with indifference and strong opinions. Heterosexuals and homosexuals alike often regard bisexuals as selfish, immoral and confused. But isn't adultery too immoral? Isn't cheating selfish? And who of us has never felt confused?

In *Dancer's Paradise: An Erotic Journey,* author Terry B. takes on the issue of bisexuality with the objectivity of an artist. The characters take on the shape of misunderstood friends, fierce objectors and torn lovers. Regardless of the reader's sexual preference, the book confronts and challenges us all to face the issue.

After all, closing our eyes won't make it all disappear. Support of same-sex marriages by the U.S. Supreme Court, an increased homosexual presence in media and entertainment and bisexuality in music videos have all contributed to an openness never seen before, although homosexuality has existed long before today. Even the Catholic church is not immune to addressing the issue.

Dancer's Paradise forces the world around us to take notice as bisexual tendencies among women seem to be more profound than ever. Many people shake their heads in disbelief to see young teenage girls walking hand in hand with other girls. Years ago, it would have been seen as something innocent but now it is looked at as scandalous. Rap videos can no longer be used as a scapegoat or contributing factor in the issue as society seeks to understand our young women.

True, misogyny perpetrated in the hip-hop community in particular is painful to witness as women struggling for acceptance today deal with it in various ways. Some choose to conform, subjecting themselves to various forms of abuse and degradation. Others wave the flag of independence, choosing to focus on careers and self rather than men. But the reasons for bisexual and lesbian relationships in the Black community go deeper.

The youth of today face the subject of sexuality head-on with a boldness once considered taboo by our elders. Sex today is used not just as an instrument of love, comfort and power but also rebellion. Women in particular are upfront and outspoken, embracing an independence no generation has ever had before. No longer does sexuality have to live in the closet. For some, that still takes some getting used to. In making the adjustment, the hip-hop generation has been forced to grow up faster, struggling with adult issues much sooner than any of us may be ready or willing to accept. Pushing the uncomfortable behind the scenes in a safe place only hinders growth and understanding and becomes the very heart of the issue for why bisexuals feel the need to hide their preferred lifestyle.

Hunted by a sense of secrecy, denial, fear and confusion through the life of bisexual woman, Debrena Allen, *Dancer's Paradise* reveals a range of emotions to which any woman, regardless of her orientation, can relate. But the most interesting factor is the fact that a man was able to tell this story as his ability to convey the emotions of a woman are dead-on. He truly is able to capture feelings from a female's perspective, emotions attributed with the search for self. Struggling with fear, rejection, criticism and guilt at some point in our relationships and search for belonging reaches a crossroads. That is life but for a bisexual woman, the drama is intensely magnified, subject to self-doubt and judgment.

In a very real and painful way, the characters reflect the many feelings of sexuality by society. Revealing the importance of honesty in sex and relationships, the book is confrontational, thought-provoking and a lesson for all. Far from just a fictional story, *Dancer's Paradise* provides an important context and dialogue for a society that seeks to dictate what is and is not acceptable in life, love and sex.

--fayemi shakur

A SPECIAL THANKS to all my chat buddies:

AsianAvenue.com

dancer_paradise	juam3344	RogueScholar	808finest
gearbolt2k	PerfectOne	TrickRix21	HappyCampa
yoshisun	sappysport	AccuritDj	eukiOne
red_herring	hmongq	KH26	sigma004
lexigal143	Punstrackster	gsxr723	jerseyjohnjohn
yhkim12	navyswim	parkdhere	lostones
vtecjimbo	SJ-GUY	yellowflash	chakabrah
CuteAsianBoy	TWO3	BLING-X-2	merjurie
BayBeepei_143	Nokia6160	A-zErO	GREY7
Worktohard	wutdadilyo	MR2Turbo	leaf1996
2HawksCircling	63t	nahya80	ronin2300
NyCzVersatiliTy			

BlackPlanet.com

mileniummonti	Letzgettheremis	KaReMeLpLaYbOy
Shy_21	Eros99	Cocoa-Sista
Jean-o	FeliciaBarnett	layzbone2000
sweetclit21	baisley163	discreetamust
bigperk22	MnMoor	onedeepbruh
twatsplita	khalif21	blacklily18
joegrinde	AnjalaBlack	d-papiny28
OOCHIE_WALLY33	KissMyKlit	Fairchild07
NAUGHTY_BUTGOOD	ando113	roadsInc
MistresDAIQUIRI	FLAHOT	queen_nubienne
Pawhitemale69	qmdtime	bigperk22
5-9-175lbsa7234	Dooyou	RISINGSUN_00
stylescommedia	SweetSpot22	GENTLE777
MellowBrooklyn		

MiGente.com

MSDrippingWet	LISALICKME	dancer_paradise
Dre-3000	mamisensual118	SlowBudgetMC
bi_freaky-lady	Latinstuntz	gomab
Taide_4U	Specialbigbooty	cityballer10
68IOU	Sooperlovin	UNI_69_24_7
DrSuess	scorpianfreak	JerZeyPrince5
Dat_GoThYc_Mami	slickspic	DeMarrCo
KaliBa	SSILKY66	spendmymoney
Jay-High	NorTh_JeRz_PaPi	knowledge255
brazilliancutie	ms_moka	waynelivas
Bklyn-Bori	Flavorish	quick2stick
Coquito_Bravo	SweetVanilla	FINESTCUBANO
Iron_Snake	DASHAFTWETTA	Escorts_R_Us_NJ
PRLOU6IX	Eros99	
BRONX_BUTTERFLY		

Terry B. would also like to thank:

Author Toni Staton Harris, Quaada Barbee, Sakinah Smith, Latoya
Williams, Rod Lee, Laura Jones, Mandy Joy, Open Eye Media (Bryan
Robles and Gabe Soto), Duane Wilkins and Asen James.

Dear Reader,

Debrena Allen is a composite character gleaned from more than one hundred interviews from women who identified themselves as bisexual or gay. Intensive research over a five-year period has resulted in this work of contemporary fiction. I have decided to make Debrena Allen the "author" of this book as a way to acknowledge all the women who have shared their experiences with me. Although this is fiction, I feel that I am simply retelling a woman's dilemma as it was told to me.

Also, Debrena Allen has been able to grab the attention of more than three thousand Internet community members who see her situation as real. With all that said, sit back, enjoy and prepare to be taken on an emotional roller coaster.

Respectfully yours,
Terry B.

Dancer's Paradise

An Erotic Journey

Chapter One

I was ten years old the day I stood with Mom in front of the Frederick Douglass Community Center.

"You sure you don't want to wait inside?" Mom asked.

I shook my head. I wanted to be the first person my new friend, Lorrie Cunningham, saw when she arrived at the center. It was the Friday afternoon for which the children had all worked so hard. But it was also the Friday that would break many young hearts. The auditions had begun with more than two hundred children from three elementary schools in Elizabeth, New Jersey.

We all wanted to be members of the Young People's Dance Theater but there was no way all of us who came out could be accommodated. There were just too many children and too few instructors. In the beginning, Mom was reluctant to allow me to audition because she felt that if I didn't get in, the failure would crush my will to dance. But Mom didn't know how competitive I was; Dad knew because we had talked about it so much, and he supported me, big time. He told Mom that if I didn't take this opportunity I would never know how good I really was.

With Mom being a lawyer and Dad a professional jazz musician, they could afford to pay for my dance lessons, but if I made the cut I could get free lessons from professional New Jersey instructors. The first Friday auditions that were held had been exciting and sad because many of the children didn't make the cut. The instructors were upfront with us as they brought us into the auditorium in groups of twenty.

"We can't use everybody. If for some reason you are not picked, it does not mean you weren't good," Mr. Fred, one of the instructors, told us.

Of course nobody wanted to hear that; we all came because we truly wanted to be a member of the theater. The fifty children who made the cut and got the callback were considered the best of the best, a small but mighty group of boys and girls, serious and competitive. Many of them, including myself, had cried the week before, but those had been tears of joy. This Friday tears would surely flow again, but not all of them would be happy ones. Some would be tears of bitter disappointment.

We had to do two things: dance in a group and then dance solo. Some children brought tapes but an old White lady accompanied everyone on an old black piano. We knew that we were going to be members of the theater, no doubt about it. We had seen much of the competition and many of those trying out looked pitiful. Most of the children were too nervous to dance their best and showed no personality as they stood before the judges.

I stood with Mom but felt that I wanted to jump out of my ten-year-old skin. I was overly excited because I had made a good friend the previous Friday afternoon. Lorrie and I just looked and nodded like we knew something no one else did. I felt I was staring in a mirror when I looked at Lorrie. We glanced at each other and talked like we had known each other in another life, like we had been separated at birth and this day was our reunion. In this "mirror," I was dark chocolate brown and Lorrie was smooth light caramel.

I liked the way she danced and she liked the way I danced, and we made the cut. We cried together, and she called my house Wednesday. We talked for almost an hour but had to stop because her mother had to use the phone. I reluctantly hung up after I told her that I would call her Thursday night. Unfortunately, I never got a chance because my parents had one of their knockdown, drag-out fights as Dad always called them. It got me so upset that I jumped between them and begged them to stop.

I cried even harder that night because after talking with Lorrie that Wednesday, I found out that her parents were divorced. I cried because I didn't want to live apart from Mom and Dad. They had to stop fighting to convince me that they were not going to divorce, that they just had a difference of opinion.

As always it had to do with Dad's work. He refused to take a teaching position—and many were offered to him—because he wanted to be free to travel and play in clubs all across the country.

"You have a family now, Stan. You have to provide stability," Mom would always say.

Then Dad would come back with, "Sandra, you think this is some kind of game? Some kind of freakin' hobby?"

3

They would go on and on with Mom talking about the fact that she graduated from Seton Hall Law School and how she should be on Easy Street. And Dad would ask her where this freakin' Easy Street was, and they would go at it for another hour or so.

But that night was just too much for me, and I couldn't deal with the thought of visiting Mom one weekend and Dad the other, like Lorrie. Talking to Lorrie made me feel so sad because it was almost like Lorrie was an orphan. It took Mom and Dad a long time to calm me down. And Mom was really scared because she thought I would make myself sick.

The next morning I was feeling a little sick. But after a light breakfast of toast and tea, I was all right. Dad was nowhere in sight. He had left early for a gig in Washington, D. C. Mom assured me that he would be back because he had brought me to the first audition and wanted to find out how well I did this time. Because Mom didn't want to upset me in any way, she let me go on and on, talking about my new friend as we had breakfast and then decided what I was going to wear.

I told Mom that I wished that Lorrie and I attended the same school but that was impossible because Lorrie lived downtown, outside of my district. That Friday afternoon Lorrie took a cab to the center. Mom had offered to pick her up, but Lorrie's mom didn't agree with that. She didn't have a car but she wanted to let Mom know that she could give her daughter everything she needed. It was a matter of pride, Mom explained to me and told me that she would like to meet Lorrie's mom. They had only talked on the phone that Friday morning.

Lorrie stepped out of the cab in a faded blue denim jumper over a full leotard. On her feet were short white socks and scuffed saddle shoes. I was dressed the same way but my clothes were newer and brighter. Still, she looked cute. She was all long arms and legs and short, kinky hair that she just couldn't seem to control.

She told me that she was tenderheaded and it really hurt when her mom combed her hair. She wanted a perm but her mom thought she was too young for one. Last week she had touched my braided hair and told me how pretty she thought it was and how much she'd like to see it down. That Friday afternoon I wore my hair like Lorrie suggested.

"I like your hair down," Lorrie told me as she looked from me to Mom.

"Thank you," I replied, and then looked over at Mom. "This is Lorrie Cunningham."

Mom touched one of Lorrie's small round shoulders and said, "Glad to meet you, Lorrie. My baby says you're a very good dancer."

Lorrie smiled shyly. I blushed because I hadn't expected Mom to share our private conversation. Lorrie nodded slowly, obviously not knowing how to talk to the tall, beautiful woman before her. Mom had that effect on a lot of people. She was so drop-dead gorgeous and smart that not too many people knew how to take her.

All her close friends were people she met in law school or those she worked with on cases. She looked more like a model than a lawyer, and I was very proud of her. Even that day, in her black body suit, blue jeans and black leather mules, she caught the attention of many who walked passed us as we stood in front of the center. I had told Lorrie how beautiful Mom was, and by the way she looked at her, it was obvious that Lorrie agreed. Lorrie looked at Mom like she was a movie star.

The week before, Lorrie had met Dad, a short, thick man with a round brown face. You'd never think my parents would be a couple but there were times when they were very nice to each other.

The best times were when my mom was sitting in the basement watching my dad play or when she sat front row center at one of his concerts. He would be onstage with his silver trumpet, and she would look at him with adoring eyes.

Dad didn't have much to say to Lorrie; he was too busy getting me out of the center after the audition. He did congratulate Lorrie as he got me into the front seat of his Honda Civic so he could get me home and get himself ready for a gig in New York City. I wanted to spend more time with Lorrie but Dad explained, he was on a timetable. Still, I did manage to get Lorrie's phone number and give her mine. I borrowed one of Dad's business cards to write down Lorrie's information.

"Girls, we really need to get inside," Mom said as she moved toward the entrance to the center.

"Mom, please, you promised," I reminded her.

Mom sighed, but she knew what I wanted. We had talked about it that morning. "Baby, can't we do it after the audition?"

I looked up at her with a small face that said, who knows what's going to happen after the audition? I might be sad, Lorrie might be sad because things didn't work out like we had hoped.

Because Mom and Dad never denied me anything, Mom said, "Okay, baby. But it has to be done quickly."

That was when I grabbed Lorrie and pulled her up the stairs. We're going to take a picture," I told her.

From her soft, black leather purse, Mom pulled out a Polaroid camera and took a picture of Lorrie and me on the gray stone steps leading to the center, leading to our future.

Although Dad brought me to that first audition, it fell on Mom to get Lorrie and me to the center each and every Saturday. After Lorrie's mom met Mom, she let Mom pick Lorrie up and take us to dance class. I often wondered how Mom swung that but all she would tell me was that she had a "heart-to-heart, girl-to-girl talk" with Lorrie's mom.

The first lesson we learned was how to dance as a group, to move with the same steps, on the same beat. The second lesson was how to work together, not as individuals. To illustrate this Mr. Fred,

5

our main instructor, danced around, twirling in different directions. He looked so ridiculous that we all had to laugh.

"Now that's how you look when you dance out of sync, when you think only of yourself," Mr. Fred told us, and then he extended his hand to Miss Molly, a beautiful red-haired dance instructor.

They danced beautifully together. They looked so good that I wanted to take a picture of the tall, slim Mr. Fred with Miss Molly. Because they danced so well I thought that they had to be boyfriend and girlfriend.

One night, during a family dinner, I asked Mom if she thought the dance instructors were going together. But before Mom could say anything, Dad laughed out loud. He laughed so hard that he choked on his food. Mom cut her eyes at him as if to say, "You behave yourself, Stan Allen."

What Mom said out loud was, "I don't think that Mr. Alston and Miss Quinn are an item, baby."

Dad stopped laughing long enough to say, "There's no way that could be possible."

Then he began coughing and laughing again. I just couldn't see what was so funny.

"They work together, baby," Mom said. "Don't you think that's enough?"

I looked over at Dad before I answered. He was still smiling as I said, "I just thought they looked so good together."

"Two nice girls together," Dad said sarcastically and began laughing again.

"Stan, please," Mom said sharply. "Let her have her innocence."

I was really confused then because I didn't understand what my "innocence" had to do with my dance instructors. And neither Mom nor Dad seemed eager to break it down for me. After a moment of uncomfortable silence, I let it go. Besides, I wanted to tell them other things about the theater. I got the lesson that Mr. Fred taught us: dancing together is always better than dancing alone.

At the theater we were taught to be courteous. At the end of every rehearsal, Mr. Fred would say, "Thank you, most excellent students," and we would say, "Thank you, most excellent teacher." And during that first year we were so hyped that we danced at home, on the streets and in school hallways. Because of the theater I became totally comfortable onstage. There were times, I tried to explain to Lorrie, when I got so much into the dance that I forgot where I was, like I was on another level, away from this world.

After a really good workout, it took a little while for me to come down from my natural high. It was a totally weird, but totally great experience. Our teachers, ten including Mr. Fred and Miss Molly, wanted us to "get the energy out and express our feelings." I had no problem with that and neither did Lorrie.

7

Chapter Two

During February we were fitted for costumes and our dance rehearsals became even more intense. In that month, Mr. Fred disappeared and Miss Molly took over. She was a good instructor but she wasn't as animated as Mr. Fred, who could make you laugh just by looking at you.

In March, Lorrie and I were selected to be part of a special master class. We and the other twenty chosen had to give up Saturday morning cartoons, vacations, Little League for the guys, Scouts for the girls, school trips and play time, but our reward was the best roles in the upcoming event of the year. We had double rehearsals every other Saturday.

During that time, mothers and fathers, sisters and brothers were allowed to watch us rehearse, starting at ten o'clock in the morning. They sat around the small rehearsal room on the second floor of the center in a mirror-walled studio and watched us dance our little hearts out. We wore sweatshirts and sneakers, jeans and leotards, ripping up the dance floor. Our families came in and out, sometimes watching us for six hours straight. It was hard work but it was also a lot of fun. Mr. Fred came back and put us through some tough workouts.

"That was ca-ca," Mr. Fred would say, his pale white face turning red as he made believe that he was choking on something nasty. "This is just not acceptable, especially when I know you can do so much better. You are the best of the best. Let's do it again. You owe it to yourself to be the best that you can be."

And we would do it again and again until we brought a smile to Mr. Fred's face. We didn't want to be seen as "ca-ca." We also didn't want to hear Mr. Fred call us slackers.

"There's no room for slackers in this company," Mr. Fred would say.

And as we got nearer to our final rehearsals, Mr. Fred would begin each one by saying, "I know I won't be able to get everything done, so I'm going to ask you to listen and dance real hard."

We listened and danced so hard that Lorrie once told Mom, "We love Mr. Fred, even when he yells at us."

I hated to hear Mr. Fred yell, and what made him yell the most was when we didn't put any energy into our dancing. Mr. Fred always called for more and more energy, like it was the fuel that would make us great dancers.

9

In May, more children were invited to watch our rehearsals during school hours. They weren't dancers, they were art students who would sew the costumes and design and build sets for the production. A music teacher from downtown wrote a musical score and put together a student orchestra to play it. During the final month, June, there were dance rehearsals during school hours and on Saturdays and Sundays. We performed our show a few weeks before the end of the school year.

By way of celebration, Dad invited Lorrie and her mom to our house for dinner. In the beginning of the evening, Lorrie's mom, Miss Edna, was real uptight, but after dinner, when Dad brought out his bourbon whiskey, Miss Edna loosened up. She got so loose that she fell asleep on the couch in the family room. Lorrie and I couldn't help but laugh because Miss Edna slept with her head thrown back and her mouth wide open. Mom chased Lorrie and me upstairs to my room as she and Dad went into the kitchen.

Upstairs, in my room, we fell across the bed and held our hands to our mouths. We tried to hold our giggles but it was a losing battle. Even with the radio on we were afraid that Mom and Dad would hear us. Once we settled down, we talked about the show in which we had participated.

We were so proud of ourselves—we both had solos in the

show, and we both got standing ovations. Being in the Young People's Dance Theater was a journey that began with auditions, then months of rehearsals. When the curtain went down, the large crowd hollered and stomped. Many of the children onstage smiled and shed tears of joy. The year in the theater was over, and that journey had ended in what Mr. Fred called a "massive success."

It wasn't until much later that I found out that Mr. Fred had begun dancing when he was five years old. He joined the New York City Ballet in his teens and performed major solos at nineteen. At twenty-one he appeared in movies and Broadway shows. He stopped dancing professionally after he injured his leg in a skiing accident. He brought the idea of the Young People's Dance Theater to the Elizabeth Board of Education. Unfortunately, the board voted to fund the project for only one year.

"I'm going to miss Mr. Fred," Lorrie said as she sat on my bed the night of our performance.

"Me too," I agreed, knowing I mirrored the sadness I saw in Lorrie's big brown eyes.

Because we weren't the kind to stay down for long, Lorrie said something to make me laugh.

"I'm gonna miss some of the kids, too, but not all of them."

I had to laugh at that statement because some of the children were not as serious as I thought they should have been and became slackers, not putting in the necessary work.

"But there is one boy I'll miss," Lorrie confessed, then leaned forward to whisper his name.

I nodded, indicating that he was one to remember. I wasn't overly excited about him but, I had to admit, he was a cute. And he attended my school.

I moved closer to Lorrie and said, "I could get his phone number for you."

Lorrie squealed, then covered her mouth with both her hands.

"You can't do that," she said.

Her reaction puzzled me, so I said, "I thought you wanted to get to know him?"

"I'm too shy. 'Sides my mother won't let me have a boyfriend.

I'm too young."

"A boy can't even call you?"

Lorrie looked at me like I was an idiot. "No. No. No way."

"If you like him?"

"I like him. But I can't let him know it."

I couldn't see how that made any sense but I didn't say anything. I didn't want to embarrass Lorrie.

As we sat on my bed, a slow song, "Choosy Lover" by the Isley Brothers came on the radio.

"I like slow songs, sometimes," Lorrie told me in a soft voice.

I preferred fast songs, like those by George Clinton, who Dad called a "funky genius." He really liked Clinton's band, especially the horn section when Clinton performed with Parliament/Funkadelic. Without a word Lorrie rose from the bed and began to dance around the room.

11

"I'm dancing with my boyfriend," she said as she shuffled around with her eyes closed.

I smiled because she reminded me of Mom and Dad when they slow danced in the family room, after Dad put on a stack of his "oldies but goodies." I would always smile as I watched them because my tall mom would kick off her shoes and still be able to put her arms on my short dad's shoulders. Dad would rest his head in the middle of Mom's full bosom and close his eyes like he was a man in paradise; he looked so comfortable, so content, that I thought he would never let her go.

The singer from the Intruders sang "Slow Drag," another slow song coming from the radio in my room, this one about getting close to a loved one.

Because Lorrie had her eyes tightly shut, she didn't see me stand up from the bed. She wasn't even aware of me until I put my hands on her slim waist. When she did open her eyes, she didn't look surprised to see me so close to her face. As a matter of fact, she looked glad to see me, like I was a welcomed stranger.

"You ever kiss a boy?" Lorrie asked me as we touched from hip to thighs and moved around the room in our long black skirts.

"I played spin the bottle at a party," I told her, but even as I said it I got the impression that Lorrie was talking about something deeper than that.

"Did you like it?"

I nodded, although I realized that I had never really thought about it. "Especially the taste," I said.

"How did it taste?"

"Like sweet potato pie."

"I never had sweet potato pie. My mom doesn't make it. I had pumpkin pie, from the store," Lorrie said.

"Well, it's kinda like pumpkin. But more like sweet potato pie with a lot of cinnamon in it," I said, then smiled.

"Taste good, huh?"

"Yeah."

"How does kissing feel?"

"Like a cool towel against your face when you're hot."

"A cool towel," Lorrie said, trying to paint a picture in her mind.

"Refreshing. Especially when you really want that particular person to kiss you. Then you get an ache in your stomach."

"It hurts?"

"Not a bad hurt, Lorrie. It's like when your parents tell you that they're going to take you to Coney Island, with all those good rides."

"I've never been to Coney Island."

"You've heard about it?" I said, becoming a little frustrated.

"Yeah."

"What I'm trying to say is that a good kiss is something that hurts in your stomach because it's something you're looking forward to."

"I think I understand. But because I've never done it, it's kinda hard to imagine."

"Well I don't know what else I can say."

"Could you show me?"

"I-I guess I could. Just so you'll know," I said hesitantly.

"I really want to know."

"Okay. But if we're gonna do this right, you'll have to close your eyes."

Lorrie closed her eyes as I moved forward to kiss her. Time

stood still, and I couldn't hear any music. I couldn't even remember if we stopped dancing.

All I could remember was the warmth of her body and the freshness of her breath.

"Girls!"

13

Chapter Three

I pulled away without kissing Lorrie as Mom's voice came up to us from downstairs. She didn't like to climb the stairs to my room if she didn't have to. Not knowing what to do, I turned up the volume on my radio. Michael Jackson came on singing "Bad."

Because the music was so loud, the first thing that Mom said when she entered my room was "No wonder you can't hear me. Baby, are you playing that music for the whole neighborhood?"

I shook my head as I turned down the volume. I found it hard to look at Lorrie. Just the thought of what we had almost done made my face hot. I felt so awkward in my room that night. I felt so strange, like I was back to taking baby steps.

I turned the music down even more and heard Mom say, "…your mother is ready to go. My husband will drive you home."

I had my head down as Lorrie said, "Mrs. Allen, can I come back again?"

"Of course," Mom told Lorrie, like Lorrie's request was absurd. "Anytime you like. Just give us a call first to make sure that we're home. Is any of your stuff up here?"

I looked over at Lorrie as she shook her head.

"Everything is in my dance bag downstairs."

"Okay, well, let's go," Mom said.

Lorrie shyly waved good-bye to me. I waved good-bye back, missing her a lot already. It was the strangest thing.

I thought about asking to ride with Dad but Mom crushed that plan when she said, "I need your help downstairs. In the kitchen."

I knew that meant washing and drying dishes and straightening up the kitchen and dining room area.

"I have to change my clothes," I told Mom.

She nodded, indicating she had no problem with me changing my clothes before I came downstairs to work. To show that I was serious, I unbuttoned the top button of my white blouse.

"I'll see you downstairs," Mom said as she left my room with Lorrie in front of her.

Instead of changing my clothes, getting into some jeans and a tee, I went over to the window. It wasn't long before I saw Dad and Miss Edna appear on the black street below my window. Lorrie came up behind them but was the first one in the car. She took the backseat. As I watched her, my heart felt like it was in my throat.

My whole body shivered, and I felt like I was getting sick, coming down with something. Tears came to my eyes as I watched my dad's Honda Civic move down the street. Suddenly I felt so lonely, like I would always be by myself. The tears stopped just as suddenly as they began because I knew I would see Lorrie again.

Another slow song came on the radio and I ran across the room to switch the station. I couldn't bear to hear another sad song. I didn't stop turning the radio dial until I found EPMD rapping "You Gots to Chill."

When Mom came back up the stairs, she found me sitting on my bed, still in my white blouse and long black skirt. She looked at me with so much love and concern that I began to cry again. That was when she sat down beside me on my bed.

"Are you all right?" she asked and held me against her hip.

Was I all right?

I didn't know how to answer that one.

Chapter Four

It was the summer of 1999. Twelve years had passed since the Young People's Dance Theater and I was faking the funk that morning at the Dominique St. Claire Dance Studio in Elizabeth, New Jersey.

It was a Friday that I should've called in sick, but as one of the Sisters of Soul (SOS) dancers it was something we just didn't do. It had been ingrained in us that no matter what, "the show must go on," like athletes who played when they were hurt. And if we couldn't make it, we knew that the show would go on without us. As my dad often said, "If you don't get yourself together, the gravy train will pass you by," and I believed that deep down in my soul. Still, I thought I could put a "fake it 'til you make it" move on my teacher and my fellow dancers.

I knew I would have to pay for my dishonesty; one always does. I just didn't know how soon or how high that price would be. What it came down to was that nobody was fooled, and I looked like a fool. And that hurt me deeply. Never mind what the troupe thought, I always did a good job of beating up on myself.

You see, I thought I always had to be perfect. And that morning I was less than perfect. I stunk!

There was a line of ten dancers, and we were preparing for our annual summer concert. In the three years that I had been with Dominique, every summer concert was a sellout success. This was the last big event before everybody had to go back to school. This year's performance was entitled "Keep On Truckin'" and "Boogie Down: A Tribute to the Music of Eddie Kendricks."

I had too much emotional turmoil on my mind to give my heart and soul to my dancing that morning. I thought I could slide by because we spent most of the morning working on ensemble pieces. But toward the end of the rehearsal, Dominique asked to see my work on "The Boogie Down," my solo turn. It was the moment I truly dreaded. I knew I had to bring my heart and soul to that moment, to put in that intense concentration, and there was no way I could fake it. Still, I tried.

The night before I hadn't gotten much sleep, tossing and turning and thinking about why my lover left me. Everything I knew about myself and relationships told me to let it go but I couldn't, and I had to pay a high price for that. I cried the night before and became agitated because I knew it was just the beginning of misery, a prelude to the flood of tears I would shed. Let it go, let it go, I told myself. But my heart and soul couldn't, wouldn't let it go.

The SOS dancers grouped themselves in a pyramid formation as the song began. We all moved together through the lyrics that Kendricks sang in a high, clear falsetto. Even though my dad was a die-hard jazz musician with a silver trumpet, he loved the horn work on "Boogie Down," a funky song written by Frank Wilson, Leonard Caston and Anita Poree. And performed with gusto by Kendricks. As a SOS dancer, Dominique insisted that we do our homework.

Not only were we supposed to know the dance steps, but also, we were supposed to know the artists and the era their music came from. "Boogie Down" was released as a single in 1974, two years before I was born.

When I stepped out of formation to do my solo, everybody knew I was in trouble. No one laughed at me because we all had our bad days. But every time I messed up, my face became hot, and I wanted to find a deep hole in the floor.

"Let's take it from the top!" Dominique shouted, and everyone knew why.

Needless to say, after taking it from the top four or five times, I wasn't the most popular sister in that studio. I began to sweat like mad, and it wasn't just because I was exercising. I was drenched in "flop sweat" because I was bombing big time. My heart and soul were just not in harmony with my good intentions.

Dominique ended some of my misery by pulling me off to the side. I trembled as she stood near me, but not because I feared her. I reacted so emotionally because I felt that I had let her and my sister dancers down.

"What's going on, Debrena?" Dominique wanted to know. Never one to hide her disappointment, she let me have it with both barrels. "If I came to the summer concert and saw that, I'd demand a refund, and I'd get it too."

"I'm sorry, Dominique." I sounded so weak that I couldn't look her in her eyes.

18

I looked down at my bare feet and when I knew that wasn't working, I looked over at my sister dancers. They were all there: LaToya Baskerville, Kammie Youngblood, Erica Harper, Tamara Tucker, Shay Epps, LaTasha Brown, Angela King, Marcy Chase, and, of course, Lorrie. And I felt they were all looking at me. That really wasn't the case. The majority of them were moving around, practicing steps to keep their bodies warm during their unexpected break.

In my embarrassment I felt like I had been stripped naked and pushed into a corner, like I was the stupid bad kid who needed to spend a whole week in detention.

"I know it's just the beginning of the summer, and it seems like we have a lot of time," Dominique continued, "but we don't."

"I know that, Dominique."

"I'm not so sure you do, especially with a performance like that."

I was tempted to say how difficult the steps to "The Boogie Down" solo were but I knew that Dominique, the creator of the dance, didn't want to hear that. I also knew that my sister dancers sympathized with me but I also knew that they were glad it was me in the hot seat and not them. No one wanted any negative attention from Dominique St. Claire.

"You know how I feel about rehearsals," Dominique gently reminded me.

I nodded because I knew that Dominique felt that a rehearsal was a performance. Whether we performed before an audience of ten or ten thousand, she expected us to give all that we had, to be sharp, to be professional.

"Debrena, you have to get it together, you know all the new girls look up to you." In a softer voice she asked, "Is it that time of the month?"

I almost laughed because I knew that Dominique was trying to give me a legitimate reason for my poor performance. But because I had my pride, I wouldn't allow myself that option. I prided myself on living my life in an honest and open manner. Anything less than that made me feel bad about myself. I looked Dominique in her pretty light brown eyes.

19

"No, it's not that," I finally said.

Someone put on "Keep On Truckin'" and the music swirled around Dominique and me as we stood in the far corner of the long, wide room. It was another Eddie Kendricks song written by Wilson, Caston and Poree and another top ten R&B hit for Kendricks, released a year before "Boogie Down." The music was a comfort to me as I stood before my dance teacher.

Dominique looked at me intently, then said, "Come with me."

As I followed her I couldn't help but catch Lorrie's eye. She was standing with Angela and Marcy. And before I left the room, I mouthed a silent "I'm sorry" to them. I felt bad because I had been with them for the past three years and knew because they truly cared about me, that my pain was theirs.

"I'm a little worried about you," Dominique told me as we stood in her office.

I tried hard to smile. "I'm all right."

Dominique looked at me like she didn't believe me. "I'm a little concerned because you've been looking so depressed lately. And the way you danced this morning—"

"I'm all right," I said, cutting Dominique off.

"If there's anything you need to talk about, anything, you know where I live."

"I know you're there for me, Dominique."

"You have my home number?"

"I do."

"Use it. I mean it, Debrena. I don't want my girls suffering in silence. You have a problem, I should be the first one to know about it. If I don't have the answer, I can find somebody who does. I don't care what it is. You hear me?"

"Thanks," I said with a smile. "But really, I'm all right."

That was when Dominique held my shoulders and looked into my eyes.

"Don't play with me, missy."

I had to laugh because the elegant Dominique St. Claire sounded so street, like a "sister from the hood," ready to kick some booty.

"Really, Dominique, I'm all right. And if I had a problem, I wouldn't have any qualms about telling you. With Mom and Dad down in Florida, you're like a second mom to me."

"And don't you forget that, Debrena Allison Allen. You know how I feel about your parents. If anything happened to you on my watch, I'd never forgive myself—or face your parents."

"When I talk to them twice a week, I let them know you're a good mother hen."

Dominique had to laugh at that. "Well, I don't know if I see myself as a mother hen but I'm looking out for you, Debrena."

"I know that. I'm secure in that."

Dominique reluctantly let go of my shoulders. "You need me, call me."

I nodded in understanding. And as Dominique sat on her desk, I took a deep breath, then released it in preparation for returning to the dance studio.

"Debrena," Dominique called as I turned to leave.

I turned back to her.

"Tomorrow is another day. You get some rest, get some sleep, whatever you need to do, downtime. We'll see you tomorrow morning."

My heart was in my throat as Dominique dismissed me.

I hit the showers and tried to get out of the building as fast as I could. Although Dominique had been gentle with me, I was totally devastated. I'm sure that if I weren't so dark I would've blushed red like a White person. But as I pulled on my street clothes, I had to admit that Dominique had done the right thing.

If I had returned to the studio and continued to mess up, my confidence would've been shot, and who knew how long it would have taken me to recover from that blow to my ego? I slammed my locker and got my booty out of Dodge City, so to speak. I knew I was defeated—you didn't have to shoot me down in the street to convince me that I was a loser that morning. But like Dominique said, tomorrow was another day. Still, I had to get through that Friday.

I rushed out of the Dominique St. Claire Dance Studio and into the street. I suffered some anxiety because I hadn't checked the clock in the hallway before I left the building, so I had no idea what time it was. I usually checked my bus schedule, looked at the clock in the hallway and timed myself accordingly. That morning, when I hit the streets, I was flying blind.

In a moment of intense self-doubt, I felt that my life was spinning out of control. *I will get it together,* I told myself as the hot summer sun slapped my face. Inside the coolness of the dance studio, I had forgotten what a monster it was outside. It was like stepping into the deepest part of hell. And although I wore loose white linen, the heat during the summer of 1999 was no joke.

I didn't want to feel sorry for myself but there was no way I could hold my head up at that moment. My wounds were too new, too raw. There was no pep in my step as I made my way to the bus stop. I prayed that no one spoke to me because I was in a mood, a mood to be alone. All I wanted to do was catch my bus, go into my house, jump into my bed, pull the covers over my head and shut out the world.

I knew I was totally off schedule when I saw the bus whip around the corner.

"Wait, wait!" I yelled as it just kept on going.

I might've had a chance of catching the driver but my dance bag got in the way. It slipped off my shoulder and fell in front of me. I almost broke my neck tripping over it. I went down but I managed to get a hand out to break my fall. But while I was stumbling, the bus picked up momentum and left me waving my hand like an idiot.

Because the bus driver saw nobody standing at the bus stop, he sped up at it, and I was the loser again. I'm sure someone on the bus saw me running and stumbling, but I guess nobody wanted to be a good Samaritan that morning. I was truly pissed because I knew that I would have to wait at least another half hour for the next bus. Going back into the studio to wait just wasn't an option for me. I knew my sister dancers would ask if I was all right, and I just didn't want to keep on lying.

As I stood there waiting for my bus, I saw Angela come out of the building with Marcy. They were talking and holding hands, but I thought nothing of it. I was too busy stepping back into the bus shelter so they wouldn't see me.

Chapter Five

About twenty-five minutes later, a car horn blew from behind me. I didn't turn around because I was sure it was some roughneck, trying to hit on me. *I'm not the one,* I thought, my back straight with a serious grip on my dance bag, murder on my mind. *Mess with me and I'll put a hurtin' on ya.*

The car horn blew again. A dark blue Toyota Camry pulled up beside me, and the front passenger window came down. I immediately knew who it was.

"You got out of there so fast I didn't even know you were gone."

"I think I embarrassed myself enough for one day," I told the driver.

Lorrie Cunningham looked real cute that Friday afternoon in her yellow body suit and long black skirt. She shook her head like she was amused by my situation—me, making a fool of myself inside the studio, then sweating like a pig in the hot sun because I was too stupid to check the bus schedule. I was just glad she didn't see me trip over my dance bag as I ran for the bus. I wasn't at all pleased with myself that particular morning, and I really didn't want to take it out on anyone. I promised myself to be nice.

Lorrie, always sweet, said, "It wasn't that bad, D."

"Lorrie, I stunk up the place!" I snapped, quickly forgetting about my promise. "I'm sure that Dominique is asking herself why in the world she picked me to do that solo in 'The Boogie Down.'"

"Dominique picked you because you're a great dancer," Lorrie assured me.

"Not today, Lorrie. Today I was 'ca-ca,' just terrible."

After a thoughtful moment, Lorrie said, "D, if I stay at this bus stop much longer, I'm going to get a ticket. You need to get in the car."

I reluctantly got in, telling myself it was just to beat the heat.

Chapter Six

"*I meant* to tell you I really like your haircut," Lorrie said once we were on the road.

I gently touched my new do. "I'll tell you, it's a whole lot easier to manage this way."

"I'll bet it is, but I'm used to long hair now."

Lorrie's hair was a wild mane of braids and extensions that ran down her back and when she danced she had to wear heavy-duty barrettes to keep the hair out of her face. On anyone else all that would've been too much, but on Lorrie it was just right. With her position as one of the top dancers with the Sisters of Soul dance troupe, under the direction of Dominique St. Claire, Lorrie Cunningham carried all that attention very, very well. Lorrie became a real bold girl once she really got into her dancing. In high school she was voted Least Likely to Succeed; she wasn't focused then.

She didn't come out of her shell until at my insistence she auditioned for the SOS dance troupe. Once a member, she became a real bold, hip swinging soul sister. In that summer of 1999, Lorrie was a natural five-ten, slim-hipped and caramel-colored, stacked beauty.

"Where are you on your way to? I mean really," Lorrie wanted to know.

"Home."

"You all right?"

Because I hate lying with a passion, I said nothing.

"I only ask because you've been looking real down lately," Lorrie continued.

I seriously thought about telling Lorrie to drop me off at the next corner.

"I didn't realize you and that White girl had gotten so close."

"We lived together for two months, Lorrie," I snapped, really irritated at that point. Because I didn't try to hide it, I wondered if Lorrie knew how close she was to a beat down. "You get a little close day in and day out like that."

"I'm sorry it didn't work out."

"Me too, Lorrie. Me too."

I really hated that the conversation wasn't flowing between Lorrie and me. We had never been like that. Lorrie fumbled around with the car radio until she came upon Anita Baker singing "Giving You The Best That I Got."

"Lorrie, how's Miss Edna doing?" I asked, inquiring about her mother.

"Real good, considering what happened to her," Lorrie told me, still turning her radio. She sounded concerned and relieved at the same time.

A year before Lorrie's mom had suffered a minor stroke.

Lorrie worked hard to support herself and her mom. I admired her for that.

"She's taking her medication and making all of her doctor's appointments," Lorrie went on. "I make sure of that, even if I have to take her. You know, D, it's sometimes like I'm the mother and she's the child."

All I could do was nod in sympathy; it was inconceivable to me how a situation like that could be. Mom and Dad were healthy, retired and living in Florida. Even if one of them got sick, they had each other.

Miss Edna had no one but Lorrie, but with Lorrie's love and dedication to her mom, Lorrie was all that Miss Edna needed.

Because the conversation was going so good between us, I decided to go into more personal territory—Lorrie's, not mine.

"What's up with you and Angela?" I asked, flashing back on my seeing Angela so chummy with Marcy when I thought that Lorrie had something going on with Angela.

Lorrie laughed bitterly, then said, "I hated to have you catch me with Angela like that."

I had caught Lorrie with her head up Angela's skirt. It was during my housewarming party on my sundeck at the back of my house. "You two didn't have to stop. I like to watch," I said, then laughed to keep things light.

"I was so embarrassed. But Angela surprised me by being so understanding. When you caught us like that, all she did was turn around, let her skirt fall down and say, 'We've really got to finish that *soon.*' Talk about a bold one. You know, she told me that she'd like to get down with you."

"We could never get down like that. Angela sees me as too much of a dance rival. She really wanted that solo in 'The Boogie Down,' thought she had it in the bag. And she hadn't even spoken to Dominique. Getting down with the get down? She could never be truly comfortable with me."

After a few moments of silence, Lorrie said, "I don't know why we never got down, D."

I hadn't realized what a can of worms I had opened until Lorrie shared that with me. I turned toward Lorrie and found her looking straight ahead, keeping her eyes on the traffic.

"You know why."

"I know what you told me, years ago."

"And I repeat, Lorrie. If I take you on as a lover, I lose you as a friend, and I can't afford to do that. I wouldn't want to do that."

"We could try it."

"No, Lorrie. Besides I know you have other girls you deal with. Girls you hung out with in high school. And there's Angela." Before Lorrie could say anything, I added, "And besides, I'm not gay."

"I hate labels."

"Yeah. You have to know where I'm coming from, Lorrie. I like men. I know you don't, but I like men very, very much."

"Not all girls will live happily ever after like that."

"I plan to."

"What about that White girl?"

"Her name is Tyra."

"You let her live with you," Lorrie said, and the bitterness in her voice alarmed me.

"That was just a temporary condition. Tyra was staying with me to save money for her own place. She was also looking for a company to dance with, to help build up her credibility. How do I look telling my parents I have someone living with me? And I would have to tell them sooner or later."

"Why don't you just give us a chance?"

"Get real, Lorrie." I didn't want to be cold or hurt Lorrie, but she had to know from where I was coming.

"I know you'll dig it, D. You know I know how to get down with a sister. Ain't no shame in my game."

"I know that. You've always been upfront, and I respect that about you."

Then Lorrie said in her most seductive voice, "Ain't no man alive who can compete with the funky magic of two women together. That's some powerful shit, D. You know what I'm talking about. That's why you can't get that White girl out of your head."

I felt a sudden lump in my throat. "Tyra was very special to me."

When Lorrie parked in front of my house, it was obvious that she didn't want to let me go.

"I know that White girl—I mean, Tyra—was special to you, D. I would never try to minimize that," Lorrie continued, both hands on the steering wheel. "Remember I was there when you two met."

It was at an audition for a traveling show and the producer/choreographer was a son-of-a-bitch taskmaster. We shook our booties for hours and none of us knew where we stood. There were a lot of good dancers there, but one of the most impressive was a White girl who shook her little boy's booty like a *Soul Train* dancer. After the audition, I got a chance to talk to her. It was an intense twenty minutes before Lorrie pulled me away, reminding me that we had another appointment across town.

"What did you two talk about?" Lorrie wanted to know.

"I can't really remember all of it," I had to admit. "We had a

few things in common. Dance classes at age ten, professional training in our teens, an off-Broadway show here and there, things like
that."

"I didn't even see her take your phone number."

"I didn't give it to her. Tyra tracked me down through the
phone book. I got a call from Stella's Diner. She called from there,
afraid to knock on my front door."

"What was she afraid of?"

"Making a fool of herself. She didn't know if I was with someone or if I was married. Or even into women."

"What did you tell her?"

"I told her to come over."

"And she came? Just like that?"

"Not right away. We had to talk some more."

Lorrie sat in her car, trying hard to digest all of this. Whenever
I talked to Lorrie about Tyra, I always got the impression that Lorrie
felt I had betrayed her in someway. I couldn't seem to get Lorrie to
understand that in my book, friends just didn't become lovers easily.

"Then she just left. Why, D?"

I really didn't want to get into that with Lorrie.

"I-I don't know, Lorrie. I really don't know," I answered truthfully, my heart heavy. "She had a key, she could come and go as she
pleased. One night I came home and the house was so quiet. I
called out to Tyra, but nothing. It was two weeks before I accepted
the fact that she wasn't coming back, even though that night all of
her clothes and things were gone."

Lorrie looked at me like she wanted to take me in her arms, to
comfort me, to protect me from the mean dyke, Tyra Woodstock.
That was when I looked at her and suddenly saw her as more than a
friend. I knew I needed a lover who really cared about me, unconditionally.

"What about you and Angela?" I wanted to know because of
this new way I was feeling. I didn't want to start something we
couldn't finish.

Lorrie smiled sadly. "I guess you haven't heard."

"If it's gossip, I'm always the last one to know."

"Marcy moved in with Angela."

I couldn't say that I was really surprised. I had, just that day, seen Angela holding hands with Marcy.

"I thought Marcy had a steady boyfriend."

"Marcy did, but since she's been hanging out with Angela, there's no time for anybody else."

"What are Marcy's parents saying about this?" I had to ask.

"They think it's just two girls living together."

I had to laugh at their naivete. "Like one big slumber party every night."

30   I couldn't help but think about all the erotic possibilities of those two together, getting their freak on. I couldn't know what Lorrie was thinking as we sat in the front seat of her car, deep in our own thoughts, but I had no doubt that Marcy Chase and Angela King had to be somewhere in her mind. If not them specifically, then girls in general, making funky magic. There was a thin film of sweat above Lorrie's upper lip, and although it was a summer Friday and hot as hell, I knew that her sweat was from more than the heat. And understand this, the air conditioning in her car was working just great.

In the final analysis, it was so hard to resist Lorrie. She was a great-looking girl and a truly creative dancer. That summer we were paired to perform "Loose Booty 2000," a new dance Dominique came up with based on one she created during the seventies called "Loose Booty." We had performed "Loose Booty" as an ensemble piece a few seasons ago, during the company's tribute to George Clinton and Parliament/Funkadelic. Lorrie had many moves that I admired and I looked forward to working with her that summer.

She was also a certified Jazzercise instructor at the Frederick Douglass Community Center. She was a Black beauty who trained hard and stayed positive, and the possibility of taking her on as a lover made me tingle. I said I didn't want to go that way but I really needed a distraction, something to blow my mind and take me out of my funky mindset.

I wrestled with my conscience before I said, "You want to come in?"

Lorrie looked at me, puzzled and surprised. I didn't want her to think I was a wishy-washy person, but felt I owed it to myself to have a good time. Ever since Tyra left so abruptly I spent many nights pleasuring myself. That type of action satisfied my flesh but did nothing for my mind or spirit. And in the final analysis, although masturbation felt damn good, it also seemed so unnatural.

Not only that but I didn't want it to become a habit. Still, a girl like me needed a little somethin' somethin', and I knew that Lorrie would understand. I didn't think I was being hypocritical even though I was about to cross a line. One I told myself that I would never cross.

31

In answer to my question, Lorrie nodded, like she was just too emotional to speak. But there was also wildness in her eyes that told me all I needed to know. I knew when I opened myself up to Lorrie; she would sex me like she loved me. That she would be a complete and thorough lover and that I would have to pull out all of my bedroom tricks to keep up with her. Her obvious excitement turned me on and let me know that Lorrie would be fun to play with.

Chapter Seven

We stepped onto the porch of my house, a split-level that I had inherited from my parents. They could've sold it, but they showed me the utmost respect by allowing me to remain home alone. I took the mail out of the box that identified this house as The Allen Residence.

Then I opened the front door and had Lorrie follow me inside. I threw the mail on the small table in the foyer, promising myself to get back to it later. In the meantime I had company.

"Your place is always so neat and clean," Lorrie observed as she stepped ahead of me. "I can't let anyone just drop by my apartment. I'm always straightening up."

I kicked off my flat shoes and walked behind Lorrie. I couldn't help but notice the shape of her womanly booty in her long black skirt. "That's because I live alone in this big house. It kind of makes cleaning up easier."

"Yeah," Lorrie said, still looking around, with her hands on her round hips.

I threw myself back into an oversized armchair, my favorite piece of furniture.

"Well," Lorrie began, "here we are."

"You have any place you need to be?" I asked as I popped the buttons on my white linen vest.

"No, no place," Lorrie assured me.

That was when I popped the buttons on my white linen, wide-legged pants. I wasn't trying to be provocative, I told myself. Just making myself comfortable in my house. After the morning I had, I needed to totally relax. I thought about a nice hot shower with a good friend as a prelude to a good time in my bed.

Beneath the vest, I wore a pale sports bra. And beneath the pants, I wore a matching thong. With a little more pushing and pulling, I was suddenly almost naked. My discarded outer garments lay on the polished wood floor like dumped laundry. Lorrie looked down on my long, smooth legs.

"You got some real pretty legs, D."

I smiled a thank-you for the compliment, and then said softly, "Aren't you going to take something off?"

Lorrie smiled shyly. "I guess I should, although I don't have much to take off."

"Take off your shoes," I suggested as I pulled my legs up and folded them underneath me, yoga style.

Lorrie kicked off her shoes. "What now?"

"That skirt has got to go."

"Okay," Lorrie said as she removed her skirt and draped it over a nearby chair.

She stood before me in her cute yellow body suit that snapped at the crotch. I knew that we were almost at the point of no return. I was somewhat nervous because I knew that by doing this, my relationship with Lorrie would never be the same. I was taking a big chance, but I also knew that Lorrie was the only friend with whom I would take such a big chance.

We had known each other since we were ten. We had been through a lot together. Still, where we were about to go was uncharted emotional territory and I had to admit that I wasn't sure if I was doing the right thing.

I looked over at Lorrie and saw that there was some hesitation in her eyes as well. She had to know what this would mean for our relationship. But I didn't see her backing down or picking up her clothes and running from me. And because she stood before me I waved her forward, using both my hands.

"Come to me," I said softly.

Then I stood to welcome her into the circle of my arms. I tingled because I knew that this embrace would take our relationship to another level. Since age ten we had been close, but never intimate. With the simple act of pressing our lips together, sucking each other's tongues, we were about to go to a place of no return: a passionate place that would burn us with its heat. I knew that after this kiss, I would never see Lorrie the same way.

It was like everything before that time had been child's play. Now we were playing adult games, and it was serious, very serious. But before our lips met something happened that snatched me out of that special moment.

34 Suddenly there was the sound of a key turning in a lock, and then the front door swung open, wide. I turned my head and saw Tyra standing there in the doorway. There was shock on her beet-red face, then deep disappointment, sadness.

"Tyra!" I called out to her.

Tyra let my spare key drop to the floor before she backed out of the house and slammed the door behind her. I wanted to yell out to Tyra that I hadn't done anything with Lorrie even though we were half-naked and our clothes were strewn all over the living room. It looked like we had really gotten into it and I couldn't blame Tyra for not wanting to hear anything from me. My head felt so tight I thought my eyes would pop out of my burning face.

I wanted to slam things and I wanted to scream. I ran to the window in my living room, just in time to see Tyra settle into the front seat of a Plymouth Voyager with bulging fenders and big headlights. There was two Black guys in the minivan, one driving and one in the seat behind the driver. All of them looked at me before the van pulled off, moving fast down my street.

I turned away from the window. My half-naked body was hot with anger and frustration. *Why can't things ever work out for me!* I screamed inside my mind. I wanted to blame somebody. I wanted to kill somebody.

"You!" I yelled at Lorrie, even though I knew I was wrong when I was doing it. "Get out of my house!" I was like a madwoman, pointing an incriminating finger at a startled Lorrie. "Right now!"

Lorrie started to say something but I wouldn't let her. I cut her off with more angry words.

"Tyra came back to me and I was freakin' off with you! I really lost her this time! She'll never come back now!"

"D-Debrena—" Lorrie began, moving toward me in her half-naked glory.

I picked up her skirt and flung it at her. "Leave me alone! Just leave me the hell alone!"

I turned and quickly walked down the hall to my bedroom.

"D!" Lorrie called out to me one last time before I slammed my bedroom door hard behind me. Then I threw my half-naked body across the bed and cried like there was no tomorrow.

35

Chapter Eight

As I lay there on my bed, I thought about my last big argument with Tyra. And the crazy thing was that it was right after we had sex. That crazy girl was trying to get me to "come out" as a lesbian.

"But I'm not gay," I told Tyra that night.

"What about what we just did?" Tyra asked me as she lay naked in my bed.

That was when I sat up and leaned back against the headboard. "What we did was just some fun, girl. Why you want to make it more than that?"

"You take me too lightly, Debrena. And you know how I feel about you."

"Don't go there. I like you. I like you a lot. But you know and I know that I still deal with men. That's not going to stop because we had a good time in bed."

"What man are you dealing with now?"

"No one right this minute, but when I see something I like, I'm on it, Tyra. And I'm not going to let you or anyone else make me feel bad about it."

"So you're one of those bisexuals?"

"Don't try to make fun of me. I'm just being real with you."

That was when Tyra turned away from me, giving me all of her long, bare back to look at. "I used to be like you."

"What is that supposed to mean?" I asked as I grabbed her shoulder.

Tyra suddenly stood from the bed, and my hand fell from her

soft, warm flesh.

"You're in denial," was her funky-ass accusation, and I didn't appreciate it one damn bit. She made me so mad I lost control.

"Don't try to pin me down like that! I'm not like you! All you want to do is lay up with some girl 24/7! All girls, all the damn time! I'm not like that!"

"I don't want to fight with you, Debrena." Tyra held a sheet to cover her naked body.

"You won't ever have to fight with me if you stop calling me gay!"

"I know, I know, you like men."

"And don't you forget that shit!"

I was so furious with Tyra that I let her take the sheet and sleep on the couch in the living room, although we normally slept together.

I fumed in bed and thought, *Where in the hell did she get that idea? Me gay? If she ever saw me get down with a man that thought would've never entered her mixed-up mind.* I was so angry that I couldn't even sleep that night. I didn't want to think about Tyra. I really didn't need her.

Thinking of Tyra I came to the realization that I owed Lorrie a big apology. I rolled over onto my back and grabbed the phone off the nightstand. I got her on the second ring.

In my softest voice, I said, "I'm sorry, boo. I should not have yelled at you like that."

"You know you a crazy bitch?"

"I know."

"What a friend you turned out to be."

"Sorry."

"Let that White girl be your friend. If you can find her sorry ass!"

"Don't do me like that. I know I messed up. I said I was sorry. You want me to get on my knees?"

"That would be a start, the way you tore your ass this afternoon."

"I was wrong."

"Dead wrong."

"And I'm so sorry."

"You know you are pitiful?"

"I know."

"Let that White girl open your nose like that."

"Don't go there, Lorrie. I had strong feelings for Tyra. But the way she left me, on top of what happened today. I got to let it go, girl."

"I'm trying real hard to be mad at you."

"Don't be mad at me. I need my best friend."

"I'm the best friend you ever had. And you treat me like shit. After all I've done for your sorry black ass! We've been rolling since we were ten, D. That should count for something."

"It means a lot, Lorrie."

"I can't believe your shit, D. That White girl comes in and you drop me like a hot potato."

"I was wrong. I'm sorry. Please forgive me."

"Yeah. Whatever."

"Lorrie."

"We could've been funky magic together."

I didn't want Lorrie to go any farther with the idea of us having sex. As far as I was concerned moving in that direction was a big mistake. I didn't think we should ever go there again. That afternoon was the result of a moment of weakness on my part. But I didn't think that it was wise to share that with Lorrie when I was trying hard to smooth things over with her.

To change the subject completely, I said, "I'm putting all my feelings for Tyra behind me. I need to concentrate on my career. I have to make some big moves; I'm not getting any younger. I have to get serious, Lorrie."

"I feel you on that one, D."

"You know we have to work on our routine tomorrow."

"Tomorrow seems so far away."

Because Lorrie sounded a little down, I said, "Why don't you join me for dinner tonight?"

"What are you cooking? I can bring some wine to go with it."

"I was thinking about Stella's."

38

"You know I can't figure out why they still call it Stella's Diner. Stella's been dead for at least twenty years."

"I believe that Slappy lets it stand as a tribute to his late wife."

"Yeah. That's sweet. That has to be it. Why don't I just meet you over there? In, let's say, fifteen minutes."

"Make it a half an hour," I told her.

"Okay."

"I'll see you then."

I hung up the phone feeling better than I had felt in a long time, like a heavy burden had been lifted. I didn't know what the future held for me, but I felt real good knowing I had a good friend like Lorrie in my corner.

Chapter Nine

When I went across the street to Stella's Diner, on the corner of Bishop and Burke, the first person I saw coming out of the eatery was Dominique St. Claire. She was smiling and dressed in a pin-striped business suit, and flanked by Marcy and Angela. Dominique hugged me and gave me a kiss on the cheek.

"I keep forgetting how close you live to this place," she said as she used her fingers to wipe off the cranberry-colored lipstick she had put on my face.

"Hello," Marcy called out to me, being her usual perky self. Her long permed, black hair was pinned up, showing off the beauty of her long, thin neck. She was a light-skinned beauty with green eyes and a dimpled chin.

Angela nodded at me, acknowledging my presence, but said nothing. She always exuded a smoky, underground type of sexiness. Lorrie had once told me how hot she was in bed but whenever I was around her, Angela seemed to take pride in not showing any emotion.

I could never see Angela getting buck wild in bed like Lorrie told me she could be. But I learned a long time ago that you couldn't judge a book by its cover, especially when that person was inspired. I suspected that Angela could be a firecracker when she got "inspired." Of course, I had no way of knowing that personally, and I didn't want to go there with Angela.

Angela was sexy, but too cool for me. I liked my lovers open and warm like Tyra. Still I couldn't help but look at Marcy and Angela in a whole new light because of what Lorrie had told me about their current living arrangement. They looked good in their dark business suits. And Marcy had a super fem thing going on with her ruffled, high-neck blouse.

"We just had a business meeting," Dominique informed me.

I nodded, knowing that this season, Angela was serving as president and Marcy was serving as treasurer for the dance company. Dominique handed her car keys to Marcy.

"You girls get into the car. I'll be with you shortly."

Before Dominique could say anything, I said, "I'm all right."

Dominique laughed. "I'm being a mother hen, right?"

41

"It's okay. Sometimes I need that. I'm meeting Lorrie for dinner."

"Look, don't hang out too late. I want all my girls fresh for tomorrow's rehearsal."

"Yes, Dominique."

She patted my shoulder before she walked away to her car.

I walked into the diner, dressed super casually in a black tank top, khaki pants and open-toed sandals. I was definitely not trying to impress anyone. A few feet into the establishment, Slappy Martin greeted me with a smile. He was behind the long white counter as he waved at me. The dinner crowd was deep but he managed to find me a table.

Slappy, with his short salt-and-pepper hair and beard, was always a welcome sight. Although he had waitresses, he always extended a personal greeting to me. I attributed that to the fact that he knew my parents so well, especially Mom who had been a close friend of his wife, Stella, before Stella and Slappy married and before Stella died of cancer.

"You eatin' alone tonight?" Slappy asked as he pulled out a chair for me.

I sat, and then smiled up at the handsome older man. "I'm waiting for my girl Lorrie."

"Ain't that that fine, long-legged, caramel treat I like so much?"

"That's Lorrie."

"Lookin' forward to seein' her again."

"She'll be here soon."

"Her man might not like that, huh?"

Because I didn't want to lie, I just laughed, like I was going along with Slappy's little joke. If any man came on to Lorrie, there might be some jealousy but it wouldn't be from a man.

"Those young bucks don't know how to treat a woman. It's an art that they don't teach in no school."

"Maybe you could open a school, Slappy."

"On the memory of my dear Stella, God rest her soul, I should. But those young bucks wouldn't use the skills right. I ain't teachin' them how to be better mack daddies. I'm talkin' 'bout a love thang."

42

I laughed at that, glad that Slappy kept it light.

"Can I get you anything now?"

I thought about telling him I'd wait for Lorrie but my stomach began growling, letting me know there was a little problem.

"Let me have a small garden salad and a peach Snapple."

Slappy nodded and left me alone at my table. I looked around the diner. I saw some people I recognized, associates of my parents, but none I knew well enough to invite over for some chitchat. This was good because I wanted to be alone with my thoughts.

Chapter Ten

I made quick work of my salad and half of my Snapple, and there was still no sign of Lorrie. I thought about calling her when a voice called out to me.

"Mind if I sit?"

I looked up and saw a fine Black brother looking down at me. He had a chiseled face, baby dreadlocks and a thick goatee. His khaki short-sleeved shirt showed off his muscular arms, and his khaki pants outlined his long, thick legs. Suede sandals completed the outfit.

He looked real neat in his urban solider gear. And when he smiled, his teeth were movie-star straight and pearly white. I had no way of knowing who the fine brother was, but he made me think of champagne chilling on ice; candlelit dinners, rose petals on hardwood floors; sexy soul music, like Brian McKnight or Luther Vandross; and full-body massages and hip grinding all night long. *You are trippin', Miss Debrena,* I told myself as I brought my booty back down to reality.

"Excuse me," I said, giving myself some time to slow my racing heart.

"Mind if I sit?" he repeated as he waved a big, brown hand to the empty seat.

"For a little while," I told him, getting a grip on myself. "I'm expecting a friend, a girlfriend."

"I was on my way out, and I knew I would kick myself if I didn't say something to you," the brother told me as he sat across from me. That was when I noticed the camera hanging from a black leather strap around his thick neck.

"That's your hobby?" I asked, pointing to the camera in the middle of his broad chest.

"My business," he told me, then handed me his business card. It read PHOTOS BY CHOICE. "I'm Choice Fowler."

I looked at his card again. It also included his phone number his fax number and his e-mail address. There was no street address.

"Do you have a studio?"

"I like to say the world is my studio." He smiled, obviously pleased with his own wit. It didn't cost me anything, so I smiled back. "But, yes, I do have a studio, in a loft, near the waterfront. I'm currently exhibiting some work there. You should come by to check it out."

Inviting me to his place already? I thought. *The brother is moving much too fast.* "You been around long?" I asked to change the subject.

"No, not really, just a couple of months. I'm from L.A."

"Lower Alabama?" I joked.

Choice just kept on smiling. "Los Angeles."

I laughed out loud and suddenly realized that I was too comfortable with him. It was as if we had met in another lifetime. It was spooky because the only other time I had felt like that was when I first met Lorrie. I looked at him and got the crazy idea to invite him across the street to my house for some wine and a bath sprinkled with rose petals. I looked over at Choice Fowler and suddenly realized how much I missed the comfort of a man.

"I'm Debrena Allen."

He put out a hand, and I shook it. "Glad to meet you, Debrena."

We had been getting on so well with the laughter and the conversation that I didn't even bother to look at my watch. But when I did, I saw that Lorrie was more than thirty minutes late for our dinner date.

"Excuse me," I told Choice as I took out my cell phone and speed-dialed Lorrie's number.

"Yes," Lorrie answered tentatively.

"What's up, girl? You didn't leave yet?" I said into the phone,

44

putting on a little show for my audience of one. "I ain't mad at ya, but you got to tell me something."

"I can't come now," Lorrie told me. "But I need to talk to you." Then she dropped the bomb. "Angela and Marcy are in my apartment."

I didn't know what to say to that. "You all right? Should I come over there?"

"I can handle it."

"Well, call me later on."

As I put my phone back in my bag, I didn't want to think about why Marcy and Angela were at Lorrie's apartment. I had had enough drama for one day.

45

"Stood up?" Choice asked, letting me know that he was still there.

I was somewhat distracted. "I guess you could say that. My girl got tied up."

"I'm sorry."

He looked so sad, I felt bad for the brother. "Why should you be sorry? You didn't do anything."

"You're obviously disappointed."

I wasn't really disappointed; I was deeply concerned because I was so afraid that Lorrie would get into a catfight with Angela and Marcy. That's what was on my mind, and there was no way I wanted to share that with someone I just met. Openness did have some limits. Still, I smiled at Choice, touched by his genuine concern.

"A lady as pretty as you should always be smiling."

"That's not always possible, Choice. You ever hear the expression, 'Into each one's life, some rain must fall?'"

"That should never apply to you."

This man just keeps touching my emotions, I thought, like there were buttons he had learned to push. I had to keep telling myself, Choice was a complete stranger.

"Thank you," I said, knowing that I had to get away from this Choice Fowler. He was just too appealing and I was too vulnerable, worrying about Lorrie and, as quiet as it was kept, worrying about myself.

"But happy all the time is just not realistic," I said.

"It can be if we work at it."

I smiled at Choice, then decided to go into my diva bag to give him a little something to remember me by.

"You want to make me happy, Choice?"

"Yes, I do," he said too eagerly. Like he thought I was going to let him do me on the table.

"Pay the bill," I told him. "And don't forget to leave a tip."

Then I stood to make my grand exit. His mouth dropped as I turned away from him and made my way to the front door.

46

In the street I laughed out loud. Before he knew what hit him I'd be across the street and into my house. I had to laugh because I imagined him searching for his wallet, putting some money on the table, and then running toward the door. But like Cinderella at midnight, that prince wouldn't be able to find me.

Chapter Eleven

I felt like a peeping Tom as I looked out of my window, my eyes on the entrance to Stella's Diner. I couldn't stop laughing as I thought about Choice fumbling to pay the bill and run after me. I knew he'd be a wreck because he wouldn't believe that I could disappear so fast. Because he had been so friendly and seemed so interested in me, I had no doubt he would try to catch up to me.

But I told myself I had no time for Choice or anyone else for that matter. I had to admit that my head was still messed up behind Tyra. I once heard a psychologist on one of those New York radio talk shows say that one should not rush into a new relationship after a breakup. Her thinking was that there needed to be a period of emotional healing. What she suggested was that one should wait at least a year before beginning a new relationship.

Even when I first heard it, I felt that a year was an awfully long time, but I did agree that there should be some time for healing. Maybe six months, but a year? Who could be celibate for that long?

I accepted that Tyra was gone, but I couldn't stop thinking about her. Like where was she living? And who were those two Black guys in the minivan? Because I didn't want to depress myself, I brought my attention back to the front of Stella's Diner, just in time to see Choice walk into the street. He looked to the left, he looked to the right, then walked away from the diner, frowning like he wanted to punch somebody.

I felt a little sorry for him. I followed him with my eyes as he walked down Bishop Street. He walked quickly and only stopped when he reached an expensive-looking Lincoln Navigator. He climbed into his ride, but didn't pull off right away. He looked around some more. I know I shouldn't have treated him like that but I didn't want to lead him on, make him think there was something when there wasn't anything. I just wasn't the one because I had some serious emotional healing to do.

After he pulled off, I turned away from the window and remembered the mail on the table in the foyer. I kicked off my sandals before I went over to collect it. There wasn't much. Some bills for me and some junk mail for Tyra. I hadn't thought she'd been at my house long enough to be on someone's mailing list, but then I realized that she had forwarded her mail from the motel where she had been staying.

When I met her, Tyra was living in a room at the Lord Sterling Motel in Elizabeth. I begged her to move in with me, just to get herself together. As far as I was concerned, that motel was a hellhole.

She had been over to my house several times before I suggested that I meet her at her place. There was a restaurant that I wanted to treat her to for dinner near where she told me she lived. I figured that after dinner we'd come back to the motel to have sex. But when I saw the small single bed in her room, which wasn't anything but a closet with a bathroom attached, I knew I couldn't have sex in there. Just the thought of that dingy little room made me feel dirty.

I wasn't looking for a roommate, but I had to get her out of there.

To get my mind off Tyra, I picked up my home phone and dialed Lorrie. I became agitated when the phone just rang and rang. When the answering machine came on, I stubbornly refused to leave a message. Of course, as I sat down heavily on my couch, my mind went back to Tyra.

I had dealt with Black guys, Black girls, but never a White girl. And it wasn't easy with Tyra, and not just because she was White. The real reason was that Tyra was a drama queen. What bothered Tyra was always a very big deal, a major production. And this was so surprising to me because we didn't start off that way.

My phone rang one evening and Tyra was on the other end. She

48

was very tentative, almost shy. "You might not remember me," she began. "I'm the White girl you met at the audition. The red head."

Of course I remembered "the red head," that very striking girl with the long hair and the baby blue eyes that almost disappeared in her face whenever she laughed or smiled. And I also couldn't forget her clean, healthy-looking skin or the smell of her perfume.

"I remember you," I told her, smiling on my end of the line.

"I was wondering if you'd like some company?"

"I would like some company."

"I'm across the street, Debrena. In the little diner across from your house."

"Come over."

"Debrena, I'm not a bold girl. Most of the time I take it real slow."

"But not this time?"

"Not this time."

"I want you over here, Tyra."

And that was how it began for us. After that wild first time I laid up under her, and we talked for hours like old friends, not like first-time lovers.

"Do you have any toys?" Tyra had asked as she rested comfortably in my bed.

"I thought you'd never ask," I had joked.

"I'm asking because I don't know how much you're into girls."

I tried to be as candid as I could because I saw this White girl as someone I wanted to get to know better. But from the beginning, she had to understand something about me. I told her straight out, the first time we got together. "I still like to ride a man every so often, but I've been pretty heavy into girls for the past two years. I really couldn't stretch out until my parents moved to Florida and left me with the house."

"How would you feel if they found out about you with girls?" Tyra asked.

"I hope they never find out. And if they do, I must be the one to tell them. Do your parents know about you?"

"My mother does, but not my father. They're not together so I don't think he needs to know. My mother has met some of my girl-friends. I took a few out to Jersey City, where I grew up and where she still lives. I told her because I didn't want her looking for any grandchildren."

"And she's cool with that?"

"Not so cool, but she knows how I am. I'm not going to change; she has to accept me as I am."

"At least you're honest with her. I think it's real important to be honest with other people, but more importantly with yourself."

I wanted Tyra to know that I was a person of integrity, that I had this really developed sense about right and wrong. Even if I accidentally took a pencil I'd feel bad about myself all day until I could return it to make things right.

I think I developed this strong sense of what was right and wrong when my mom would take me to church. Dad would never go, and it even got to the point when my mom stopped going and used Sunday mornings to read the Sunday *New York Times* in bed. But when she did take me I really concentrated on all that the preacher had to say, especially about sinning and its consequences. As a little girl I made sure that I never did anything wrong because I wanted to go to Paradise.

I wanted to be a "good girl," according to all that I had heard at church. As I got older, I found other things to do with my Sundays, but I never let go of my desire to do the right thing. I wanted Tyra to know how important it was for me to be a good person.

Chapter Twelve

I wanted to learn everything I could about Tyra, the White girl in my bed. Every time we had sex we would talk long into the night afterward. One night she said something I thought was really funny at that time.

"At least your folks don't have to worry about you getting pregnant," Tyra said.

It sounded so weird but I'm sure it was in the context of the after-sex conversation that we were having. I laughed like it was the funniest joke I had ever heard. For some strange reason, Tyra made me feel nervous, and a little sad. I thought that maybe I was being selfish, that I was not giving my parents what they really wanted from me. I knew my parents wanted grandchildren even though they never came out and said it.

Just talking with them on the phone, I sometimes got the impression, especially from my dad, that grandchildren would be the thing that would give my parents much comfort in their later years. It was like grandchildren would complete the circle of their lives. And I knew, being their only child, I was the only one who could do that for them. But with the way I was living my life, there was no possibility of grandchildren.

With Tyra's offhanded remark, I got the feeling that I was letting my parents down, that I wasn't living up to their expectations. And laying up under Tyra or any other girl wasn't getting me any closer to grandchildren. As a matter of fact, if I followed Tyra's example, I'd be a stone-cold lesbian, where there'd be no room in my life for a man, no possibility of grandchildren. And the way that Tyra talked about herself gave me the impression that she was stone-cold lesbian from day one and maybe even looking for a "wife." I had to let her know that I wasn't the one for that, but it seemed a little premature to get into that conversation with her.

The way I figured it back then, and she seemed to agree, was that she was staying with me just until she could save some money to get her own place, hopefully a big step up from the hole-in-the-wall she had inhabited at the Lord Sterling Motel. After all, I told myself, this was just some fun for me. And even though I wasn't involved with a man when I met Tyra, I wasn't opposed to that type of hookup and took the Pill faithfully, because whenever I got with a man I didn't want to fuss with condoms and contraceptive foams. Still, I couldn't deny the fact that I was totally involved with the White girl I found in my bed during that summer of 1999.

"Have you always been into women?" I had asked her.

"I've had high school boyfriends, but never any big sparks. Never any super-heavy affairs."

"But you like dildos?" I observed.

"Does that make me weird?"

"I know a lot of girls who are into dildos and vibrators."

"I like vibrators, when I'm by myself, but when I'm with a girl, I want a strap-on," Tyra told me. "Can I see your strap-on, Debrena?"

That evening I got out of bed and searched through the bottom of my lingerie drawer. I came out with my dildo and harness. It was a long black dildo with some serious thickness and leather straps I could secure around my waist and up between my legs like a thong.

"That's a nice one," Tyra said as she sat naked in the middle of my bed and, nonchalantly, rubbed herself between her widespread thighs.

I held up the black dildo and black leather harness and let Tyra admire it. I had bought it impulsively at a sex shop in New York City. Tyra held out her hands to hold it, and I reluctantly let it go. I had never let anyone use the dildo on me. Tyra grabbed it like an old friend. She stroked it, fondled it and then licked the fat head.

"You know how to suck it," I had to tell her.

"I told you, I've had some boyfriends, all through high school. When I got into college, although I didn't stay long enough to graduate, I got into girls heavy. I don't want anything to do with men now; too many games. Too many lies."

Because I didn't want to get into all that with Tyra, I said, "Suck it, Tyra. Show me how you work it."

Tyra sucked it, sucked it good. Her technique was a turn-on. The way she wet it with her mouth sent chills up and down my spine. She used her long, pink tongue to lick up and down the full length, then she deep throated most of the nine-inch dildo.

53

"Girl, I know the guys miss you," I said between giggles.

"That's not all I can do," Tyra assured me.

Keep it light, I told myself, but I wasn't sure if I was talking to my new lover or myself. I'm sure I could've gone on and on reminiscing about Tyra if the phone hadn't rung so loudly in my living room. It was Lorrie calling, and she wanted to stop by to talk with me. Without hesitation, I invited her over.

When Lorrie arrived I lead her into my kitchen, which was where we had our most intense one-on-one conversation. Lorrie wore a short black denim jacket and matching short skirt over a black leotard. As she sat across from me at the kitchen table, I searched her face for any signs of physical abuse. There wasn't a mark on her caramel-colored skin.

"What's going on?" I wanted to know. "Why did Angela come to your place with Marcy?"

For some reason, which I couldn't put a name to, I just knew it had to be more than just a social visit. I tried to be patient and let Lorrie tell the story in her own way.

"Marcy wanted the meeting," Lorrie told me, giving me a crooked smile. "She had asked Angela about me before, but Angela refused to go into our history. I'm ancient history, D."

"Obviously Marcy didn't think so."

"I was the only one she knew about. Most of the girls Angela messed around with moved to New York City."

"So what did Marcy want from you?"

"All the gory details."

"And you told her?"

"Of course not; besides, there wasn't much to tell. We weren't that close. That time on your sundeck was the most intense we've ever been, and that was two years ago."

"That was heavy enough. And Angela did say she wanted to finish it. I heard her say that before I went back into the house to my housewarming party."

"We got together after that and had dinner at Malika's Place."

"Isn't that the new restaurant uptown?"

54   Lorrie smiled. "That's the one. After that we went to her apartment. I had a good time with her and wanted to see her again."

"You told Marcy that?"

"It was what Marcy came to hear. But my time with Angela was very brief. We got together a few more times, but I-I just couldn't go as far as Angela wanted me to. I wasn't looking for a girlfriend."

"And Angela was?"

"I don't know. I don't think so. But when we got together she wanted me to be more enthusiastic, more into it. She wanted us to get down like we were making love."

"And you couldn't do that?" I asked, looking at Lorrie twist her face like she was in pain.

"D, I can't make love if I don't care about the person. Do you love everybody you get down with?"

"No. I can't lie like that. But sometimes I see a girl I like, and I just go for it. I'm not looking for a forever lover. It's the same with some guys I've been with. It's just fun for me."

From the look on Lorrie's face, it was obvious that she thought it should be more.

"Well, it's always a little more than that for me," Lorrie let me know. "Anyway, Angela just wasn't satisfied with the way I performed in bed."

"Did she say that?"

"Not in those exact words. But the last time we were together, she suggested that I not even bother to take my clothes off."

"That bad?"

"We touched and kissed but I was, uh, distracted. Angela said I should be where I really wanted to be."

"What did you tell her?"

"I told her that that wasn't possible."

"How long ago was this, Lorrie?"

"About a year and a half."

I was surprised, shocked really, because I couldn't see Lorrie being celibate for that long. "I really thought you were dealing with Angela on the regular."

"A lot of people thought that. But I don't care what people think. They don't know my heart."

"Is that all that Marcy wanted to know? That you were once involved with Angela?"

"More or less. Marcy's in love with Angela."

"Just like that?"

"It doesn't take a long time to fall in love."

"I'm just a little surprised. Earlier today you tell me they moved in together, now you're telling me that Marcy is in love with Angela."

"Marcy just wants to make sure that the field is clear. If I'm not in there, Marcy feels Angela is all hers."

"And what does Angela say about all this closeness?"

"She didn't say anything in front of me. She followed Marcy into my apartment and they sat on my couch. Marcy did all the talking."

"And she didn't feel like a fool?"

"Marcy held Angela's hand while Marcy interrogated me. D, I almost laughed in the girl's face. She was too intense, like a *NYPD Blue* detective."

"Is this the first time Marcy dealt with a girl?"

"As far as I know."

"And you answered all her silly questions?"

"All the ones I could. I wasn't about to give dates and positions, but I did tell her that we enjoyed ourselves."

"But that wasn't true, was it? I got the impression that—"

Lorrie cut me off. "I enjoyed it, D. I just wasn't all into it, like Angela wanted me to be. I wasn't looking for love. Not there."

"And Marcy was satisfied with what you told her?"

"She hugged me and kissed me before she left."

"Did Angela hug you and kiss you?"

"Angela only hugs and kisses when she's about to get down. She stood near the door while Marcy did her Miss Grateful number."

"Sounds pathetic to me," I said, half-joking.

But I guess that Lorrie didn't see any humor in the situation because she didn't even crack a smile. She even looked a little sad, a little pathetic herself. Because she was my best friend, I wanted to reach out to comfort her, but I didn't want to start anything I wasn't prepared to finish, so I held myself back.

"Well, I'm just glad it didn't turn into a catfight," I said, trying to bring an end to the conversation.

Lorrie stood to leave. "At least Marcy's happy."

I stood. "You know I'll never be able to look at Marcy and Angela in the same way. Not after all that you told me."

Lorrie didn't say anything.

"How long you think it's going to last?" I asked Lorrie as we walked to the front door.

"Angela's not ready to settle down," Lorrie told me, then pulled her jean jacket around her, like she was cold. "Like someone else we know."

I knew she was talking about me, but I didn't rise to that bait. If I was to get into anything with Lorrie or any other girl, they had to know where I stood. I wasn't looking for a girlfriend. Besides that, I had met a real cute guy that evening. And although I had no plans to do anything with his business card, that little interlude at Stella's told me something about myself.

I was more than ready to lose myself in the loving arms of a man. I had to laugh to myself, knowing how good that would make my parents feel. That would definitely make me the daughter they dreamed I was. But I didn't know if I could make that kind of sacrifice for my parents. Still, giving my parents grandchildren would be like giving them blessings from Paradise.

But I felt that deep down inside that just wasn't me. And I couldn't fake the funk like that.

"You get some rest," I told Lorrie as I opened the front door. "We have rehearsal in the morning."

"I can pick you up," Lorrie suggested, and I knew if I turned her down, she'd be crushed.

To prove to myself that I wasn't completely selfish, I said, "Sounds good to me."

"I'll call you in morning."

A sad-faced Lorrie hugged me, then kissed me gently on my cheek. As she stepped out into the dark, still night, I watched her from my front porch. She walked quickly to her car and didn't look back at me until she sat under the steering wheel. Lorrie waved shyly at me then blew her horn before she pulled off.

57

When I finally got into my bedroom, I threw myself across the bed. I was too tired to take my clothes off. I felt used up, emotionally drained, like there was just too much pulling at me. I looked over at the clock and saw that it was 12:01, the first minute of a new day.

Chapter Thirteen

Tamara Tucker said yes.

Shay Epps said yes.

LaTasha Brown said yes.

Kammie Youngblood said yes.

Erica Harper said yes.

LaToya Baskerville said, "It seems like a great idea. Yes."

I voted yes and Lorrie did the same.

Marcy didn't have to say anything because it was her idea. And Angela, standing beside Marcy, just nodded in agreement, which was what everyone expected.

"So, we'll do it," Dominique St. Claire said to seal the deal. "We will do the calendar as a fundraiser for the fall season."

"Who will take the photos?" Little Erica wanted to know. At five-four, she was the smallest girl in the company and we quickly branded her the nickname Little Erica.

When she once told me she wore a size zero, I couldn't believe it. I didn't realize they made clothes that small for women. But what she lacked in size, she more than made up with her big mouth. Erica was on top of all the gossip. And I don't mean that in a malicious way. She always had her ears open, and she was never shy about repeating what she had heard. Still, she was the cutest thing with her light skin and curly black hair. She was a great dancer who began every rehearsal with a prayer.

Dominique smiled at Little Erica. "We have someone lined up, and you'll meet him soon."

"Is he a cute guy?" Kammie wanted to know.

I laughed because I didn't see what that had to do with anything, but Kammie was persistent. She asked again, "Is he cute?"

At five-ten, standing near Little Erica, Kammie was impossible to ignore. In a tiny cropped top, she had boobs for days and a tight waist. And her belly button stuck out like a knob of flesh above her baggy black shorts. Below that she was all shapely legs and bare feet.

"I don't see what that has to do with anything," Dominique said, echoing my exact thoughts, "but he's not hard to look at. I think he's what you girls call 'eye candy.'"

Everybody laughed at that, except Kammie who was deter-   59
mined to let everybody know that her concerns were not frivolous.
"I'm asking 'cause the cuter the photographer is, the more I'm inspired. My pictures for the beauty pageant were so good because the photographer was so darn cute."

Then Kammie Youngblood gave her winning smile, one guaranteed to win future beauty contest. And I had to admit, she was a stunner with her mocha-colored skin; long, straight hair; muscular arms and legs; and big, brown, almond-shaped eyes.

"The photographer is from NTA," Domnique let us know.

As a former Miss Black Teenager, Kammie got the highest scores for poise, swimsuit, beauty and talent. Dominique discovered her on the stage of Harlem's Apollo Theater, although Kammie was a New Jersey native, specifically from Elizabeth.

We hadn't even begun the day's work when an overly excited Marcy told us that Dominique wanted to speak to us as a group. She really didn't have to run the idea about the 2000 calendar as a fundraiser by us, but Dominique always wanted us to have a sense of ownership of the company when it came to policies or decisions that would affect all of us. If the Nelson Talent Agency was involved, it would mean that the project would be professional and expensive. But maybe not too expensive because Dominique was close friends with Carrie Nelson who owned the talent promotion agency, along with her daughter, Dany Nelson.

My only concern was how revealing the shots would be. I never minded showing a little skin for the cause but I told myself that I wasn't going to get scandalous. But I had to wonder if we'd be pre-sented as professional dancers or hot chicks. I had no problem with being a hot chick, but I didn't want to have my sexuality exploited to make some money for our dance team. I felt secure in the fact that Dominique, like my mom who was from Dominique's generation, always did everything with good taste and style.

For example, our costumes were always colorful, but never revealing. Never so tight that you felt like you were naked onstage. Yet, all the SOS dancers were proud of their bodies, but not one of us wanted to be seen as just a body. We had brains, talent and skill, and we wanted everyone who came to any of our recitals to know that. We were crowd pleasers, not dick teasers.

I was toweling the sweat off my face when LaTasha came over to me. At five-ten she could look me straight in my eyes. She was a big girl with wide shoulders, and I had no doubt that she intimi-dated most people. But it was established long ago that I was not in that number. Everybody knew if you pushed me, I'd push back, twice as hard.

"Are we still going to get together?" LaTasha asked, coming at me with the laser beams she called eyes.

"I said we will, LaTasha."

Her light brown eyes seemed to glow as she stood before me. "I really want to get this, Debrena."

"LaTasha," I said, like I was talking to some child.

"Yeah."

"LaTasha, I said I would work with you and I will."

She stood before me in a gray sweat-stained tank top cut off at the bottom to reveal her tight waist. "'Cause Shay asked me to remind you."

I heard her loud and clear but I got the impression she was speaking for herself. I nodded in understanding but I knew that the girl was not finished with me.

"I really want to do good," LaTasha let me know. "I believe we got the routine down, but I want you and Lorrie to look at us before Miss Dominique sees us."

LaTasha hung out with Shay and Erica. They wanted me to critique the routine they were working on for the upcoming summer production. Lorrie called them the Three Hood Rats because they were all born and raised in a downtown housing project. When Dominique met them they were more jocks than dancers, and played a mean game of basketball. But because they were so into their strong bodies and loved funky music, they became more than decent urban team dancers.

"Like I said, LaTasha, if you girls are willing to stay at the studio one day after our regular rehearsal, I'm more than willing to work with you."

I knew that nothing I said at that time could erase all of her anxiety but I also knew that it would be a long day at the studio if I didn't give her some reassurance. And because I had been there in my early days with Dominique, I was a lot nicer to LaTasha than she deserved because her pushiness was a stone-cold turn-off.

"Okay, but don't go easy on us," LaTasha said unnecessarily, and I almost lost it right then and there. *Who does this girl think she's dealing with?* I thought. She almost got on my last nerve! "Even if we complain. Don't let up. Be like Dominique, Debrena."

I could never be like Dominique St. Claire, I wanted to shout out to LaTasha. Dominique was a dance legend, a diva for sure. When she began her dance company in 1975, I wasn't even born. With all the time Dominique put in, with no professional training, there was no way I could match that. But I could show Dominique that I appreciated all the time she had invested in me by helping out anyway I could.

That was why for the past five years, I had been donating my time to costuming and coaching. Sometime ago I began sketching out my costume ideas and sharing them with Lorrie. She encouraged me in this direction, like I encouraged her to pursue her interest in stage makeup. She was the one who hooked everybody up backstage or when we had our girls' night out on the town.

That usually meant dancing the night away at some club. She was so good at hooking us up that I called her a makeup artist. I even encouraged Lorrie to apply for a part-time job at NTA. Because we were always looking for extra cash, I told her that photographers down there had to need somebody who was good at doing makeup. I didn't think that Lorrie took me seriously until she showed me some Polaroids with the different styles of makeup she had mastered.

All her models were SOS dancers; still there was no denying her talent as a makeup artist. As for my coaching, I never got tired of helping my sister dancers improve their technique. They all had the talent but the self-confidence wasn't always there. That was where my coaching came in. I was more than happy to assist them. Even with hood rats like LaTasha who didn't know how to ask for help.

62

Before she left my presence that afternoon, LaTasha pinned me down to a day and a time after rehearsal. Because she was so pretty, I found it hard to be angry with her.

Chapter Fourteen

Oh, that feels so good," I exclaimed, the pleasure coming from my feet and spreading like a wildfire throughout my body. I truly felt like I had died and gone to Paradise, and all Lorrie was doing was giving me a foot massage. It was Lorrie's idea, and I let her do it with the thought that I would return the favor. It was the evening after a full day of rehearsal, and I really needed it. And Lorrie really gave it to me as she sat between my bare legs.

We were in my living room, and she was making me feel, oh, so good. I tried not to moan too loudly because we were not alone. I opened my eyes and saw Tamara come into the living room with some goodies from the kitchen.

"Where are your clothes, girl?" I asked because when I let her into my house earlier she was covered from shoulders to ankles in an unflattering bulky white sweat suit and ratty-looking white sneakers. When I saw what she wore under that getup, I was somewhat surprised.

"I'm dressed," Tamara let me know, her voice squeaky and defensive. But not too defensive because she knew I was joking with her; I wanted her to be comfortable in my house. As quiet as it was kept, I enjoyed looking at her in her skimpy outfit.

Lorrie, who sat on a small wooden stool at my feet, looked over her shoulder at Tamara who boldly walked around me in a well-washed black body suit and nothing else. The one piece was so well worn it was almost sheer, emphasizing fat nipples and a thick V between her shapely thighs. I appreciated her even more when she turned her back toward us. She had a high, round African booty, and she knew it, telling me once that the guys from her high school nick-named her Sweet Cheeks. Of course, I would never call her that but I had to agree with those guys. And it was good that she had so much in the back because her chest was almost flat.

Still, she was a beauty with her shoulder-length dark brown hair and thick eyelashes over dark brown eyes. She was three years out of high school, no longer a child.

"She is dressed," Lorrie said, then turned her attention back to me. She put my feet into a yellow plastic pail of water.

"Barely dressed," I said as Lorrie continued to massage my feet. In Tamara's small hands was a bowl of microwave popcorn.

"Don't get any of that on my floor," I scolded her playfully.

"Relax, Debrena," Tamara told me. "I got this."

Tamara sat across from me in my favorite armchair. She then shoved another fistful of butter-soaked popcorn into her wide mouth, which was fascinating because her lips were so thin over her small white teeth.

"Nobody's coming over for another two hours or so," I let her know, although I knew it didn't make any difference to her. She was obviously where she wanted to be and totally relaxed.

I had invited my sister dancers over for an afternoon of relaxation. And I had to admit my reasons weren't totally selfless; I figured the more people I had around me, the less I would think about Tyra. I also had to admit that I was a little fragile and vulnerable during my emotional recovery. Still, I didn't think I could last a year without it. I had to laugh to myself because I didn't think I could last six months without sex, especially with little honeys like Tamara prancing around my house half-naked.

Lorrie took my feet out of the water and patted them dry. "I think D is asking you why you came over so early."

"I like hanging out with you guys," Tamara informed us.

"You sure you didn't come over for a free pedicure?" I asked, still teasing Tamara while looking down at Lorrie and all the spa products she had around her.

"We do that to each other at my place," Tamara said, then smiled.

She lived in a two-bedroom apartment with Shay and Kammie.

"I just had to get out of the house," Tamara told us. "They're great girls but a change of scenery is always good. You know what I'm talking about."

On my CD player, which was plugged into my downstairs sound system, was Eddie Kendricks' *Ultimate Collection* CD blaring but not too loud. And even though "Girl You Need a Change of Mind" was almost eight minutes, it came and went too quickly. I thought about getting up to start it again but I couldn't move because Lorrie began to clip my toes.

That was when Tamara came over to look at my feet. "Why the square shape?" she asked Lorrie.

"Because the square shape is much healthier," Lorrie, the professional, schooled her. "It prevents ingrown nails."

That sounded good to me and I said nothing as Lorrie worked oil into my cuticles.

Still standing near us Tamara said, "I guess y'all heard about Marcy and Angela?"

I looked down at Lorrie, and she looked up at me. I knew I hadn't heard anything about those two, not since they paid Lorrie that evening visit, but I was sure that that was old news that Tamara knew nothing about.

"Marcy locked Angela out of her own apartment," Tamara told us, eager to dish the 4-1-1.

"How is that?" I wanted to know as Lorrie began to buff my feet. "If I'm paying rent on my spot, there is no way anybody is locking me out."

"I heard that," Lorrie said and chuckled, and I realized that I said it a lot more forceful than I intended to.

"I mean, if I'm paying I set the rules," I said, trying to clean it up a little bit.

"Marcy doesn't like Angela running around on her," Tamara explained. "I guess if they're living together, Marcy feels that they're exclusive."

"Marcy doesn't know Angela as well as she thinks she does," Lorrie said, putting in her two cents.

"Angela came home late, and Marcy wouldn't open the door," Tamara told us. "Angela had to call the building manager."

"And Angela got back in," I said, adding my happy ending to this dyke drama.

Lorrie was making me feel so good by moisturizing and massaging my feet that I felt like singing "Joy to the World."

"The building manager opened the door, but Marcy had the chain on," Tamara said, then laughed out loud.

Lorrie chuckled as she ran her fingers up and down the center, then back and forth beneath the balls of my feet.

66 "And who told you all this?" I was curious to know.

"Big mouth," Tamara said, like Erica's big mouth always spoke the gospel truth.

"You can't believe everything you hear," Lorrie cautioned Tamara.

"I know, Lorrie," Tamara said. "But I believe that. I saw those two in the locker room, kissing and squeezing on each other's bare butts when they thought nobody was looking."

Lorrie looked up but said nothing. I was about to say something when Tamara hit us with a hard one.

"I can't understand what would make two pretty girls go that way," Tamara thought out loud.

There wasn't anything I cared to say to that. Lorrie got real busy painting my toenails with peachy-pink polish. As I leaned back on the couch, I realized that Tamara Tucker didn't know as much as she thought she did.

Chapter Fifteen

When LaToya and Shay walked into my house with grocery bags in their arms, Lorrie asked, "Shay, I know you didn't forget the tape."

Shay looked over at LaToya and laughed out loud. "And if I did?"

"I'd send your rusty ass back to get it."

"Toya, Lorrie doesn't have any faith in me," Shay said, still smiling.

"You play too much," Lorrie said, her arms crossed beneath her breasts.

"I know you, girl. Like my momma used to say, 'you'd forget your head if it wasn't attached to your shoulders,'" Lorrie said.

When Shay stepped farther into the house, Lorrie put a hand in Shay's chest.

"Is this any way to treat a guest in Debrena's house?" Shay asked, looking past Lorrie at me. "Don't trip. I got your movie. My daddy recorded it."

Lorrie put out a hand. "Hand it over."

Shay reached into her bag and handed Lorrie the videotape.

Lorrie took the tape and playfully said, "Bitch."

"Takes one to know one," Shay said, just as playfully. A smiling Lorrie took the *Temptations* movie from her.

LaToya handed her grocery bag to Tamara who also grabbed Shay's bag and took them both into the kitchen for me.

"How's it going?" Shay asked me.

"Okay," I told her.

"Who's here?" Shay wanted to know.

"Just us so far," I told her, indicating Lorrie, Tamara, me and now her and LaToya.

Tamara returned to the living room with another bowl of popcorn, looking at Shay's short blond hair. Shay had recently dyed it, and she was striking, the color really complimenting her gold skin tone. She was five-seven and had all the hips and boobs that Tamara could only dream about.

68

"That smells so good," Shay said, looking hard at the bowl of popcorn in Tamara's lap. "I want some."

Without being invited, Shay tried to sit on Tamara's lap and dig into the popcorn. Tamara just wasn't having it. *I'm going to have to put a sign on that chair,* I thought as Shay and Tamara carried on like Bebe's kids in my favorite chair.

"If y'all break that chair, one of y'all is going to have to pay for it," I told the two crazy chicks.

They both laughed, Shay a lot harder than Tamara who was really trying hard to get Shay off her lap. And she didn't stop trying until Shay was on the floor.

"I don't want you sitting on me, Shay," Tamara told her, suddenly sounding serious.

Shay hit the floor with a loud thump, but the way she giggled, it was obvious that her natural cushioning kept her from hurting herself. Still, she hit the floor pretty hard.

"I don't want no girl hanging all over me," Tamara fired off.

From the floor, Shay said, "But I love you, Tamara."

A shocked Tamara snapped, "I'm not gay!"

"You shouldn't knock it if you haven't tried it," Shay continued, still in spirit of mad fun, speaking to Tamara as she lay on the floor.

Suddenly Tamara stood. "Shay, you are disgusting! I'm not into that freaky shit!"

I raised my eyebrow and looked over at Lorrie. She gave me a sly smile. LaToya stood near the door, like she wasn't sure that she wanted to join this "all girl party." She had her thick hair pulled back into a ponytail. The hairstyle made her forehead look big but there was no denying her natural beauty. And because she wore no make-up, I could almost count the freckles across her wide face.

They were all new girls in the company. That was one reason why Lorrie and I were so eager to help them.

"Shay, you need to stop with all that gay mess," Tamara told her, and it was obvious that she was not playing.

"You know I'm just messin' wit' you," Shay told Tamara.

"That shit is not funny, Shay. I don't play like that."

"I know you're not gay, Tamara, and you know I'm not."

That was when Shay got off the floor and tried to console Tamara but Tamara just wasn't having it. She pushed Shay away.

"You're really serious about this," Shay said, sounding a little hurt.

"I'm not going to stay here if you keep up with that gay mess."

"Okay, okay, my bad," Shay said apologetically. "I didn't know you were so sensitive."

Tamara used both hands to wipe the tears from her face.

"Do you know I almost didn't join this dance team behind that?" Tamara told Shay as Shay rose to her feet. "Every time I talked about dance, everybody pointed me to Marcus Salley. You know why?"

Shay stood beside Tamara and shook her head.

"There are girls and guys in the Marcus Salley Dance Company," Tamara explained, emphasizing her point with a finger aimed at Shay, but I got the feeling it was also pointed at Lorrie and me. "Dominique is all girls."

"So?" LaToya said, obviously ready to defend Dominique's professional reputation.

"All girls, Toya?" Tamara said forcefully, like there was no way we could not see her point. "All girls together, 'they got to be doin' each other' is what some people think."

"Bullshit, Tam!" LaToya said, her face suddenly red. "We're athletes. We work out together. We shower together, do the locker room scene like the guys. Anybody says there's something more than that is sick, just sick. You hear me?"

69

"Some people think that," Tamara said in a much calmer voice.

"Well, they think wrong," LaToya said, her voice suddenly soft. "I'm not about that, I've never been about that. And if anybody says I am, then they're in line for a serious beat down."

"All I can say is just look at Marcy and Angela, the way they carry on," Tamara said, like a lawyer resting her case.

"I heard the rumors but—" LaToya began and didn't seem to have enough steam to finish.

"Look, I'm not one to spread anybody's business," Tamara said, cutting LaToya off, like she wanted to be done with this who's gay, who's not business. "But Erica told me about those two, and Erica has no reason to lie."

"I got to talk to Erica about this," LaToya said, obviously disturbed.

"I'm not lying, Toya," Tamara said.

"I didn't say you were, Tam. But this demands some further investigation."

"I don't care what they do behind closed doors," Tamara said. "I just don't want everybody talking junk about the SOS crew."

"I still want to talk to Erica," LaToya persisted.

"If you do, don't tell her that I said anything. All I'm saying is that if Angela and Marcy need to keep it on the down low, okay. But I just don't want that mess hanging over me. I don't want anybody questioning my womanhood."

"I heard that," Shay said as she dug her hand into Tamara's popcorn, nodding like she was in the amen corner.

I took a peek at Lorrie as she shook her head, as if to say these girls are bugging. I knew this conversation would be revisited. And that made me nervous and somewhat angry. I definitely didn't want to get into anything like that that particular evening. *Damn,* I thought, *all I wanted to do was chill, eat some junk food and watch the* Temptations *TV movie.*

Chapter Sixteen

I want to finish it," Lorrie said long after the girls had left.

I took a long, hot shower and came into my bedroom wrapped in a thick gold towel. Lorrie had everything for my massage on my night table.

"This has turned out to be a real spa day for me," I said as I lay facedown on my bed.

My whole body tingled when Lorrie ran her moist fingers on the back of my neck, just below the hairline.

"You are so stiff here," Lorrie said, telling me something I knew all too well.

I really enjoyed having my sister dancers over to my house, but there were some hairy moments. One good thing was that Marcy and Angela decided not to make an appearance. With everyone there, I knew that the fallout would've been heard from near and far. And I agreed with Tamara, I, too, didn't want a whole lot of people talking about our dance team.

Still, I needed to relax. That was one reason that I accepted Lorrie's most generous offer to help me clean up after the girls had left.

"That shit with Tamara," I said and exhaled loudly. "Why did she come out like that?"

"She's new to many aspects of the dance world," Lorrie said as she worked my shoulders. "She's new to our crew. She hasn't learned that people will talk even when there's nothing to talk about."

"Tamara is an excellent dancer. I'd hate to see her drop out behind some mess like that."

"D, you're so tense here."

"I'm trying so hard to relax."

"You must relax. We have so much to do."

"I know, Lorrie. That's good. Right there, so good."

"Lower?" Lorrie asked.

"Yes, yes."

"Let me know if I'm being too rough."

"You're good, Lorrie. You know, we have to keep these girls together."

"We'll work with LaTasha and Erica and Shay."

"Not just them."

"All the girls," Lorrie said.

"Yes."

"They all seem eager to do well."

"I know," I said in agreement with Lorrie. "That darn LaTasha is so aggressive."

"She'll be all right."

"But Tamara is not like that. LaToya is not like that."

"Neither is Kammie. I like her a lot," I had to add.

"They're all serious dancers. Dominique wouldn't have picked them if they weren't."

"I know that, Lorrie. I just feel that this summer concert has to be the best."

"I can't believe that the Dominique St. Claire Dance Studio is celebrating its twenty-fifth anniversary."

"I talked to Dominique recently, and she can't believe it herself."

I wanted to say more but I couldn't say anything because Lorrie worked my lower back so good, really digging into it and pressing out all that tension. All I could do was moan.

"I'm gonna push this towel down," Lorrie said.

There was nothing I wanted to say about that. I just arched my body as Lorrie dug her fingers into my spine. It felt so good that my legs began to tremble. She was a great makeup artist and an excellent masseuse, giving her two big things to fall back on if dance didn't work out.

At that moment I envied her, and I got a little scared, knowing that I had nothing to fall back on. All I knew was dance. That's all I ever wanted to know. If I couldn't make it with that, there was nothing else for me.

Because I didn't want to depress myself, I let my body melt beneath Lorrie's magic fingers. By this time, the towel was spread out beneath me, leaving my bottom bare.

"Lorrie."

"What's up, D?"

"I need you to help me keep this company together."

"Hasn't Dominique done that for the past twenty-five years?"   73

"She has but we're the only two from the old crew; all the other girls are new. And Dominique has been doing so much running around lately," I informed Lorrie.

"I'll help you, you know that. Just relax now."

Her voice was a whisper in the room, her hands moved over the rise of my booty. The oil dripped between my cheeks, making me hotter and hotter. And I couldn't have been wetter between my legs. *Do it, do it,* I silently pleaded. It felt so good.

Then I came to my good senses. It would have been good to cum, but then I would've had to deal with the guilt of knowing that I had used my friend. I wanted to let it all hang out but I had promised myself not to go down that "Lover's Road" with Lorrie. It was so hard, especially with my booty bare in my bedroom, hot with Lorrie hands on me. But I had to be strong, I told myself. I had to be strong for Lorrie and myself.

Suddenly I pushed myself forward, rolled over on my back and then sat up in the bed. Lorrie looked at me strangely as I rested my back against the headboard and pulled my knees up to my chest. I knew there was no way I could completely cover my nakedness but my sudden move gave me some distance from Lorrie's erotic intentions. I knew I was acting like a wishy-washy bitch but that was the only way I could fight the battle raging inside me. I felt to give in would not be good for Lorrie or myself.

Lorrie looked at me with sad eyes. "I think I should leave."

She said that but she made no move to go.

"Please, don't," I said, touching her arm.

She looked at me, wanting me to say more.

"Leave in the morning," I suggested.

"What's going to happen if I stay?" Lorrie wanted to know.

"I just don't want to be alone tonight."

"Is that all?"

"That's all I can handle."

Lorrie nodded like that was all right, but we both knew it was far away from what she really wanted. Or what she expected. Because she understood me not wanting to be alone, Lorrie laid with me spoon fashion, my back to her front, under a light sheet. She put her arms around my waist and let me fall asleep.

Chapter Seventeen

Lorrie left in the middle of the night. I found it a little hard to look her directly in her eyes the next morning when she came to pick me up. Although we hadn't crossed the line, I felt we had gone way beyond friendship. Lorrie had not become my lover but the early-morning tension between us signaled that it was only a matter of time. After sleeping in my bed with the smell of Lorrie's skin in my bedsheets, I couldn't shake the feeling that we had turned a corner in our ongoing relationship.

It was like a prelude to something more, and there was so much I needed to say to her. But I swallowed all of that, letting it sit in the bottom of my stomach like a lead weight. So, when she came to pick me up, we rode in her car, listened to the radio and made small talk. The only topic of substance we tackled was my hair. Lorrie suggested that I think about adding some highlights.

I explained to her that I didn't want to think about that because I was going low maintenance all the way. That I was more than happy with the way it was.

Once in the dance studio, we walked up the stairs to the second floor. There was an elevator but none of the dancers ever rode it. The long boxy elevator was for visitors. All of our in-town performances were at the Frederick Douglass Community Center where many of us, including Lorrie and myself, moonlighted as exercise leaders or hip-hop dance instructors. The second floor on the corner of Livingston and First streets was for dancing and the business of the Dominique St. Claire Dance Studio.

As founder and artistic director of the company, Dominique held court there, sometimes seven days a week. "This is your home away from home," Dominique once said to me. I got the impression that she spent more time at the dance studio than anywhere else.

"This is her home," Lorrie once told me and, somewhat reluctantly, I had to agree.

There was something elegant and sad about Dominique. She was a diva but life didn't seem as full as it should've been for her. From all the time I hung around her, and from conversations with my parents, I got the sense that she spent a lot of time alone. It was obviously her choice, but it seemed so sad to me that this beautiful, vibrant woman didn't have anybody to be with.

It was as if life had passed her by and there was nothing to keep her going. There was no doubt in my mind that she had many sweet memories but I always felt that life was an ongoing adventure, not a place where you stopped and stood like a spectator watching a New York style ticker tape parade.

I once tried to explain this to Lorrie but all she said was, "You're getting too deep for me, girl."

I just wanted her to see why we should feel a little sorry for Dominique. And I wasn't sorry that I had shared my deepest thoughts with Lorrie, because although she said she didn't quite understand, she listened to me, and that was more important than anything else was. As we walked up the stairs, Lorrie kept going on about my hair.

"Now you're a makeup artist and a hairstylist?" I asked sarcastically as I pushed through the double doors that lead into the studio.

We came in dressed in our dance clothes so there was no need for us to visit the locker room. Everybody was there and I immediately noticed Dominique huddled in a corner with LaToya, Erica and Shay. Dominique wore black leggings and a skintight leopard top. The girls around her wore colored tops and black biking shorts.

Lorrie and I greeted all the girls. We hugged and kissed like we had been apart for days when the reality was that it was only the day before we were together, all except Marcy, Angela and Erica. The ten girls of the company were as close as family because that was the way Dominique wanted it; she always reminded us that we were "all in this thing together." She had handpicked us, and she always told us that we were the "best of the best."

We had no doubt that we were the best because Dominique worked us hard and never let us think we should give less because we were performing for a small audience at the Frederick Douglass Community Center or a large crowd on the road. "You give your all every time you hit the performance floor" was Dominique's motto. And that thought was deeply implanted in our minds, our bodies and our souls. When the SOS dancers performed for the Dominique St. Claire Dance Studio, we always danced our hearts out.

Chapter Eighteen

I bet your ears were burning this morning," Dominique said when she got over to me. I looked around for Lorrie and found her deep in conversation with Tamara and LaToya. Because I wasn't sure what Dominique was trying to tell me, I knew I looked clueless. But Dominique was always patient with me. "I've been talking about you all morning. First to your mother."

"Mom called you?"

"No. I called her."

"About me?"

"No, not about you. I told her that you're doing okay. I called her to give her an update on Cheeba."

I knew that "Cheeba" was an affectionate nickname for chore-ographer Marcus Salley. His intimate friends like Mom, Dominique, Slappy Martin and Slappy's late wife, Stella, called him that because as a young man Marcus Salley smoked more than a little marijuana. "It was his recreational drug of choice for a long time," Mom once told me. But she wasn't condemning her friend, she was just telling it like it was. I also knew that Marcus Salley had been in and out of the hospital during the past year.

"I told Sandra that Cheeba is not doing so good," Dominique went on, her big brown eyes sad. "Not good at all."

I felt bad because I hadn't spoken to Mom or Dad in two weeks. *I have to give them a call,* I told myself.

"Sandra wanted to come home right away," Dominique let me know. "But I told her Cheeba is holding strong. He's back home now, able to do some things for himself. He doesn't want to be a burden to anybody. He's so thin now."

I nodded, trying hard to understand as best as I could. Everyone who knew Marcus Salley knew that the founder of the Marcus Salley Dance Company had been diagnosed with HIV in 1985. It was now June of 1999 and he was still holding strong.

"But I wanted to talk about something good for you, Debrena."

I gave Dominique my full attention.

"You ever hear of Walter McCary?"

A thrill ran through my body. "Oh yes! I have all of his CDs. Even from the early days when most people accused him of trying to sing Black."

Dominique laughed, and then frowned, obviously amused and saddened by the narrow minds of some people. "The man sings from his soul. That makes him a 'soul singer' in my book. Race has nothing to do with it."

All I could say to that was a silent *amen.*

Walter McCary was White but there was no denying his soulfulness. I had to sell Lorrie on him because she, like many brothers and sisters, wanted to dismiss him as just another Michael Bolton. But I felt that Walter McCary was right up there with Chico DeBarge, Brian McKnight, Joe, Kenny Lattimore or Eric Benet, all of whom were hot that summer.

I once read in *Billboard* magazine that Walter McCary considered himself a "student of soul music." And I had to give him props for that.

"I also got a call this morning from Janis Wilson," Dominique told me.

I had heard of Janis Wilson but had no idea what she looked like. She had been a dancer with the company long before my time. She had moved to California and got involved in the music business. First, as a singer, mostly backup, then as a manager for many up-and-coming West Coast artists. As I stood there, I still couldn't see what any of that history had to do with me.

"She's working now as Walter McCary's personal assistant," Dominique said. "She's in town, at the Plaza. She's going to stop by today. She's looking for dancers for Walter McCary's next video. I recommended you and Lorrie."

I felt like jumping up and down! I didn't do that but I smiled so hard my cheeks ached.

"She can't promise anything," Dominique made it clear. "But she will check you and Lorrie out and see what she can do for you two."

I couldn't stop smiling.

Dominique held up a finger. "No promises now."

"I know, but just the thought of her coming will make me dance my best."

"You would do that anyway, right?"

"Yes, Dominique. You know what I mean."

She smiled, then said, "I know what you mean. Let me go and tell Lorrie the news. Then we'll get into our work."

I danced away from Dominique and began my isolations, my warmups. I did them from head to toe. When I was on my hand isolations, I looked over and saw Dominique talking to Lorrie. I winked at Lorrie when she finished talking with Dominique. She gave me a shy wave and a big smile.

I finished my isolations on my toes, and my body was warm inside my black tights and yellow body suit. As a group, we went through our routines with Eddie Kendricks' stirring voice floating over us from powerful hidden speakers. And somewhere behind the two-way mirror that ran the length of the dance floor, Dominique watched all of us. I had no way of being sure, but I felt that Janis Wilson was looking at Lorrie and me and ready to tell Walter McCary what great dancers we were.

Chapter Nineteen

Well into the rehearsal we were all dripping with sweat, but still smiling because we were so deep into our passion. Not once did Dominique come from behind the two-way mirror to correct us. We did our pivot turns, crossovers, hip swivels, plies, all in unison for our ensemble pieces, moving as one, like a great dance company should. The last half of the rehearsal was devoted to work on our individual projects.

"I don't want to do too much more here," I told Lorrie. "Let's get out of here, grab some lunch."

Lorrie nodded, and then stood with her mouth wide open, like she was looking at something she just couldn't believe. I looked over my shoulder to see Dominique coming over to us, and she was not alone. *This has to be Janis Wilson,* I thought. She looked ghetto fabulous in a scalloped-edged halter and a full skirt, showcasing her thick bare legs and Lucite sandals. There were diamond studs in her ears, and she wore her hair in sexy, dark brown ringlets.

Dominique made all the introductions.

"You two were just great," Janis Wilson gushed.

Standing there with Lorrie, Dominique and me, Janis was the shortest, but her figure was impressive with small, well-shaped breasts; a thick waist; and round booty. She looked like a California girl who worked out but not as much as she should've. Janis was a little thick around the middle, and if I saw her on the street, I would've never imagined her to be a former dancer. Still, the girl had a lot of energy about her, and she came across that afternoon as positive and eager to please.

"I want to know more about this thing with Walter McCary," Lorrie said, her face shiny with excitement.

Janis smiled at Dominique, and then turned toward Lorrie and me. "Well, I really believe that 2000 will be Walter's year. He's been in the background much too long."

"What about that cover story in *People* magazine?" Lorrie asked. "Wasn't that just a week ago?"

"That was great," Janis agreed, "but it was mostly about Vonda." Vonda was Walter McCary's blond, superstar-model girlfriend.

"We want Walter to blow up in 2000," Janis shared with us. "His new CD is doing well but we want it to reach number one."

82

"What song is the video for?" I wanted to know.

"The video will be for a song Walter wrote for Vonda, 'A Dream.'"

" 'A Dream,' " I shouted. "That's my favorite song on the CD. I love dancing to that song."

"Like I told Dominique," Janis went on, "I can't promise anything."

I nodded but in my mind I was entertaining the very real possibility of my dance career taking off big time.

I barely heard Janis say, "I have to look at some other dancers. Some in New York and some from Marcus Salley."

I was not intimidated by the mention of the Marcus Salley dancers or even the New York dancers. There were very few dancers who could hang with the Sisters of Soul; as for the New York dancers, it didn't matter who they were because SOS were world-class dancers. We had no problem learning from another choreographer. We had talent, energy and creativity from jump and all our training with Dominique just made what we had even better. We were ready for the world.

When Lorrie and I stepped out from this great group, I knew that we could hold our own. I was so excited because all my years with Dominique had lead me to this great opportunity.

"The auditions will be in the Grand Ballroom of the Plaza Hotel," Janis told us.

I didn't have to tell her that Lorrie and I would be more than ready.

Chapter Twenty

When Lorrie and I walked into the Plaza Hotel's Grand Ballroom, I got the feeling that something just wasn't right. The big hall seemed so empty because there was no one there except for the deejay and Janis Wilson who stood beside him. On the long table in front of them the deejay had his two turntables. Janis and the deejay stood there, looking like two lost children in that big, high-ceilinged room.

I came in with Lorrie beside me. She was dressed in a Showbiz black top and Capezio red jazz pants. I wore a Funky Diva fuchsia top and Showbiz black leggings. We both wore New Balance sneakers, the hot footwear for all urban dancers that summer.

"There's Janis," Lorrie said, but I had already seen her.

Before she came over to us, Janis whispered something to the deejay, and music suddenly came out of the big black speakers he had at opposite ends of the long table. I recognized the music as the instrumental version of Naughty By Nature's "Jamboree."

"What's going on?" I asked Janis.

I just wanted to get the show on the road. I had spoken to Janice earlier that morning, and she had made me promise to be on time. I was there, ready to go, and it didn't seem like anything was about to happen anytime soon. I almost caught an attitude.

"Marcus Salley is running late," Janis told Lorrie and me.

I didn't say anything about that but Lorrie smirked.

"Sometimes these things can't be helped," Janis said, more to Lorrie than me.

I was down for whatever. That morning she had also told me

that she had gone to a Marcus Salley rehearsal the same day that she saw Lorrie and me. I didn't ask her which two dancers she had chosen. I didn't ask because I didn't believe it really mattered. I felt we would knock them out of the box.

Now that I was in the ballroom, I just wanted to dance. That was when the choreographer walked in. He was a small-boned White man dressed in black linen shirt and pants, a wide brown belt and brown leather mules.

"I got lost looking for the men's room," he announced to us, and I disliked him from the get-go.

He was just too loud in his gayness. I had no problem with anybody's sexual orientation, but I felt that each person should keep it on the down low. He probably was a nice guy but I was so turned off by his obviousness that it just added to my overall irritation. *Lorrie is not like that,* I told myself, *and she never tries to hide her sexual preferences.* She never took out a public ad to announce the fact that she was a "lesbian virgin." She had never had a man.

And besides that, I felt a man should always carry himself like a man, even if he was gay. Anything else just didn't sit right with me. After Janis made the introductions, Harold, the choreographer, switched himself over to the deejay. Because there was really nothing to say, Janis walked away from us and returned to her purse, which was under a chair across the big room.

"One of your boys," I whispered to Lorrie as I tilted my head toward the choreographer.

"You don't know that," Lorrie whispered back, joking with me.

"Lorrie, please," I whispered. "As my dad would say, 'that man's a flaming faggot,' and you know it. Any moment I expect him to sing, "Y.M.C.A."

My little joke made Lorrie laugh. "And I guess that makes me a 'flaming lesbian?'"

"Don't play with me, Lorrie. You know what I'm talking about. You can do your thing, but don't do it so freakin' loud."

"You sound homophobic, and I know you better than that."

"I'm not homophobic; I just hate to see a man that obvious. Hasn't he ever heard about keeping it on the down low?"

"I don't care what he does in his bedroom, I just hope he's a good choreographer, with a good eye for talent," Lorrie said.

"Me too, I'm just saying—"

Before I could finish my thought, the Marcus Salley dancers came into the ballroom. There were more than two of them. It was like a mob scene at the entrance.

"Marcus Salley in the house," I sarcastically whispered to Lorrie.

Lorrie cracked up, laughing out loud. *So much for keeping it on the down low,* I thought as Janis got out of her seat and walked toward them. I was about to tell Lorrie to follow me to a seat across the room when I noticed something that took my breath away.

85

"Those two guys," I said as I grabbed Lorrie's upper arm.

"What two guys?" Lorrie asked, trying to squirm out of my grasp.

"In the doorway."

Her eyes found the two slim Black guys in dancer's clothes. "You know them?"

"They were with Tyra when she left my house that last time."

Because they were Marcus Salley dancers that could only mean one thing, and I knew I wasn't ready for that reality. *Could it be?* I thought.

Chapter Twenty-one

The sudden movement of the choreographer momentarily distracted me.

"Good. Everybody is here. Now we can begin," Harold said as he sashayed across the room.

I turned from him and looked toward the entrance to the Grand Ballroom, and I got the second shock of that afternoon. Tyra Woodstock walked into the ballroom, looking as beautiful as ever with her long red hair in a ponytail that trailed down her straight back. She wore a Showbiz baseball tee and Capezio jazz pants. And on her feet, of course, were New Balance sneakers.

"I can't believe that she's with Marcus Salley," I whispered to Lorrie.

"Well, I'll tell you this, it's a shrewd move on that company's part," Lorrie whispered back.

"What do you mean?" I wanted to know.

"Having a White dancer in a Black company looks real good around funding time."

I became indignant. "Tyra is a good dancer; she's not a token."

"I'm just saying how some people think."

I still didn't like that idea. Tyra stood between the two Black guys as most of the group of about twenty-five moved across the room to find seats. As the Black guys talked to her, her blue eyes found mine, and we looked intently at each other. There was no way we were going to greet each other, and there was no way that either of us was walking out of the hotel.

I just prayed that I didn't have to go up against her. I told myself as a new member of the troupe, if that was indeed the case, they wouldn't throw her into the latest competition. But then I realized that Marcus Salley had to put its best foot forward. With a sinking feeling I had to face the reality that Tyra was good, real good, and if she was with Marcus Salley, and that dance company really wanted the video, that they would have to go with their best shot, their most experienced dancers.

"Talk to me, D," Lorrie said. "You're scaring me, girl."

"I'm okay," I assured her.

"We're here to kick some ass," Lorrie reminded me. "Don't choke on me."

Still looking straight ahead, I said, "I don't choke."

As the Marcus Salley spectators took their seats, Janis walked over to us with long leg, dark-skinned Marcus Salley dancer, Catina Moore and Tyra in tow.

"We got this," Lorrie told me as the three came toward us.

"I'm sure you know one another," Janis began, "so I won't go into any introductions. But I have to say this: Harold will lead you through a routine, then you're on your own. He's been the choreographer for Walter's last two videos, and he's good, real good. He sets high standards and will only be satisfied with your best."

I nodded, knowing exactly what Janis was saying. Although she was giving us this shot, it was up to us to make the most of it. It was the best against the best and I, personally, had no problem with that. Suddenly, it was the four of us in the middle of the floor, until the choreographer joined us.

"This is a simple routine," Harold told us. " A little combination I put together last night in my hotel room at two in the morning because of my insomnia."

Then he nodded to the deejay and the music began. Having a live deejay at an audition seemed like a waste to me, especially with him playing one song over and over. And even though I loved Q Tip's "Vivrant Thing," I thought all that musical muscle was a bit much.

"It's just a simple little thing," Harold said, and then began to dance and count.

On one, he stomped his right foot and on two, he dropped his left hip with his palms up, swaying right-left-right-left on one and two. On count three, he stepped out with his left foot and on count four, he dropped his right hip, his left arm at his side. On count five, he jumped forward, then came back with his feet together and his right arm up. On six, he pressed his hands down his hips like he was pushing down a tight girdle and then bent his knees.

Harold was up straight on count seven, as he brought his right foot behind his left with his arms up straight; his palms cupped right over his left, his hips pumping forward. On the final count, count eight, he stepped out to a wide parallel, then fell into a "Suzi-Q" to finish his "simple routine."

"We got this," Lorrie whispered again as Harold went through his routine again. Then it was our turn to dance.

Before we began I thought about what Dominique told us about dancing to lyrics:

"This is where the dancer takes on the role of an actor telling a story, using technique and emotion. We sing with our facial expressions and body dynamics. There must be a connection between the dancer and the music."

We didn't start right away because Catina had to bend to tie her sneakers. Then it was on. I stood in the front with Lorrie behind me to my right. Tyra was in front with me to my left, with Catina in back of Tyra to her left. I never thought I would ever have to go against my former lover but there was no way I was even thinking about holding back.

The music dropped and I gave no thought to Tyra or Catina, or even Lorrie for that matter. I became a slave to the music. I had taken the choreography into my eyes and mind and implanted it within my body. Because we were real women, all the sexy moves that Harold thought he was doing were magnified to the point where our dancing became a sexual come-on.

The music played and we danced, repeating the routine over and over, becoming more intense with each repetition. I looked over to Janis and saw her jump out of her seat with her mouth wide open. If she said something I couldn't hear it because the Marcus

Salley entourage was applauding their homegirls so loudly. *Lorrie and I need big mouth Erica here,* I thought as the small group in the ball-room began to sound like a basketball crowd. They knew they were being treated to a special show, one they would talk about late into the night.

I didn't look at Tyra but I could feel her beside me. I knew she was dancing as hard as she could but it really didn't matter to me at that point. Whatever we had, I was determined to bury in the dust that afternoon. Holding back was not in my thoughts, and whether Tyra was a Marcus Salley dancer or a go-go dancer meant nothing to me. I felt like I could dance forever.

89

Somewhere during our third repetition I felt the crowd shift to the point where there was a small group of Marcus Salley support-ers chanting, "Go, Debrena! Go, Debrena!"

I appreciated the props but I didn't get all overconfident. I danced even harder, making the crowd's energy mine and shooting it back out to them through my creativity. Harold, the choreogra-pher, had given me some steps but by the end of the audition, I had made them my own. And when I went into my final Suzi-Q, there was a big smile on my face.

Chapter Twenty-two

"D, *you* were amazing," Lorrie told me as we sat in her car in front of my house.

The humbleness in her voice made me blush. "You too."

Lorrie shook her head. "I did what I could. I hung in there tough. But you stole the show, with your bad self. You even had some Marcus Salley dancers rooting for you, girl. I don't see why Janis and Harold have to get back to us. They should let us have it on the spot."

"I just remembered what Dominique told us about lyrical dancing," I said.

"No lazy arms, no arched back, no strained face. Don't flex your feet, don't drop your pelvis," Lorrie said, recalling all that Dominique had taught us.

I laughed because Lorrie was so on point with everything that she said. It was obvious that she, too, had listened closely to Dominique.

"When that White girl walked in, I was afraid you were going to lose it," Lorrie said.

"It's over with her. I've done all the crying and asking myself why things didn't work out. I'm moving on with my life. Whether or not we get this video opportunity, I'm moving on," I told Lorrie.

"I heard that," Lorrie exclaimed. "You want to do something tonight?"

I really didn't but I didn't want to say no to Lorrie right away, somehow, after all we went through that afternoon, that seemed rude. Especially when she was still on a performance high.

"We could see the *Wild Wild West* with Will Smith or *In Too Deep* with L. L. Cool J," Lorrie suggested.

I really wasn't in the mood for either film. "Those rappers are taking over the big screen," I had to say.

"Maybe we can go out dancing or to dinner," Lorrie said, obviously picking up on my lack of enthusiasm.

I laughed then said, "No more dancing for today."

"Okay, look, I'll call you later. If you want to do something we will."

We left it at that, then I went into my house.

Once inside, I breathed a sigh of relief. I was still a little shaky as a result of the audition but at least that was behind me. Then loneliness came down on me like a heavy, dark curtain. After the adrenaline rush of that afternoon had faded, I had to deal with the fact that I was alone. I really felt that I was over Tyra but I had to admit that the "healing process" was not over.

I still had emotional cuts and bruises to which I had to attend. And the only person I could think to reach out to was Lorrie, even though I knew that it would take her about half an hour to get home. On the foyer table was a pile of clothes I had planned to take to the cleaners. Earlier that day I had put the clothes on top of the mail.

When I picked up the clothes to get the mail, something dropped to the floor. I bent to see what it was. I stood with a business card in my hand. It read PHOTOS BY CHOICE.

That evening I got two phone calls—one that was expected and the other that was totally unexpected, strange even. Lorrie said she would call and she did; she still wanted to do something with me. I let her know that going to the movies was totally out but dinner sounded like a possibility. But I had to admit, after the day that I had, chilling out at home alone seemed like the best plan. I suggested that Lorrie call Shay and Tamara because they were always ready to hang out.

Lorrie told me that she would think about calling them but it was obvious that she wanted to be with me that evening. I knew I

91

wouldn't be good company if I weren't really into socializing. Before Lorrie hung up, she told me that she would be by the next morning to take me to rehearsal. I agreed to that.

A couple of hours later, around midnight, the phone rang again.

"Debrena, this is Angela."

She had to identify herself like that because I would've never recognized her voice. Over the phone, it was deeper, more sensual. In spite of my history of keeping Angela at a distance, I was beginning to see her in a new light, a little closer to how I imagined that a former lover like Lorrie might see her, as a hot chick. Behind the voice was the sound of a party. I decided not to ask her about that.

"Hi, Angela."

"I'm calling because I need you to do something for me."

"What can I do for you, Angela?" I asked.

"Well, not just for me. More for me and Marcy."

"All right."

"I'm sorry Marcy and I couldn't make it to that little get-together at your place."

"It's okay. Things come up."

"Erica told me all about it. What I'm calling about is that movie y'all watched."

"*The Temptations?*"

"Yeah. Marcy and I would really like to see that. I'm sure that Dominique will be talking about it at one of our sessions."

"I wouldn't be surprised if she did."

"Do you still have the video?"

"I have it but it doesn't belong to me," I said.

"I know it's Shay's, but can I get it from you?"

"I'll still have to ask Shay."

"Better you than me. Shay is not always so nice to me. She won't say no to you."

"You're making this a lot more complicated than it really needs to be."

"Just ask Shay. Please."

"I'll get the tape for you, Angela."

"I'd like to pick it up at our next rehearsal."

"No problem."

"Great. Marcy and I can look at it that night."

"Okay."

"Thanks, Debrena. Maybe I can do something for you some-day soon."

After I hung up, I got a strange feeling that my brief conversation with Angela was about more than some videotape. It was too late, and I was too tired to think much about it, but I felt like I had been manipulated in some way. But to what end? What did Angela want from me? I didn't have any answers, and as I got ready for bed, I didn't try to think too much about it.

93

Chapter Twenty-three

The next morning, I noticed immediately that Lorrie didn't look too happy.

"What happened?" I asked as I settled into the front seat of her car.

I wrapped my arms around the brown paper bag with the video-tape for Angela. I figured I'd give it to her and only tell Shay if she asked me for it. Before I could get my seat belt on securely, Lorrie pulled out into the traffic.

"I did what you suggested," Lorrie told me, sounding like following my lead had gotten her into some bad trouble.

"You went out dancing last night?"

"At the new Club House, with Tamara, Erica and Shay."

"Did something happen at the club?"

"Janis Wilson was there."

"Did you speak to her?"

"That was the problem, D. That chick acted like she didn't even know us."

"Who was she with?"

"Three wild and crazy chicks."

"How were they so wild and crazy?"

"Dancing all up on one another, like they were in the bedroom, making all the guys in the club notice them."

"Some girls like to get all that attention."

"Not like that," Lorrie said indignantly. "Made themselves look like sluts."

"What was Janis doing while all this was going on?"

"Janis left before they really showed out."

"And you never got a chance to say anything to her?"

"D, when she came in, I tried to catch her eye," Lorrie told me, obviously irritated. "It was like she just looked right through me. Then she went into the back with her girls. I thought about going over to her but she seemed so preoccupied. I didn't want to spoil Miss Prissy's night out, being that she was so into herself and all."

"Maybe she just didn't see you, Lorrie."

"Oh, she saw me. She just wanted to act cute. If she's gonna be stank like that, I really don't want to have anything to do with her music video project."

95

I had to laugh because I felt that Lorrie was getting all heated up over nothing.

"It ain't funny, D. You know I don't like to be played like that."

"I've been to the Club House many times. It's real dark in there."

"Not that damn dark."

"Maybe she was just keeping a low profile."

"It wasn't like I was going to hound her about some damn autograph. She ain't no damn celebrity."

"Maybe she was too much into her friends."

"So busy that she couldn't see me?"

"Maybe."

"D, don't make excuses for that skank."

I laughed again. "Come on, Lorrie. Be fair. Give Janis the benefit of a doubt."

Looking straight ahead, Lorrie said, "Janis dissed me, plain and simple. Ain't no excuse for that."

With Lorrie coming at me like that, I knew not to say anything else on that subject. We didn't say anything to each other as we rode to the studio. Once there we went into the locker room. I looked around and saw everyone but Angela. I walked over to her locker and opened it.

I put the brown paper bag on the top shelf, then closed it back. None of us ever put a lock on our lockers—we trusted one another like family. As I opened my locker, I took a peek at Lorrie. Knowing she was still upset, I didn't want to make her feel worse. She caught me looking and smiled shyly at me.

I was pulling on my dance clothes when Lorrie came over to me. Before we could say anything to each other, Dominique stuck her head into the locker room.

"Ladies, we would like to begin sometime today."

Because she was smiling so brightly, I knew she wasn't upset with us; she was just anxious to get everything started. Among the stragglers were LaToya, Erica, Lorrie and me.

96

"Forgive me for being such a bitch," Lorrie whispered to me.

"I understand," I said as I pulled on my shorts.

"Let's talk after rehearsal," Lorrie suggested, and I nodded.

"Hurry up, girls," Dominique said. "There's someone I want you to meet."

Lorrie went on ahead of me; I still had to get into my sports bra. Just before I slammed my locker door shut, Angela came into the locker room.

"I put the videotape in your locker," I told her.

Angela smiled like I had given her much pleasure, and then walked over to me and gently touched my shoulder as she walked past me.

"I'll get it back to you tomorrow," Angela promised.

I nodded. We walked out of the locker room together. When I came into the rehearsal hall, I got the shock of my life. I found Kammie talking to Choice, smiling all up in his handsome face.

The thought of them talking about me sent a chill down my spine.

Before I could recover from my shock, Dominique said, "I'd like to introduce you to a young man whom we'll be working with."

Dominique then motioned for Choice to stand beside her. As he walked toward her, he caught my eye. I was the one to look away.

"This is Choice Fowler," Dominique told our group. "He's a photographer with the Nelson Talent Agency. Carrie Nelson, the owner of NTA and a dear friend, asked Choice to meet with Marcy, Angela and me a little while ago.

"We discussed the idea of Choice doing a thirteen-month cal-endar as a fund-raiser. Choice wasn't sure if he would be available, but with some juggling on his part, which I appreciate so much, he will be able to take pictures of all of you."

Everyone clapped after that, some more enthusiastically than others.

"Any questions?" Dominique asked as Choice stood by her side, smiling.

He looked at me again as some hands went up for questions. I looked to where I thought I'd find Lorrie but she wasn't there.

Chapter Twenty-four

After rehearsal I couldn't wait to get home to call Choice. Because Lorrie was on cleaning detail at the studio that afternoon, I had to take the bus home. I had to blast him out for giving me such a shock. Or at least that was my excuse.

"Why didn't you tell me?" I asked as I sat yoga style on my couch.

"I guess you don't like surprises?" Choice said mischievously.

"Surprises? I almost had a heart attack when I saw you in the studio. How did that all come about?"

"Dominique told you most of it. I'm doing a favor for Carrie Nelson. She asked me and I couldn't say no. She's done too much for me."

"And you had no idea I was with Dominique St. Clarie?"

"No idea. We never talked about anything like that. I would've remembered."

"I guess it's a small world."

"I never thought I'd see you again. You did leave rather abruptly."

"I'm sorry about that. It's just my strange sense of humor."

"I wasn't laughing, Debrena."

"I was wrong. Maybe there's some way I can make it up to you."

"You can."

"Nothing crazy now."

"No, nothing like that. But I want to see you."

That wouldn't be a good idea, I thought.

"You still there?"

"I'm thinking."

"Do you find my company that repulsive?"

"No, nothing like that."

"I want you to come over to see some of my work."

"Your photography?"

"Yes. In my loft."

"If I came I couldn't stay long."

"I won't keep you any longer than you want to stay."

After he gave me the address, I told him that I would take a cab to his loft. Of course, he offered to pick me up at my house, but I said no because a cab ride would give me some time alone to think. I told myself that a relationship with Choice was impossible; all I wanted to do was get deep into my career, to make up for all the times that I wasn't as serious as I should've been.

99

I could've gone out for more auditions or taken more master classes, but I had been content to dance with the SOS troupe and be considered big fish in a small pond, knowing in the back of my mind that I needed to challenge myself to realize my full potential; to be that big fish in a big pond.

I even had to admit to myself that I really wanted the Walter McCary video shoot. But that left me open for massive disappointment. If I told myself I didn't really care if I got it, then my discontent would be something I could handle. But if I told myself I really wanted it, then didn't get it, there would be no way for me to hide my deep dissatisfaction.

It was like when I was a child; I used to play this little game with myself. Mom and Dad would promise me something special, like a trip to Coney Island or Asbury Park or something like that, and I would act nonchalant about it, like I really didn't care one way or the other. But when the Great Day came, my parents were shocked by my enthusiasm and amused by all the big smiles and tight hugs I laid on them.

Mom would always shake her head and say, "I didn't think this was a big deal for you."

At that time I didn't know how to explain myself to my obviously confused parents. As an adult I still had problems with getting my hopes up just to have them crushed under the mind-numbing weight of rejection or failure. It was enough to make a grown woman cry, and I didn't want anybody to see me weak like that. I didn't want anybody to know that anything in this world meant that much to me. I needed to go to Choice to take my mind off all my troubles.

When I got to his loft, he greeted me with open arms. He even offered me something to eat.

"I have some goodies left over from my last showcase. A little wine. Some cheese and crackers, some fruit."

"Let me have that. I'm starvin' like Marvin."

Choice laughed, and then went off to get me some food.

When Choice came back, I was looking at a very interesting photo of a naked Black woman sitting on the lap of the fully clothed Black man. But from the look in the woman's eyes, it was obvious that the man would soon be naked with her.

"It should be the other way around," I suggested to Choice as he handed me a small white paper plate filled with chunks of sharp cheddar cheese, wheat crackers and purple grapes.

"The man should be nude?" Choice asked me.

"For a change."

"Rumor has it that women do not like looking at nude men."

"Choice, that's not a rumor, that's a bald-face lie!"

"What about you? If I'm not being too personal, do you like looking at men in the nude?"

I popped a grape into my mouth, chewed it and then said, "It depends on the man."

"What about me?"

Right then and there, I felt that Choice was challenging me, and the thought sent a chill throughout my body; I loved a challenge. To give myself some time, I put a chunk of cheese on a cracker, then popped it into my mouth. After I finished chewing, I looked him straight in the eyes.

"I'd love to see you naked."

Choice laughed to cover his sudden embarrassment; he obviously didn't expect me to come at him like that. I wanted him to know that he had a bold soul sister on his hands.

Then he said, "I'm usually the one telling women to take their clothes off."

"Well, Mr. Fowler, that's about to change."

Chapter Twenty-five

Choice led me deep into his loft, past conventional furniture settings and work areas and a library. In the bedroom was a flat bed covered with a stark white sheet and a multitude of colorful pillows against a high headboard. Soft track lighting gave the room an other worldly dimension, like one had just stepped out of reality and into a fantasy one created by the extremely sexy Choice Fowler. The only other furniture of note was a nightstand, a papasan chair and an elaborate sound system that dominated the far corner of the room.

And although it was still light outside, the heavy dark drapery gave the room a perpetually nighttime feel.

"It's very comfortable in here," I told Choice.

Then I walked past him to look at his CD collection. It might've been a man's room but the singers Choice had collected spoke to the heart of a woman. In an impressively high CD tower was music from Brian McKnight, Chico DeBarge, Barry White, Joe, Kenny Lattimore, Walter McCary, Dru Hill, D'Angelo, Keith Washington and Marvin Gaye. I pulled out two CDs by Chico DeBarge and loaded them into the system.

Choice stared at me in my modest outfit, a dark blue chunky linen tank top, white drawstring-bottom skirt and single-band sandals. I wasn't dressed for seduction but I knew how to improvise. I pulled down my thin shoulder straps to leave my shoulders bare and kicked off my sandals.

"Strip," I told Choice.

He just smiled at me. "Just like that?"

"I don't play games."

"I like that about you."

"Take it off. You can talk to me later," I told him, my hands on my hips. "Take it all off."

Chico DeBarge's music was a sexy presence in the room as Choice unbuttoned his shirt. His chest was wide and muscular with remarkable definition. His waist was dramatically tapered and his stomach was flat with an impressive six-pack. When he pulled down his pants I saw his smooth, muscular thighs, round knees and thick lower legs, and it all made my mouth water.

Choice Fowler had it going on all over!

103

"Aren't you going to take off something?" Choice asked.

"You're not finished," I reminded him as he stood before me naked, except for a pair of Tommy Hilfiger boxers, dark blue, trimmed with red and white.

With no embarrassment, Choice pulled off his boxers. He was well hung, even in his relaxed state. And I couldn't wait to see that thick pole raised in excitement. I began to smell my perfume in his bedroom, and the crotch of my thong became damp. I knew he had to know that I was more than ready, but he didn't rush me.

Choice got props for that.

"Lay down on the bed," I directed.

As he did that, I sat in the comfortable papasan chair.

"You really like to look," Choice noted as I sat.

"Give me something to look at," I boldly suggested.

Choice looked at me strangely, obviously puzzled. He had no idea how wild and crazy I could get.

"Get that bat ready for some hot action," I told him in my sexiest voice as I sat yoga style.

Choice looked at me like he just couldn't believe what I was asking him to do.

"Get comfortable, Choice. Turn yourself on. I want to see you rise."

Choice lay on his bed, naked with his legs spread wide.

"Stroke it, Choice. Let me see that thing grow."

Choice's eyes were dead on me as he stroked himself. Soon he was closing his eyes and really getting into his solo deal.

"Don't forget the balls, Choice. Use your left hand to play with the balls."

Choice moaned loudly as he brought his left hand down to his testicles. His right hand stroked his manhood; his eyes were slits as he looked at me. He was a man in pain as he took his pleasure.

"Do you have condoms?" I asked as I stepped out of the chair.

"In the drawer of the nightstand," Choice told me as he continued to stroke and squeeze himself.

He looked at me, a man silently pleading for release.

104

"Soon, baby, soon," I promised as I opened the drawer and found the box of condoms, lubricated Gold brand.

I took out three and laid them on the top of the nightstand. Then I joined him on the bed.

"I'm going to do you right," I whispered into his ear, assuring him that his sweet torture would come to an end soon.

Choice moaned as I let my fingers do the walking up and down his hot thighs. "On your stomach," I told him.

Choice groaned as he turned over. I looked down on his well-shaped booty.

"Get on all fours," I directed him gently.

Choice did what I asked, and his reward was me gently stroking his hot behind. Then I knelt on the bed and licked the small of his bare back, still stroking his hot body. Suddenly Choice became weak in the knees and collapsed on the bed.

"Come on, baby. You're killing me," Choice groaned.

"Soon, baby, soon. I'm going to ride it," I told him. "I'm going to ride it good."

When I let him turn over on his back, Choice looked at me like I was the answer to all his prayers. That was when I stood up in his bed. With Choice watching me, I lifted the front of my long skirt. He gasped in appreciation as I reached up with both hands and pulled down my soaking-wet thong. I let it fall down to my ankles, and then I stepped out of it and kicked it away from me.

I bent down to grab his manhood. It was hot and thick in my hands. I stroked it, and Choice moaned beneath me. I stroked him with one hand and with the other rubbed the pre-cum fluid that leaked out of the fat head. Choice Fowler was ready to engage in some serious throw down.

And as quiet as it was kept, so was I! I grabbed a foil package, ripped it open and took out a condom. I pulled the protection over his throbbing erection. I wanted him in the sex position known as The Buck, his legs spread wide and me riding him like a cowgirl. A lot of men don't like this position because it leaves them feeling too vulnerable, but I felt that Choice could handle it.

The way he moaned and groaned and moved his hips told me that he was more than ready for me. I pushed my skirt up until it became a thick belt around my naked hips, then I stepped to him, no teasing. I even thought about giving him head, but I was too mad horny for any detours; I needed that big pole all up in me. Choice grunted loudly when I grabbed his manhood with both my hands.

"Give it to me," he begged. "Please."

I squeezed him once then released him.

"I'm going to give it to you," I promised as I put my hands on Choice's upraised knees and lowered my wet bottom into his crotch.

I screamed like the nasty girl I was as Choice ran right up in me. I used his knees for balance as I screwed him good! I took that man into my slick, wet opening and worked my hips like a lap dancer, moving in and out, up and down, round and round as that thing hit all my sweet spots! I felt like the queen of the universe as I used Choice like my favorite dildo. I screamed as I came but continued to bump and grind, drowning him with the thick cream flowing out of me.

I can't tell you who was hollering the loudest as we did our nasty love dance. Suddenly Choice grabbed my hips and lifted me a little. Not off his manhood, because I couldn't have that, but enough to let me know that he wanted me on my back. I closed my eyes. Before I knew it, I was looking up at the ceiling with Choice firmly between my thighs.

I found him staring down at me. He looked into my eyes, and I stared into his eyes as we went at it like champs. I just had to wrap my legs around his waist. I knew no shame as Choice's hands moved

105

from my hips to my booty as he rocked me. My nipples began to tingle, and I got that scooped out feeling in my stomach, like all I had in me was about to be snatched out.

And I cried out, "Do it, baby!"

And Choice did it, again and again.

As I surrendered my all to him, tears came to my eyes. I gave him all that I had tried to hold back in one heart-wrenching orgasm that left me drained until I felt Choice cum inside me. And then there was a big knot of emotion that I served up to him like a block that he smashed with the hammer between his thighs.

106   Something exploded in the darkness inside my head, and I shattered into a million pieces.

Chapter Twenty-six

I took the coward's way out. As Choice slept in his bed, I moved around in the darkness of his bedroom, gathering my clothes. Because I didn't want him to wake up, I dressed outside his bedroom. It was only then that I realized that I didn't have my panties in my bundle of clothes. With no thought of going back into his bedroom, I pulled on my clothes and went to the front of the loft, looking for a phone. I found a scrap of paper and wrote a cute note, something for Choice to remember me by, as if my performance in bed wasn't enough. I knew that I blew his mind; there was no doubt about that. That's why I could never see myself as a lesbian. I enjoyed the heat, smell and thrust of a man too much.

What gay woman could say that?

I called a cab. And because I didn't want the driver to blow his horn for me, I ran downstairs to meet him. I stood in front of the building. It was about fifteen minutes before I saw the bright yellow lights of the cab cut through the early-morning grayness. I ran out into the street, waving my hands to attract the cabdriver's attention. In front of my house, I paid the driver and blessed him with a nice fat tip.

I was floating on air as I walked inside. I breathed in deeply to inhale the smell of Choice still on my body, recalling the intensity of our first-time sex. I was funky, and there was an aching between my thighs where Choice had stretched me with his manhood. But it was a good ache, and I knew a nice, hot shower would ease the pain and make me feel like a brand-new person. I took off my clothes right there in the foyer and proudly walked naked through my house to the bathroom. After a long, steaming-hot shower, I went into my room and threw myself across my bed. I laid there with my thighs spread wide and my legs dangling over the edge. For a wild moment, I felt Choice moving in and out of me. I even ached down there, imaging us together, and I became wet, ready for him again. *That was some good sex,* I thought before I drifted off to sleep. Just what I needed, and I didn't know if we'd ever get together again.

Chapter Twenty-seven

But we did get together, for dinner, for a movie and for more sex. Because I spent so much time with Choice, I didn't have any extra time for Lorrie. I saw her regularly at rehearsal but I knew that we needed more time than that. It had almost been a week since we had been together, and it was mainly because I was blowing her off.

"What's going on with you?" Lorrie wanted to know when she finally caught up with me at the dance studio.

That was the moment I dreaded.

I had nightmares about this confrontation, and I still didn't know what to say to her.

"I've been real busy lately," I said lamely as Lorrie stood before me, her hands on her hips.

It was after rehearsal, and she was dressed in a multicolored body suit and a short black skirt. Her shapely legs were long and bare. On her feet were black leather sandals. If she weren't so angry with me, I would've told her how good she looked that afternoon. To avoid her I had begun taking a cab to and from the studio. But I knew I couldn't duck and dodge her forever, especially when there was work we needed to do together.

"If we're gonna do this "Loose Booty 2000" we have to spend some time together. You know, practice?"

I know that, Lorrie," I said defensively. "And we will."

"Not if you keep on blowing me off and not returning my phone calls."

With all the sarcasm dripping from Lorrie's lips, I knew trying to excuse my rude behavior would be a losing battle. I owed her more than this raggedy behavior. She was my best friend, the only girl I ever called in the middle of the night just to talk. I had shown my natural Black booty, and Lorrie was more than ready to kick it for me. I knew when to back down, especially since we were standing a few feet from Dominique's office.

I also couldn't tell Lorrie that the only reason I was there so late was to meet Choice. We had made plans to spend the day together. This was so important to me because Choice had told me that he would soon be traveling to Los Angeles for a very important business opportunity connected with the Nelson Talent Agency.

I would never stand in the way of success, but I felt the need to be around him 24/7. Still, I could've gotten together with Lorrie after rehearsal but when Lorrie saw my outfit, she could tell that dancing was the farthest thing from my mind. I wore a wide-brim hat, lime green tube top, wrap skirt, open-toe sandals and gold and silver bracelets.

"You better get your head out of your ass," Lorrie told me, "if you want to do anything with me."

At that moment I would've preferred that Lorrie punch me in my face. In no uncertain terms, she called me a slacker, a fool who just couldn't get it together. And Lorrie knew how much I despised slackers.

"I'll get it together," I promised. "Just don't call me a slacker."

Lorrie's words were hard on me. "I haven't called you anything yet!"

"No. But you're building up to it. I can see it in your eyes, in your stare. You want to blow up all over me like a live hand grenade."

"I can call you three times a day and you can't call me back once? What's up with that, D?"

At that point, when I saw tears in Lorrie's eyes, I thought it was best to let the girl go off on me, to blast me out good and get all that poison hate out of her system. I had never known Lorrie to hold her feelings in, especially when it came to how she felt about me.

"Look, uh, maybe tomorrow," I began. "We can stay after practice. I'll get the key from Dominique and ask her to let us stay. We'll lock up afterward."

"Don't do me any favors," Lorrie told me, then abruptly turned away from me, like I was not worthy of her time or energy.

I felt bad about that. But before I could say anything, Dominique came out of her office. She was dressed real cute in a white sleeveless pleated shell and a long denim pinwheel design skirt. She said, "I need to speak with you two. Lorrie, you first."

My friend moved like she couldn't get away from me fast enough.

I was so hurt.   111

When Lorrie came out of Dominique's office, she wasn't very happy. I knew enough to give her some room as she came down the hallway. Lorrie walked past me quickly as she made her way down the corridor. I watched as she entered the locker room and slammed the door behind her.

"Debrena," Dominique called out to me before I could move toward Lorrie.

I followed Dominique as she walked into her office.

"I hate to be the one to bring bad news," Dominique said as she sat upon her desk. "Please, sit down."

I sat with my legs together and my hands in my lap.

"That's one of the things about this business," Dominique began, "not everybody gets what they go after."

My heart dropped to my stomach, and I tried to prepare myself for the worse news.

"Janis called?" I asked in my impatience.

Dominique nodded.

"Janis can't use us? She's found somebody better?"

Before Dominique could say anything I rose to my feet. My plan was to go to Lorrie in the locker room, where we could comfort each other and maybe cry together. Our love for dancing made the rejection even more painful. It was like Janis was telling us that we were not qualified for something that we were born to do.

At least we can comfort each other, I thought. I knew I had to get out of Dominique's office as soon as I could.

"Where are you going?" Dominique asked, speaking to my back as I stood near the door. I refused to turn around because I didn't want her to think I was a sore loser, but I hurt so bad, and I knew the pain was written all over my face.

"You said they couldn't use us," I painfully reminded her.

"Debrena, please sit."

The only reason I sat was because of my deep respect for my teacher.

"They couldn't use Lorrie. I didn't say that they couldn't use you."

I smiled in spite of myself. "They want to use me?" I asked.

Dominique nodded, her smile sad. "Janis called me this morning. There's been a change in the direction of the video. As Janis explained it to me, they want one girl to be the center of attention. They want to try something different."

"They want to use me?" I repeated, not knowing if I wanted to jump up and down or cry my eyes out.

"Music videos are where it's at today, Debrena. When I was coming up, they were too new and expensive to be a big thing. Now everybody's making them; music videos can send a dancer's career through the roof."

"But Lorrie."

"I'm sorry about Lorrie. I tried to let her down easy but you know and I know, and Lorrie knows, rejection is part of this business. Something else will come along for Lorrie. Something she would be perfect for. I try to make you all understand that."

"But it still hurts, Dominique. It hurts so bad to be rejected like that."

"I know, Debrena. I've had my share of rejections. It's always disappointing. But at least they picked someone from our company. I believe that's something to celebrate."

I agreed with Dominique but I couldn't help but think *poor Lorrie*. "It's going to take a little time for her to see it like that."

"I know," Dominique said softly, sympathetically.

I stood there, wondering what I could do to make Lorrie feel better.

"One more thing," Dominique told me as I again rose to leave.

"Janis wants you to call her. She wants you to join her for dinner this evening."

That was when Dominique handed me a slip of pink paper with Janis's cell phone number on it.

I took it and put it in the deep pocket of my skirt. I looked Dominique in the eyes and said, "Thank you. All your good training has paid off."

"You're a great student and a great dancer," Dominique told me as she came off her desk.

I moved into the circle of her arms, and we held on to each other.

113

"A great dancer," Dominique repeated and then kissed me on the forehead.

Over a lump in my throat, I said, "I'll make the company proud" as we came out of our clinch.

"I know you will, Debrena."

Out of Dominique's office, I hurried down the hallway to the locker room.

"Lorrie," I called out, praying that she would still be there. I looked around and found no one. But the door to my locker was wide open. And on the top shelf was a folded note. I pulled it down and read:

Debrena,

THE WAY YOU DO THE THINGS YOU DO has me on *CLOUD NINE*, and it's not *JUST MY IMAGINATION* so *GET READY* 'cause here I come, and *I AIN'T TOO PROUD TO BEG*.

I want you to be *MY GIRL*.

The 1 who really loves u.

I smiled as I put the note into the pocket of my skirt, touched by the creative use of song titles from the *Temptations* movie. As I slammed my locker shut I told myself that Lorrie deserved a house call.

Chapter Twenty-eight

When I came out of the studio, Choice was there waiting for me, sitting up in his big black Lincoln Navigator.

"What's wrong?" he asked me after I climbed up to join him.

I thought about lying to him. Instead I said, "You know me too well."

That was when he gently brushed my cheek with his big hand. Suddenly my mind went to the note I had found in my locker. It was something someone who cared would do. Something Choice would do but I knew there was no reason for him to go into our locker room.

"You're so sweet," I told him, thanking him for being there for me.

I told him about being chosen for the video but I didn't say anything to him about meeting Janis that evening for dinner.

"That's what you want, isn't it?" Choice asked. "That kind of recognition?"

"Of course I do. But Lorrie didn't get anything."

"Lorrie will get something else," Choice assured me.

"That's the same thing that Dominique said."

"It's true, Debrena. I just hope that Lorrie doesn't act funny toward you about it."

"Lorrie is my best friend, Choice."

"I know that, but feelings can change behind something like this."

The thought of losing Lorrie's friendship made me nauseous. Choice couldn't help but notice. "I'm not saying it will happen.

But you can't be naïve in any competitive business. Your friend today could be your enemy tomorrow."

The thought really scared me. "Not Lorrie, Choice. It would never go down like that with Lorrie."

Choice held up his hands defensively. "I'm not saying it will. Please understand me."

"You're just saying be careful. You're saying that because you care about me. You're so sweet like that."

Choice smiled, and then said, "I hope you still think I'm sweet after I tell you about what I have to do today."

I just couldn't stop the roller coaster of my emotions. "We won't be able to spend any time together?" I asked, more than a little concerned, and pouting like a spoiled child.

115

"Not as much as I would like," Choice said, and he really looked disappointed. "Not as much uninterrupted time as I promised you. You know I have to go away to L.A. in a couple of days."

"Don't remind me," I said as I turned away from him, looking out of the window as if there was something out there I wanted to see. "You know I'm going to miss you like crazy."

That was when he touched my shoulder, and I turned toward him. He kissed me, just a quick meeting of our lips but it was just what I needed. Then he explained himself, saying, "I have to meet with Carrie and Dany this evening at NTA."

Because I had my meeting with Janis that evening, I didn't feel as bad as I could have. As a matter of fact, Choice's news was welcomed; it gave me more time to decide what I'd wear to my dinner meeting.

"I know we had planned to spend all day and night together," Choice began but I put a finger to his lips to stop him.

"Don't worry about it," I told him.

"I want to spend the time with you, Debrena, especially with me going away soon. The business shouldn't take more than a few days, but whenever I'm out in L.A., something always comes up to extend my visit."

"You go and handle your business," I told him, "and get back as soon as you can."

Choice looked at me skeptically. "You sure you're all right with this evening meeting of mine?"

"I'm okay with it because you're going to call me as soon as it's over."

"You know Carrie Nelson can be a little long winded. I could get out of there real late."

"No matter what time it is, you'll call me. And I'll have something tight, hot and wet just for you."

116

Chapter Twenty-nine

Janis and I decided to have dinner at Algarve Barbecue Restaurant and Take-Out on North Avenue in Elizabeth. Since Janis had been away in L.A. for the past three years, she really missed the charcoal grilled T-bone steak. I always liked the tasty, melt-in-your-mouth ribs.

"What would you like to drink?" Janis asked before the waiter came over to the table. She had met me at my place in a limo so we arrived at the restaurant together.

"I don't drink," I told her.

Janis nodded like she was taking notes. "Not even a little wine?"

"Any kind of alcohol gives me a fuzzy head," I told her. "I don't like to feel like that."

"Miss Always in Control," Janis commented as she raised her delicate hand for a waiter. When he came over she asked him to give us a little time with the menus.

"But for right now, we'll have two Heinekens," Janis ordered.

"Two Heinekens?" I asked Janis. "I told you I don't drink."

Janis smiled like she got her hand caught in the cookie jar, then placed a finger against her lips as if to say, *Play along with me.* For that reason I said nothing when the waiter placed a beer near my elbow, with a tall frosted glass.

"They're both for me," Janis confessed, "but he doesn't need to know that." Then she sat back smiling like she had really gotten over.

After we ordered our food, including a chicken finger appetizer, Janis got down to the business of Walter McCary.

"Like I said, when I first met you at the dance studio," Janis said, after making quick work of her beer in one greedy gulp. "The year 2000 is going to be Walter's. The video is a big thing, especially with your involvement, but an even bigger thing is what will happen in September."

Of course I had to ask, "What's happening in September?"

"Have you ever heard of The Taste of Chicago celebration?"

I had to admit that I had not.

"It's an annual event with great concert lineups in addition to food from all over the city," Janis explained. Then she put the empty green bottle and glass in front of me, like I had drunk it. She grabbed the other bottle of beer and glass that were originally in front of me. I marveled at the way Janis put it away; it was like she had what my dad called a hollow leg.

"You want some of these?" I asked Janis as the waiter placed my order of chicken fingers in front of me.

Janis shook her head, obviously more than satisfied with her liquid appetizer. "This September, Walter will perform at Grant Park in the Petrillo band shell. This event will be cosponsored by the Mayor's Office of Special Events, V-103 and WGFI-FM."

"It sounds real nice," I commented as I dipped a chicken finger into marinara sauce.

"More than nice, especially for you, Debrena. As the dancer featured in Walter's latest video, everybody is going to want to see you in person. And when Walter performs 'A Dream,' you'll be there onstage with him, dancing your little heart out. With a good manager behind you, you can go anywhere you want. All you have to do is have a vision. Do you have a vision for yourself, Debrena?"

Because Janis was throwing so much at me and caught me off guard, I came across a little lame. "I want to do more than just dance," I said, still dipping and chewing.

Janis took that in, but moved on as if what I wanted wasn't important at all, definitely not as important as Walter McCary. "Since his debut in 1992, Walter has released four multiplatinum albums. Recently he's received American Music Awards, several Blockbuster awards, along with multiple Grammy nominations.

Walter always had a vision, he never wanted to be a one-hit wonder." With that said, Janis finished her second beer.

As I digested all that she told me, Janis called the waiter over for two more Heinekens. "Me and my friend are very thirsty," she told him as he took away the bottles and glasses. He again placed a setup in front of me, a beer and a glass, and the other in front of Janis. The waiter said our orders would be ready soon and left as Janis drank from her new bottle of beer.

Ten minutes later, Janis said, "Walter is no joke."

"I've always respected Walter McCary, the man and his talent," I let her know. I would've said more but that was when the waiter placed our food in front of us.

After the waiter left and I dug into my food, Janis said, "Forget about that blue-eyed-soul-brother bullshit. Walter McCary is the real deal. And not just on the music front. He is involved in many charitable causes like VH1's Save the Music; the J Martell Foundation for Leukemia, Cancer and AIDS Research; and he's a member of the Red Cross Celebrity Cabinet."

I heard all that Janis told me but I was a little distracted noticing that she barely touched her meal. It was like she was inhaling her beer; another bottle was emptied as we continued to talk.

"Do you understand what I'm saying, Debrena?" Janis asked as she made the switch, putting the empty glass and bottle firmly in front of me and taking my setup.

"I heard you loud and clear."

"But do you understand?" Janis asked with emotion, and her intensity rocked me. She looked at me as if a wrong answer would result in a serious beat down for me.

"Walter and the people behind him, the record company, his managers, are not just about the music," Janis wanted me to know. "Today it's about music and image. Walter is not perfect—no man is,—but he has to come across as squeaky-clean. The public can never know anything to tarnish that squeaky-clean image."

She captured my complete attention, making me feel like I was being recruited for some top-secret mission. I felt like I had to somehow convince her that this mission was not impossible for me.

"I really appreciate this opportunity, Janis. I won't let you down. I know how to keep my nose clean."

"We all have our dark sides, Debrena. I have mine, and I'm sure you have yours. And no doubt, Walter has his; an artist with all that magnetism has to have a dark side. I'm not saying that Walter is into having sex with underage groupies or anything like that, but even if he did, the public can never know that."

"I'm sure that would blow up his spot with the Red Cross," I said somewhat sarcastically.

Janis smiled at me like I was her prized pupil. "Exactly. But this image goes beyond just what Walter does. It extends to the people around him."

Janis knew she had my full attention. I waited anxiously for the punchline.

"I have a question for you, Debrena," Janis said as she motioned for me to lean toward her. I did as she wished and felt like I was a member of some grand conspiracy. "I have to ask this, especially for Walter and his people. As for myself, I say live and let live."

"But for 'the cause' you have to ask me this question?"

Janis smiled like I had given her another correct answer. I felt like I had gone to the head of the class and would surely bring home an A to my parents. I felt I was prepared for anything but what she asked me nearly knocked the wind out of me.

Chapter Thirty

Are you gay?"

Janis's question made me sit back and let my folded hands touch my lips. At that moment I felt like Janis was a private investigator who had just spread out a pile of incriminating photos on the table before me.

"I thought the policy was 'don't ask, don't tell,'" I said, trying to be cute and buy some time to compose myself.

There was a mischievous glint in Janis's eyes. "That 'don't tell, don't ask' bullshit is for the armed services."

"Yet you ask me that?"

"For Walter and his people," Janis assured me.

"For the record: I'm strictly dickly."

Janis nodded, but surprisingly, she wasn't smiling. "Like I said, live and let live."

I quickly added, "I have a boyfriend. Do you want to meet him?"

Before she said anything, Janis finished more than half of her fourth beer. "I'm sure he's a great guy."

I picked at what was left of my entrée, a little nervous because I didn't know how far my dinner conversation with Janis would travel. Would Walter McCary have to know everything we talked about? "You're asking a lot of questions for a video shoot."

"We're talking about a lot more than a video shoot, you have to know that."

I couldn't say that I completely understood her.

"Where do you see yourself in the next five years?" Janis asked.

I had to laugh because it was a typical interview question.

"I'm not joking, Debrena. And please don't say married with children. You say that, and our business is done and it was nice meeting you."

"My career comes first, Janis."

"That's what I want to hear."

"I want to dance in high-quality videos. Maybe one day choreograph a few. Maybe even direct."

"Why stop at directing music videos? A music video director Millicent Shelton directed *Ride,* a feature film starring Malik Yoba, from TV's *New York Undercover.*"

122

"I could do that."

"I don't see why you can't."

"You'll help me?"

"All the way, girl. You're not the only one with ambitions."

"I know you want to be more than Walter McCary's personal assistant."

"You bet your sweet, round ass I do."

To get away from any more discussions about any hint of gayness, I flipped the script to where we were talking about Janis's ambitions. "Why didn't you follow through on the dancing?" I asked.

Janis laughed but it wasn't a happy one. "I'm a realist, Debrena. I loved being a part of the SOS dance troupe but when I found myself in the back row at each performance, I knew I wasn't one of Dominique's star students."

I felt bad for her. "Did you quit?"

"My parents knew they were wasting their money. They're old-school realists. Still, I wanted a career in the arts. If I couldn't dance, I could sing."

"So you sang?"

"At weddings, fashion shows, talent searches. I even made it to the Apollo, into week two. I would've gone for a third week, but lost to a cute ten-year-old who sang 'Got to Be There' like freaking Michael Jackson."

It was then that I got the impression that Janis's trip down memory lane wasn't going to lead to a very happy destination.

"I wasn't too devastated because there's no winning against a cute ten-year-old singing like Michael Jackson, everybody knows that. I came back to the Apollo with three wild chicks from Harlem. We brought the house down; sang the hell out of 'It's the Real Thing' and 'I've Learned to Respect (The Power of Love)' by Angela Winbush." Janis smiled broadly at that bittersweet memory, and with eyes half closed she went on. "We went to California together. Sang at some clubs and were *thisclose* to a record deal. Then everything fell apart. First, we couldn't decide what to name ourselves. Then one girl got married, one got homesick and the other decided that she wanted to direct movies. I sang a little backup for Walter because I needed some income, and then I found myself as Walter's personal assistant, traveling around with him, making sure that he was always comfortable, making all kinds of hotel reservations and getting his food."

123

Suddenly Janis stopped and looked at me, wide eyed like she just realized where she was. I got the impression that was the end of Janis Wilson's intimate portrait. She looked at me glassy eyed, then looked down at her food before finishing her last beer. "I guess I'm going to have to ask for a little doggy bag."

I nodded because there was a full meal before her.

"A doggy bag. And I don't even have a little doggy."

The way she said it sounded so sad, like there was no one in this world to comfort Janis Wilson.

Chapter Thirty-one

Lorrie lived in a two-family house owned by her mother. Because they had had such bad luck with tenants, they decided that Lorrie would move into the upstairs apartment and her mother would remain downstairs. As I stood on their front porch I rang the second-floor bell, then the bottom bell, and then I pushed open the front door. In the hallway, I found the door to the downstairs apartment wide open as always; whenever I came over I rang both bells so that Miss Edna would know that someone had entered her house.

"Hello, Miss Edna," I called out as I stood near the staircase leading to the upstairs apartment.

Miss Edna, Lorrie's mom, shuffled to the front door. She was frail, and her face was twisted from the stroke she had suffered a year before. She still visited the doctor regularly but she had not fully regained the ability to walk. There was some improvement; her walking was much better and her speech, although a little slurred, was more understandable.

"Lorrie's upstairs," Miss Edna told me as she stood in the doorway of her apartment. She wore an oversized housecoat and well-worn house shoes.

"I just wanted to say hi to you before I went up to spend some time with Lorrie," I explained as I looked at her.

I felt a little sorry for her because I knew she didn't receive any visitors and her life was spent sleeping, eating and watching TV soap operas. Lorrie took her out to dinner at someplace like Red Lobster or Sizzler at least once a week but most of her time was spent in her apartment.

Miss Edna was a small, shrunken brown woman and the only man she ever had in her life was Lorrie's father who divorced her when Lorrie was nine years old. My heart went out to Miss Edna, and I prayed that I would not end up like her, alone and without the love and comfort of a lifetime partner. I prayed that I would always have someone to comfort me, like Mom comforted Dad, like Choice was now comforting me. With so many emotions stirring in me, I impulsively reached out to Miss Edna. I hugged her and felt her bones beneath her thin skin. Her frail body was perfumed with White Diamonds, a fragrance she always wore.

"Lorrie's upstairs," Miss Edna repeated once I released her.

"I know," I said as I looked up the staircase and found Lorrie standing at the top of the stairs, looking down at us.

"Debrena's here," Miss Edna called upstairs, not knowing her daughter was watching us.

"I know," Lorrie called down to her mother, her voice so gentle and patient it touched my heart. Miss Edna might not have a man, but it was obvious that she had the love of her daughter.

"You have a nice visit," Miss Edna said to me, and then to Lorrie, "You put my numbers in?"

"You know I always do," was Lorrie's reply.

"Lorrie don't think I'll ever hit big but one day, you'll see," Miss Edna said to me around a gap-toothed smile. "I got to get back to my stories."

With that said, Miss Edna disappeared into her apartment, leaving the front door wide open.

"Come on up," Lorrie called down to me. I noticed she had her hair pulled up in a messy knot atop her head.

"Did she ever hit?" I asked as I walked up the stairs.

The door to Lorrie's apartment was wide open. I followed her inside.

"She hit a few times," Lorrie told me, "but nothing big." Lorrie was watching the latest music videos. She had the sound of her big-screen TV on low so that she could hear what was going on downstairs in her mom's apartment. She always did that. "She's been playing the same number combination, 1-2-2-0 straight and box, for years."

125

Once, Lorrie and I talked about this habitual numbers playing and agreed that it was a waste of time and money, something that we would never do. We wanted to determine our own financial futures, not leaving anything like that to chance or luck. We wanted to be "large and in charge" and we came up with that whole concept when we were children dancing together.

"Congratulations, D," Lorrie said as I sat down on her big leather wraparound sofa. She kept the TV on, glancing at it occasionally as we spoke.

"Thank you," I said, looking at her soft, pretty face, searching for any sign of insincerity. "I really thought it would be you and me together."

Lorrie tried to smile; she didn't quite make it, and my heart went out to her.

"I've been thinking about some way to get you into the mix," I told her as she sat beside me on the sofa.

Lorrie turned away from me. "D, they don't want me in that. They got who they wanted."

"I was thinking that at the shoot they'll need a makeup artist," I shared with Lorrie. "I'm thinking that makeup artist could be you."

"I appreciate you for looking out for me," Lorrie said, still not looking at me. "I really do. But that's your shot. You worked hard for that, you earned that."

"But I know while I'm dancing, I'll be looking for you at my right."

"Do your thing, girl. Make us all proud."

I smiled. "I will do that."

Then Lorrie turned toward me. "I'll have to admit that I was so hurt when Dominique told me that I didn't make it. I got mad because I felt that Janis could've told me at the club, but then I thought it's not done that way. But I'm glad for you, D. Just be careful around Janis."

"What do you mean?" I asked, still trying to keep things light.

Lorrie looked at me like she couldn't believe that I didn't know why I should be wary of Janis. "She dissed me, D," Lorrie said forcefully. "There's no doubt in my mind about that. I'd bet my mother's life on that."

I didn't want to say anything to upset Lorrie any further, but I did feel that she wasn't being fair to Janis. "I'm sure there's some way you can be involved," I had to say. I had to hold on to that hope.

"You don't believe me, do you?" Lorrie said, obviously agitated. "Look, I'm not saying this because Janis didn't pick me. In something like this, she probably has little say. I understand that, I accept that. All I'm saying is that no matter what happens, my concern is always for you. It will always be that."

I found myself defending Janis. "She's all right, Lorrie. In the past couple of days, I've spent some time with her. She's been more than kind, more than generous. She's even offered to manage my career. She sees me as more than a dancer; she has a vision for me."

127

"What vision do you have for yourself, D? That's what you have to stay focused on. You have to keep your eyes on the prize. Like my mother, every day she plays her numbers, and no matter how silly we think it is, she sees herself as another Curtis Sharp."

I had to laugh at that, recalling Curtis Sharp, the Newark man who went to pick up his first check as a lottery winner with his girlfriend and his ex-wife with him. "What would your mom do with all that money?"

"I don't know," Lorrie had to admit. "I don't even think she knows but it gives her something to look forward to, each and every day. It doesn't cost me much to put her numbers in, to keep that hope alive."

"I'm making the future happen for me, Lorrie. I'm doing that each and every day. I'm not looking for someone to give me a million dollars; I'm making my millions dollar by dollar. I know you understand that."

"I do, D. I just want you to keep that in mind. It goes day by day. I just don't want you to see Janis as a shortcut to fame and fortune."

"I'm no slacker, Lorrie. I'm more than willing to pay my dues."

"That's all I'm saying, D, pay your dues, pay them in full. Just don't let Janis make you think she has all the answers. She's not the boss."

"Walter McCary is. I know that. I'm clear about that."

"Have you met Walter McCary yet? Have you even spoken to him?"

"It's not like that, Lorrie. Janis is his personal assistant. I'm working through her. When it comes time for the shoot, I'll meet him."

"I guess that's the way it is. All I'm saying is be careful."

I stood to leave, somewhat disappointed in my friend. "You know you have to be real with yourself, Lorrie. I detect some sour grapes here."

Lorrie stood beside me, refusing to be intimidated. "I don't know how you could fix your mouth to say some weak shit like that. It's not sour grapes on my part. It's love for you, D. It's my concern for you. I don't give a good goddamn about Janis Wilson!"

I had to admire Lorrie for standing her ground. Still I had to say, "Your concern is underwhelming, you know? I can take care of myself."

Lorrie sighed deeply, and it was obvious that she had had enough of me. "Okay, D. I see there's no talking to you now. You got that stardust in your eyes. I still wish you the best, and if you need me I'm here."

I couldn't even look at Lorrie when I said, "I'll see you around."

I made a quick exit.

As I stood at the bus stop, I felt like crying because I never thought that success would mean leaving Lorrie behind. Once I got on the bus, I pulled the note I had found in my locker from the pocket of my skirt. The song titles: "The Way You Do the Things You Do," "Cloud Nine," "Just My Imagination," "Get Ready," "Ain't Too Proud to Beg," "My Girl," and then the ending from "The 1 who really loves U." As I folded the note and put it back in my pocket, I really felt bad because one of he reasons I had gone to see Lorrie was to thank her for the sweet note; in my mind she was the only one who could've written it.

128

Chapter Thirty-two

After it was over, Choice held me in my bed. "I'm too open to you," I told him as I foolishly tried to hide my face in his hairy chest. "I'm too vulnerable when it comes to you."

Choice stroked me. His hands moved up and down my body, then to the small of my back. "I'm going to miss you," he told me.

I hated the fact that he was going to L.A. but I couldn't tell him that, I didn't want him to think I was some clinging female, especially when I was trying to keep things light the night before he was to leave.

I also didn't want to be affected by his overwhelming manly presence. And I sure didn't want to be affected by his words. I felt like a wimp because I couldn't help myself. I had let him touch me too deeply. His words touched my heart, especially the "miss you" part that made me mush inside.

I didn't want to melt but there was no way I could escape his piercing gaze, a look that always commanded my complete attention. I wanted to run, I wanted to hide, I wanted to save myself, but there was no place I could go. I was beginning to think that this was where I needed to be.

I told Mom about Choice when I called to talk to her and Dad down in Florida. Dad wasn't available but Mom was and because she sounded so alone, I wanted to give her the impression that her little girl was doing all right with her career and her love life. She was so happy to hear about Choice and me. It was so traditional but I was letting my mind move in that direction. Mom couldn't wait to tell Dad. I knew he would be happy too. Still, there was uneasiness, restlessness inside me. I attributed it to separation anxiety because I had gotten so use to the comfort of my man.

"I want to talk," I told him that night. "I need to understand this thing between us."

"We're compatible, Debrena. What's wrong with that?"

"I don't know if I'm ready for a relationship," I had to admit.

"Why can't we just take it one day at a time?"

"I don't know. That sounds good. But I feel like I want to fall at your feet whenever you come through my door, like I have to have you inside me whenever we're alone. Like I'm under some sex spell. I can't put myself through all that. I can't allow myself to be used like that."

Because I found myself getting agitated, I sat up in my bed. I pulled my legs up and sat naked, yoga style, beside Choice. "Am I making any sense?" I had to know.

Choice rubbed my thigh. "Debrena, I like you. I like you a lot. You're the sharpest sister I've ever met."

I was flattered, but I felt I had to put him straight, to keep us grounded. "Can you really say you know me? We've been together less than a month and that's between me getting ready for my summer dance concert and your photography work for NTA."

"I know being with you like this feels right."

"I don't know, Choice. I just don't know. I just don't want to get hurt."

"Neither do I. Let's not spoil this. Let's just ride this out and see what happens."

I nodded slowly.

"Besides, when I get back from L.A., we'll be working together on that calendar project."

I smiled, warmed by the sweet thought of Choice taking my picture for the calendar. As he lay near me, I wanted to give him a night to remember. I also wanted him to get some sleep. I didn't want to wear the brother out, but because my center was moist, I had to ask, "Can we do it again?"

Choice smiled up at me from my rumpled bed. "If you can get it up," he told me, spreading his bare legs wide, "you can have it."

130

Chapter Thirty-three

With Choice gone, I found myself spending more time with Janis. I saw Lorrie every day during the week at the studio, but her attitude toward me was icy cold. We did some work on our dance duet but the conversations I had with her just didn't flow. I was somewhat upset because I had never had a problem speaking with Lorrie. But now it was somewhat difficult.

Janis filled my weekends just right. Although I talked with Choice during the week from L.A., he had no idea when he would be back in Jersey. I missed him a lot and even told him so. His advice to me was to keep busy. That was easy during the week but on the weekend…

The weekends would've been a killer if it weren't for Janis. She went out of her way to keep me entertained. Industry parties, movie premieres, breakfast, lunch and dinner were just some of the amusements we enjoyed together. And even with all that, I didn't know what to expect next.

One Saturday, Janis called me bright and early and told me to get dressed. She said "dress casually" and that to me meant a clean T-shirt and jeans.

Janis knocked on my front door and I opened it to let her in.

"Smile, you're on *Candid Camera*," Janis said as she stepped in the foyer.

"Where did you get that?" I asked, referring to the mini-camcorder she held. "If I had known I was going to get my picture taken, I would've dressed up."

"You're dressed up enough," Janis told me. "But you have to do more than just stand there. This is a movie camera."

"What do you want me to do? Dance?" I asked, still standing in one place.

With mild irritation, Janis placed her camcorder on the foyer table. "You need me, Debrena. I'm going to make you a diva."

"I always thought I was a diva," I said and noticed that Janis was dressed in a ruffled-front denim halter mini-dress, showing a lot of smooth bare leg. On her feet were red leather slides.

132 "You are a diva, an ebony diva, but you can be a super diva if you work with me," Janis said as she checked me out from head to toe.

I felt self-conscious, like I was a fashion misfit. Because Janis was my "unofficial manager," meaning we hadn't signed any kind of contract, I let her push me into directions I would've never even thought about going just a few short years ago. Janis made me more conscious of my overall appearance. She even had me wearing makeup. It was light but before the summer of Janis Wilson, I only wore it onstage or for special occasions, like going to see Dad play at some slick New York jazz club or a night out on the town.

"You always look good," Janis told me. "You're a beautiful girl. But I'd like to make some adjustments to your outfit." That was when Janis spun me around so that my back was to her. "You have the perfect round ass."

I actually blushed. "I guess I'm supposed to say thank you?"

"You can thank your parents for an ass like that," Janis said with a laugh in her voice as she pulled my T-shirt out of my jeans.

"Hey," I protested as Janis's cold hands went up my bare back.

"Some adjustments," Janis said as she unhooked my bra. "You don't need that."

"I need some support," I let her know as Janis pulled my bra down from under my shirt.

"I'll give you support," Janis assured me as she grabbed the back of my tee, pulled it up and tied it in a fat knot behind my back. With that simple adjustment, she made my tee into a halter. I felt a little self-conscious because I was sure that every man that I saw that

Saturday would be drawn like a magnet to my dark nipples. But Janis wasn't finished with me.

"Lose the belt," she told me.

"The jeans are a little roomy," I told her as I unbuckled my belt.

"They need to hang lower," Janis said as I put my belt on the foyer table.

The jeans sagged down, exposing the tops of my baby blue panties.

Janis stepped back to look at her handiwork. The frown on her face told me that she wasn't completely satisfied.

"What?" I asked, not knowing how she wanted me to look.

"The panties have to go," Janis told me.

"You're crazy," I told her, then laughed, a little embarrassed and a little warm from the intensity of Janis's eyes on me.

"Trust me."

I must be crazy too, I thought as I popped the buttons on the front of my jeans before pushing down my baby blues.

"I love it shaved like that," Janis said as she looked at my crotch. The panties fell down my legs to join the puddle of my jeans around my ankles. I had to kick off my sandals to become completely naked from the waist down. When I pulled my jeans back up, they sagged on my hips and rested below my navel.

"The ebony diva," Janis said as I stood before her.

The crazy slut, I thought as she walked all around me.

"I'm not taking off anything else," I told Janis.

Janis smiled, then said, "You're perfect now. Just perfect." Then she picked up her camcorder and aimed it at me. "Remember this is a movie camera, Debrena. You have to say something."

"What should I say?" I asked with a little attitude.

"Tell me your name," Janis suggested as she stood with half of her face hidden by the silver-and-black camcorder.

"My name is Debrena Allison Allen, and I'm a dancer."

And because Janis had told me to do something, I began to dance, a little move I saw Aaliyah do in one of her music videos: I rolled my stomach and shook my hips.

I felt that Janis was pleased with me because her camcorder was

133

dead on my every move during my impromptu performance. But the seal of approval came just before we stepped out of my house, which was when Janis said, "Debrena, you are the baddest."

I blushed again.

"Let's get you out of here," Janis said. "I'm taking you someplace to make you even more beautiful."

Chapter Thirty-four

Janis and I were naked together. It was her idea, and I went along with it without any protest because I had to agree with her rationale. "We owe it to ourselves," Janis said with a big bright smile on her face. "We are two hardworking sisters."

Because we were two hardworking sisters, Janis had us limoed to Harlem, New York, where we spent the day at the Cynergy Day Spa and Wellness Center. Our spa experience began in the Jacuzzi. I kept my eyes closed as the water swirled around us.

"Debrena?"

"Yes?"

"Do you have a nickname?" Janis wanted to know.

"You mean like Sweet Cheeks or Hot Momma?" I asked, opening my eyes as I laughed at my own silly cleverness.

"No, silly. I mean like Ginger or Pooh Pooh."

I had to laugh at that. "Of course not."

"Sometimes parents give their children nicknames like that," Janis told me.

"Not my parents; my parents love me. They would never stick something like that on me. Lorrie calls me D."

"Like D-E-E?"

"No, just D. The letter D."

"I'll have to think of something."

I raised my eyebrow at that, feeling that Janis was doing too much to change me. "Come on, Janis. How much of my life are you going to change?"

"Don't you want to be successful?"

"You know I do."

"Well, to be really successful you have to become a brand name."

I didn't want to sound stupid but I needed to know what she meant. "Why do I have to develop a brand name?"

"When I say Stevie, whom do you think of?"

"Stevie Wonder."

"Smokey?"

"Smokey Robinson."

"Mariah?"

"Mariah Carey."

"Toni?"

"Toni Braxton?"

"Diana?"

"Diana Ross."

"Babyface?"

"Kenny Edmonds."

"All brand names."

"I understand. But don't you think D is enough?"

"I'll have to think about that."

Then Janis went on to suggest other things I could do with myself: pluck my eyebrows; wear purple eye shadow and blue mascara; color my hair, which was something that Lorrie suggested; wear deep dark glossy lipstick. But I had to stop her when she suggested hazel contact lenses.

"I thought you said I was a beautiful girl," I reminded her as we stepped out of the Jacuzzi.

"You are," Janis said as she patted herself dry with a big white fluffy towel.

"So why are you trying to give me a complete makeover?" I had to ask as I dried myself off as well.

"I'm just trying to enhance your natural assets."

"There's nothing natural about me rocking some hazel contact lenses," I said, and then laughed at the absurdity of that. "I'd look like The Sister from Another Planet if I let you talk me into that."

And although I was making a joke, I couldn't get Janis to laugh. I couldn't even get her to crack a smile. "Sometimes you're a little too intense," I commented as we walked toward the twin massage tables that had been set up for us.

"I'm just trying to do my job, Debrena."

I touched Janis's smooth bare shoulder. "I know that, girl. And I do appreciate it. It's just that I feel funny paying so much attention to myself."

"When you're in the public eye, it's all about image," Janis reminded me. "The public wants you to be perfect, every hair in place. They want you to be larger than life, anything less is disappointing to them. And you don't want to disappoint your public, Debrena; if you do, they'll turn on you and you'll be on that show *Whatever Happened To.* You know what I'm talking about?" 137

I sighed deeply, already tired of this superstar-making machine. "I just want to be me."

"You can be you when you're too old to do this, when you can't dance anymore and your tits sag down to your knees. Then no one will want to look at you and you can be you all you want."

The picture Janis painted was like someone throwing a bucket of cold water in my face: I got a sudden glimpse of how far I could go all the way to the top.

"I want you to be hot, Debrena," Janis told me as we lay facedown on our individual massage tables. "As hot as I know you can be."

I looked over at Janis and tried to smile. I wanted to be hot but I didn't want to burn out.

"And think about all the good things I've introduced you to," Janis went on, obviously back in her element. "Think about how much you like Gucci, Prada, Sergio Ross, Dolce and Gabbana."

I liked all those fashion designers but the thought of all that didn't give me any real comfort.

Chapter Thirty-five

Because I had been working so hard at the dance studio and meeting with Janis every night to talk about some aspect of the video with Walter McCary, which never got started, I decided to take a day off. This meant sleeping late, phone off the hook, lounging around in bummy clothes, one of those days. But of course, someone had to knock on my door. I had no intention of opening it but I was curious as to who was on my doorstep. I sneakily peeped through the blinds to see who was on the porch, and when I saw who it was, I screamed.

I screamed because I never expected to see Mom and Dad on the doorstep that afternoon. I opened the door and ran into the loving arms of my smiling parents. I couldn't hold them as tight as I wanted to because Dad held a bulky black garment bag in front of his wide torso. Our group hug turned into grunts from Dad, moans from Mom and screams from me. "Why didn't you tell me you were coming up?" I asked Dad.

"I wanted to," Dad told me as he put the garment bag on the couch, "but your mother wanted to surprise you. You know how much she likes surprises."

"I do," Mom had to admit. "I like to give and get surprises." She sounded like a little girl. "We would have been here sooner but your father wanted to drive up."

Dad smiled broadly. "I told her it would serve her right if you were entertaining your boyfriend in the bedroom."

"You are so fresh," Mom said and playfully slapped Dad's shoulder.

"My little girl doesn't do things like that. Debrena is a virgin, right, baby?"

Mom held me and I squirmed in her arms. She laughed as she placed little kisses on my blushing face. My parents always had a raunchy sense of humor, and I was taught that a woman should share a healthy sexual appetite with her man. I had never caught Mom and Dad getting it on, but I knew that they still had a desire for each other.

"You still seeing that Choice Fowler?" Mom asked as she kicked off her sandals. She smoothed down the back of her burnt orange sundress as she sat beside Dad on the couch.

"He's still around," I told Mom, almost forgetting that I had mentioned him during one of our infrequent phone conversations. I didn't see any reason to tell her that he would be back in Jersey any day now.

"I want to meet him, Debrena. We're not going to be here long. We came up to spend some time with Dominique and peek in on Cheeba; you know he's back in the hospital?"

I didn't know but that summer, Cheeba seemed to be in the hospital more than he was home.

"And we have tickets to *The Lion King* on Broadway," Dad quickly added. "One of my old running partners is playing in the orchestra."

"Choice is in L.A.," I told Mom, "on a business trip."

"I don't know anything about this boy," Dad said, turning toward Mom.

"Stan, remember I told you that he's a photographer from L.A., working up here with Carrie and Dany at NTA." Then Mom turned toward me. "Has he taken any pictures of you yet?"

Then they went on from there, both of them, asking question after question until I felt like I was standing before a firing squad. Every shot was like a blow to my heart. The more we talked about Choice Fowler, the more my heart ached for him. They only stopped when I excused myself to shower and dress now that my lazy day had come to an end.

Chapter Thirty-six

While Mom and Dad got comfortable in the living room, I showered then went into my room to get dressed. I pulled out a pair of denim jeans and a black long-sleeved top. After I dressed I took a long, hard look at myself in the full-length mirror. I didn't look happy, as·a matter of fact, I looked pale with sadness. And it wasn't anything easily identifiable, just an overall crappy feeling that I attributed to the fact that I was missing Choice.

I missed Lorrie even more. I even wondered if she felt the same that morning at rehearsal. Did she look for me in the locker room? Did she turn her head every time the door to the studio opened? Did she even ask Dominique where I was? How could a girl that I laughed with, cried with and almost made love to diss me so hard?

"For a lady in love, you look miserable," Mom called from behind me.

I turned my sad face toward her as she stood in the doorway. Love? Was it love that I was feeling for Lorrie?

"You know it's love when you're miserable one minute and ecstatic the next," Mom said, and I knew she wasn't talking about Lorrie. She walked up behind me and put a comforting arm around me. We looked in the mirror together. "I can see the love, Debrena. That's why you have to work it out. Whatever it takes, whatever it is, work it out, baby."

I felt like crawling into Mom's lap and crying like a baby. Why did I ever have to grow up? Why become a woman and go through all this? "I just want to be happy, Mom."

"You will, baby," Mom assured me, "once you sort everything out. But you have to talk, communicate, understand each other, go as deep as you need to go."

"I know all that, Mom. But it's not easy. I don't think it's ever going to be easy for me, and that scares me. I feel that I'll always be alone no matter what I do."

"That's the way it is for a woman. Your dad is a good man, but still sometimes I feel all alone."

Mom held me tight but I didn't feel that she could ever hold me tight enough. "It gets better, right?"

Mom smiled at me, and then said, "It gets worse."

We laughed together as Mom sat beside me on my bed, hugging me like I was her baby girl, and I was so glad for that.

Then it was Dad calling, "Sandra!"

"I told him that I'd only be a few seconds," Mom told me as I reluctantly let her pull away from me. "I really came up to tell you that there's a surprise downstairs for you."

I had to laugh. "You and your surprises."

"This is a biggy."

"Mom, what surprise? You and Dad showing up like this is more than enough."

"We just want you to be happy, Debrena. To live your life the way you want to live it, to be in love. To be happy."

I thought about Lorrie, and I had to admit something to myself. "I am in love."

Mom hugged me again, like I had given the right answer to an important question. She looked like she wanted to cry. As we stood from the bed, she said, "He's here."

I was clueless. "He who?"

With the biggest smile, Mom said, "Your young man."

"My young man?"

"Choice. Choice is downstairs, baby. Waiting for you."

I was shaken to the core. I felt happy. I felt sad. I felt giddy. I felt sick. I felt like laughing. I felt like crying. When I got downstairs with Mom beside me, Dad said, "You have a very fascinating young man here."

Choice smiled as he basked in the strong light of Dad's praise and acceptance.

I wanted to jump on Choice right then and there, to screw his brains out, to smash him into Silly Putty, make him do my will so my parents would know that their daughter was no virgin.

"Debrena," Choice called out to me.

You'll pay for this, I told myself as Choice put both of his arms around me. There was a sudden joy in a distant part of my body because no matter how I felt about him just popping up like this, I was still holding Choice, and that always made me feel so good. I closed my eyes tightly and hugged him back. Before he could kiss me, I pulled away. It was so hard but I did it. I had to. I didn't want to melt all over him in front of my parents.

"Why didn't you tell me you were back in town?" I asked, playfully scolding Choice.

"I wanted to surprise you," Choice told me, and Mom and Dad laughed out loud.

"You people are going to kill me with your surprises," I said. "No more surprises, okay? No more surprises for a million years!"

They all laughed.

I didn't know I was such a comedian. "I'm serious," I told them but it didn't make any difference, they just kept on laughing.

Chapter Thirty-seven

I walked Choice out to his Navigator.

"You bum," I said as I playfully punched his shoulder. "When did you get in to town?"

"I just came from the airport," Choice told me, and it made me feel good that he was so anxious to see me. "I haven't even gone home yet."

"Why didn't you call me from the airport?"

"I tried but your line was busy."

I didn't want to tell him that I had purposely left the phone off the hook.

"But I did call the studio."

"I decided to chill out at home."

"I see that. With your parents."

I didn't want to tell him that little reunion wasn't planned; he seemed so pleased by the idea of me being at home with my parents. "You have to call me later," I said.

"What about your parents?"

"They'll be visiting friends, and they have tickets to a Broadway show."

"How long will they be staying?"

"I don't see them staying more than a couple of days, probably just this weekend. It's Friday now. Knowing Dad, they'll be gone by Sunday night."

"Then it'll be *you and me,* " Choice said and that sounded real good to me.

You and me, I thought as Choice smiled at me. In my heart, I knew it was not that simple. That day I had admitted something to myself that I knew I had to deal with. Choice was back but I knew I had to speak to Lorrie as soon as possible. But what would I say to her? I knew I just couldn't come out bold and tell her how I felt. It scared me so bad because I didn't know how she would react to my truth. How did I want her to react?

"You all right?" Choice asked as he leaned against his Navigator.

"Yeah. This has been quite a day, with my parents coming to visit and you coming home."

Before Choice could say anything, a long, white limo with deeply tinted windows swung around the corner and came down my street.

Choice jokingly said, "Who's the celebrity in your neighborhood?"

I didn't know how to tell him it was me.

The impressive white limo parked in front of my house, and the White chauffeur stepped out to open the door. Janis smiled as she stepped out. She wore a sand linen shell top with matching pants and open-toe pumps.

Her smile turned to a frown when she saw Choice beside me. I looked at Choice, and he didn't seem too happy to see Janis. *What's going on here?* I thought as Janis came toward us.

"Hello, Choice," Janis said, her eyes cold.

"Janis," Choice acknowledged. "Still on top of the world, I see."

"That's the only way I ride," Janis told him. I got the impression that if I weren't there, they would've came to blows. "You look naked without your camera. You're still dibbling and dabbling in that?"

"I'm still into it, but I wouldn't call it dibbling and dabbling."

"One day you'll grow up and get a real job."

"Like you have the nerve to call what you do real?"

"I'm working with Walter McCary now. I'm sure you've heard of him."

Choice nodded but I knew he could do more to insult Janis. The reason he didn't, I felt, was because I was standing there. "I didn't know you were working with Janis," Choice said to me, turning away from Janis.

"On the Walter McCary project," I said.

· "Look, I've got to run," Choice told me, looking hard at Janis, "but I will definitely call you tonight."

Choice stepped into the street to get to his truck.

"That could be a great man if he wasn't so small minded," Janis said as Choice climbed into his ride.

"I believe Choice has a great talent," I said as we watched his Navigator move quickly down the street. "I never would've guessed that you two knew each other."

"In another place, in another time. I don't deny his talent, Debrena. But it takes more than talent to make it," Janis said coldly, then she looked at me and tried to smile. "That's where a good manager comes in."

"Like you?"

"I'm willing to work hard for you, Debrena. You'll never be sorry you met me. I believe in you as an artist, a talent and a person. I got that get-up-and-go-for-it attitude. I'm here for you, Debrena. I think I've already proven that, but are you here for me?"

"What do you mean, Janis?"

"Something we talked about before."

"A contract?"

"Right. I think it's time, Debrena."

"We haven't even done the video yet."

"That's a done deal. I'm looking toward the future. I see you doing ad campaigns for Pepsi, FUBU, Dark & Lovely and Kawasaki, not to mention TV and films. I've already got a call from *XXL*. They want to spotlight you in the Eye Candy section of their magazine. I believe in you, Debrena. Do you believe in me?"

"I do, Janis."

"Come, sit in the car."

I got into the backseat of the limo with Janis, and the chauffeur closed the door behind us.

"Would you like to go for a ride?" Janis asked, her smile back on her face.

"My parents are in the house," I explained. "They're home for a surprise visit. Probably just for the weekend."

"You told me they were both retired."

"Yes, but Mom more than Dad. He still travels and plays."

"I'd like to take them out for dinner before they go, show them a real nice time. Would that be possible?"

"I don't see why not."

"One big, happy family. I come from a big family, Debrena. Even have a twin sister, but we were never close." From her large brown Dooney & Burke tote bag, Janis pulled out a black leather folio. She opened it so it rested across our laps. In the seam of the folio was a silver-and-gold Pilot ink pen. "What do you think of the name 'D. Allen.'"

"I don't know," I said honestly.

"Well, you better get use to it because after today that's who you'll be."

I didn't know what to say about that. I recalled our conversation about brand names and now I had one. If it would sell me to the public as a media superstar I figured I had to get use to it.

"It's just a standard contract, nothing fancy," Janis continued. "All it says is that I'm authorized as your representative to further your career in the direction we just talked about."

As I took the pen from Janis, my first mind told me to let Mom read the contract before I signed anything. Being an entertainment lawyer before she retired, I knew she would go over this contract with what she called "a fine tooth comb." And being her daughter I knew that was the right thing to do, but because Janis had done so much for me, I didn't want her to feel that I didn't trust her.

I signed and then Janis signed.

"I'll get you a copy of this," Janis promised me as she closed the black leather folio.

Chapter Thirty-eight

Even though my parents were in town, staying at the house, I still found myself at home alone on a Friday night. They went out with Dominique, and I didn't expect them back until much later that evening. I had wanted to spend some time with Choice, especially after that strange scene between him and Janis. I wanted to find out more about Janis from Choice, and I wanted to have a face-to-face conversation with him, but because he was tied up in his dark room, I could only talk to him on the phone.

"Why can't I come over?" I asked, although I already knew the answer.

"I told you, I have to develop these prints. Carrie needs them as soon as possible. That means like yesterday."

"And I can't just sit there until you're finished?"

"We tried that before, Debrena."

I had to laugh at the memory of my last time at his loft. He told me he had work to do and I tried to behave myself. "I'll keep my hands to myself," I said into the phone. "This time." The last time we ended up naked on the floor. He never did get back to his work.

"Debrena, how can I trust you? How can I trust myself?"

"We just have to exercise some self-control."

Choice had to laugh at that. "That's a great idea, but it's a little too late to start that now."

"I did want to talk to you," I told him, making my voice soft and sexy.

"Talk," Choice encouraged.

"I like to see your face when I talk to you."

"I'll see you tomorrow."

"I really need to talk to you now."

"Go ahead, I'm listening."

"Take me off that darn speakerphone."

"I need my hands free."

"It's about Janis, Choice." The silence was so thick that I thought he had hung up. "You still there?"

"Yes, Debrena."

"Say something. You don't like Janis?"

148

"It's a little more complicated than that."

"Tell me."

"I don't want to influence you in any way. But I will say this: Be careful."

I felt a chill run down my spine because that was the same thing that Lorrie told me. I had to ask, "Is Janis the big, bad wolf?"

"I'm not saying that. All I'm saying is that Janis is out for Janis."

"She won't help me?"

"She'll help you as long as it suits her."

I found myself getting defensive. "Why can't you just be happy for me? You're just saying that because you don't like her."

"Debrena, it's not about me not liking Janis. I'll give her the benefit of the doubt. Maybe she has changed. It's been at least three years since I've seen her. When I met her she was singing with a group of girls in little clubs all over Cali."

"Was she any good?"

"I thought the group was hot, but talking with Janis after their first set, it was obvious that she wanted more than that for herself. She wanted more control over her career. I took some pictures of them at the club I worked at."

"You sure there's not anything more between you and Janis?"

"No, Debrena," Choice said, like he was losing patience with me. "She's just not my type. That's not how I know her."

"I'm listening."

"The crazy thing was that I wasn't supposed to be there that first night. I was one of the club's roving photographers. We all dressed in black T-shirts, black pants and black sneakers. I had switched with another photographer because I wanted a nice long weekend. Janis came across as a sister who had to have it her way no matter what."

I didn't like the way that sounded coming from Choice's mouth. "Why must an ambitious woman always be seen as pushy?"

"Don't bite my head off, Debrena. That was just my take on her."

"It sounds like you're calling her a bitch."

"I didn't say that. Maybe *aggressive* would be a better word than *pushy*. She came at me like she just had to have me. That turned me off. I'm a man, I like to do the pursuing. I let her know that I just wasn't interested."

149

"Why? Were you involved with someone else?"

After a pause, Choice said, "I told you, she's just not my type."

He just didn't sound convincing but I didn't push him because I didn't want to argue or have him stop talking to me. I wanted to know more about Janis, and Choice could tell me things that she probably never would.

"She even gave me her business card," Choice went on.

I found that odd. "A business card for her singing group?"

"No. It was for her. She wanted to move onto artist management," Choice explained. "She found the girl group thing too unstable. She saw a much brighter future for herself in artist management."

At that precise moment I thought about the contract I had signed with Janis, but I didn't say anything to Choice about it. "Did you call her or see her again?"

"I never called her, but I did see her again, at the club."

"Sounds like she really wanted to get with you."

"I wasn't flattered."

"You make her sound like a stalker."

"It wasn't that deep, Debrena."

"But something happened between you two, Choice. The way you looked at each other in front of my house today. That wasn't actually a look of love."

"It's not what you think, Debrena."

I resented the idea that he thought he could read me so easily. "Tell me."

"One night, there was a girl at the club. She looked like a model, tall with a tight body and a beautiful face, dimples and high cheekbones. I saw her, and I had to say something to her. I had to take her picture whether she wanted to pay for it or not."

"Did she let you take her picture?"

"Like I said, I would've taken it anyway. But, yes, she let me take her picture. I took two; I kept one for myself. We talked during my break. She was new in Cali and trying to get some film work. She told me she had gotten a manager, and things seemed to be opening up for her."

"Did you get with her, Choice?"

"Not the way I wanted to."

"In what way did you get with her?"

"I won't lie, I wanted her, and I thought she wanted me—until we got to my apartment."

Although I wanted to hear this story, I got a rotten taste in my mouth. I didn't want any other woman getting down with my man. "Go on," I said reluctantly.

"A little candlelight, a little soft music, a little wine," Choice went on, setting the stage. "Because we knew what we were there for, we stripped down to our bare skin."

I had to let him know, "I'm getting very jealous, Choice."

Choice chuckled softly. "No need for that. This story doesn't have a happy ending, thanks to Janis Wilson."

I was totally confused then. "Janis showed up?"

"Janis sent the girl to me," Choice said with anger in his voice. "Janis told the girl that she would get her some film work if she was 'nice' to me."

I just couldn't believe what Choice told me; it sounded too much like a soap opera. "Janis pimped that girl."

Choice gave a bitter laugh. "Out in Cali, it's you do something for me, I'll do something for you. Janis felt because she had sent this beautiful girl to me that I owed her a little something."

I got a little uncomfortable as a result of my new insight into Janis. "Owed her something like what?"

"I never asked her. Whatever it was it was totally out of the question, I don't get down like that."

"Did the girl stay?" I asked out of curiosity.

"For a little while, but when it was time to seal the deal, she got cold feet. She began trembling like a leaf, afraid she wouldn't be able to satisfy me, ashamed because she had allowed Janis to talk her into having sex with a stranger and afraid that she blew her career because I would tell Janis that I wasn't satisfied with her. The girl looked so miserable and depressed that I told her to put her clothes on and go home. She begged me not to tell Janis, her so-called manager, how things really went down. She wanted me to give Janis a glowing report. You know, mission accomplished."

151

"Did you tell Janis that?'

"Janis came into the club the next night, smiling like she really had something on me. She asked me how I enjoyed her little 'gift.' I cursed her out and told her that I was not a charity case. She got an attitude, called me ungrateful, and we went at it for a few minutes. She just couldn't see how she did anything wrong. That's the scary part." After a pause, he added, "Don't let her use you, Debrena."

Although I knew that Choice meant well, I caught an attitude. "You think I'd let her pimp me like that? Do you think I'm that stupid? Or that needy?"

"No. You're too smart for all that," he said, but I still felt like he was patronizing me. "But there are other ways someone like Janis can use you and hurt you."

I was really angry at that point. "Choice, I don't believe you think I'm that freaking naive!"

"I know you're not naive, Debrena. Just be careful is all I'm saying. Maybe Janis has changed, I don't know."

"Choice, Janis invited my parents out to dinner! Does that sound like someone who is trying to use me? Hurt me?"

"I don't know, Debrena. You asked me what I knew about Janis, and I told you."

"Thank you very much," I said sarcastically, wanting to hurt him.

Terry B.

"I don't care about Janis. All I care about is you."

He sounded sincere, but I just wasn't buying it. He sounded too much like Lorrie, another person who just couldn't seem to be happy for me. All they could say was be careful, be careful, be careful, until it became some silly chant. I had had enough of that. "I can take care of myself," I said, and then slammed the phone down.

152

Chapter Thirty-nine

Janis's word proved to be her bond. She said she would take my parents to dinner and she did. Even Dad was impressed with the limo that Janis came to pick us up in. The place she took us, Amy Ruth's on 116th Street in Harlem, New York, was fabulous and historical.

"I had the pleasure of eating here when they first opened," Dad said as he sat beside Mom and across from Janis and me.

"When was that, Mr. Allen?" Janis asked, giving Dad a chance to tell one of his stories.

"Amy Ruth's was established in 1998," Dad said but I got the impression that Janis probably knew that. But because she didn't say anything, Dad drew us all into his story. "I came out of retirement to play at the Lenox Lounge between 124th and 125th streets. Back in the day, Miles Davis and John Coltrane played there. Now, Roy Campbell leads a Monday night jam session."

Janis smiled like Dad was the greatest man who ever lived. She was a pretty young woman giving Dad her undivided attention, and he just sopped it up like he was dipping a biscuit into gravy.

Mom looked at me as if to say, "Will you just look at that man? He is in his glory." And it was obvious that Mom wasn't mad about that. As a matter of fact, she encouraged him with her attention to Dad's story, although she had probably heard it a million times.

"I brought in a great quintet, which was Tobias Fox on piano, Tommie McKenzie on bass, Rickey Joyce on drums, James Holloway on tenor saxophone, and me, Stan "The Man" Allen on trumpet,"

Dad went on. "That's one group that I wished I had made a record with, but the group was too good to stay together. Everybody was in such demand for studio work. It was Tommie who got me some studio work with Al Jarreau. We did a lot of standards at the lounge and some originals, written by Tobias and me. Back then, people came out to hear the music; now, the music is just background for some loud drinking and foolish conversation. We played the weekends, and every night we'd do about three encores. And when the club closed we'd jam until about 7:30 A.M. Then we'd go over to Amy Ruth's for breakfast. My favorite meal was a cheese omelet with stone-ground grits that were brought in from Dothan, Alabama. They called it home-style southern cuisine."

Dad sat back like he had a meal, but that was not the case because we hadn't ordered anything yet. Because it was a Friday, the specials were fried coconut shrimp, Louisiana chicken jambalaya and pan-seared, herb-crusted jumbo scallops.

"I didn't know you had such a history with this place," Janis said, gushing all over Dad.

"Not just this place," Dad informed her. "I was born in Staten Island, but Harlem was my stomping ground and not just the clubs. I spent a heck of a lot of time at The Studio Museum and the Schomberg Center for Research. I even attended Abyssinian Baptist Church when Adam Clayton Powell led the congregation. I'm talking about senior not junior. Now Reverend Calvin O. Butts is the pastor and he ain't doing too bad of a job from what I hear."

"I heard that their gospel choir is out of sight," Janis said, the eager student to Dad's little Black history lesson.

"I'm not surprised. Just carrying on the tradition," Dad said, almost as if he had forgotten that we had come to eat. "After the Apollo Theater, Abyssinian Baptist is the most popular landmark in Harlem. Tourists come from all over the world to enjoy the services."

During a brief pause in the great conversation Dad was having with Janis, Janis signaled for a waiter. We placed our orders and of course Janis ordered the same thing Dad did: Louisiana chicken jambalaya.

At Amy Ruth's there were no alcoholic beverages on the menu, so we all had freshly squeezed lemonade.

"Janis, I really want to thank you for giving my baby this fine opportunity," Mom said between dainty bites of her baked catfish with white rice and steamed okra. "I always knew it was a matter of time before my baby got her big break."

Janis pointed her fork at me. "Debrena is great, Mrs. Allen. There were many girls in the running but when I saw Debrena dance at Dominique's studio, I knew she was something special."

Dad was so busy eating that all he could do was nod in agreement.

"But I do have one concern," Mom said, and that simple statement made Dad stop eating. "My baby tends to take too many things at face value."

"What do you mean, Mrs. Allen?" Janis asked, looking so sincere it seemed like she was ten years old. I had seen Janis in action around her show business peers, and I knew that she didn't like anyone to question her judgment. I knew that if it weren't Mom who was talking to her, she would've exploded in anger in that restaurant.

"I don't want my baby to look back on this video-making experience and feel ashamed," Mom finally said. "Young girls in those videos are portrayed as having the morals of an alley cat. I don't want to see my baby portrayed like that."

Dad just had to say something. "Sandra, Janis is a class act, and I'm sure the people involved with her are the same. Walter McCary, although not my cup of tea, is a very well-respected musician in the industry. I know because I've asked around. None of the musicians I've worked with have played with him, but their children, fine musicians in their own right, have good things to say about him."

"I listen to the radio, Stan. I know who Walter McCary is. And I have watched some MTV. The videos on that station are scandalous."

"Don't be such a prude, Sandra. Even Doris Day had her sexy moments in the movies."

"Sexy is one thing, and I have no problem with that, but half naked for no good reason is something else," Mom said forcefully.

155

"Mrs. Allen, I assure you that Debrena will not have to do anything that she is uncomfortable with. If she says no then it's no, and I'll be there to back her up."

"Do I have your word on that?" Mom pushed.

Janis smiled so broadly that I thought she would damage her cheeks. "You have my word. But understand that Debrena is a very beautiful girl and there's no way that the camera can ignore that."

"I have no problem with anyone appreciating my baby's beauty," Mom said, "but I will not have her exploited."

"Sandra, please," Dad said, "you act like you want Debrena dressed in a gunny sack."

156

"Stan, you know I'm not saying that. I'm thinking about my baby's future in this business. If she starts out with all that sexy stuff, that's all that they'll think she can do. My baby is a talented dancer, and I don't want anybody to overlook that."

I wanted to say, "Mom, they hired me for my dancing," but I knew when Mom and Dad went at it, nobody—and I do mean nobody—wanted to get in their way.

Janis wisely let them go back and forth, and although the discussion got heated, it never got loud or disrespectful. My parents were the king and queen of healthy debates.

Janis seemed highly amused. "I plan to have a long relationship with your daughter, Mrs. Allen. A long, professional relationship, and the video is just the start. The money is in versatility, and I plan to capitalize on that in terms of Debrena. I understand your concern."

"I hope you do, Janis," Mom said, "because I'm thinking about my baby's future too.

"I do understand that, Mrs. Allen. I assure you that Debrena's video debut will be professional and tasteful."

Mom still didn't seem convinced, but she did smile when she said, "I'll have to trust you on that."

"Anybody for dessert?" Janis asked.

Mom and I split a good-sized piece of red velvet cake. Janis, although she barely touched her entrée, ordered banana pudding. Dad, being the big man that he was, ordered carrot cake with raisins and nuts and destroyed that treat in five bites.

Before we left, Mom and Dad went off to find the rest rooms.

"She's tough," Janis said when Mom was out of sight.

"Mom doesn't mean any harm," I had to say.

Janis turned toward me, still smiling. "I wouldn't expect anything less, Debrena. I know girls are exploited in this business. She's a good parent. She loves you, she cares about you. I wouldn't expect anything less."

When Janis said that, I thought about how she had probably done her share of exploiting naive girls. I couldn't ignore what Choice had told me, but I also couldn't let his story scare me away from a golden opportunity. Because I felt I knew of what Janis was capable , I promised myself to keep my guard up around her. I'd let her drink all the alcohol she wanted, but I was determined to stay sober.

157

How could she hurt me if I was always in control of myself?

"Debrena, I need to talk to you about something," Janis said, looking around like she wanted to get this out before my parents came back to the table. "It's about the video. There has been another change in its direction."

"Not again." I sighed, almost ready to give up.

Chapter Forty

The next day Janis met me in the lobby of the Plaza Hotel. I wore a light trench coat over my dance costume. "I'm getting a little tired of this," I told Janis.

"I'm sure it'll be the last time," Janis had to say to prevent me from saying "take this project and shove it." I wanted to do the video but all the delays and false starts had me taking time from rehearsals for the summer dance concert that was just around the corner; it was July and the concert was scheduled for August. Like Dominique had once said, "It seems like a long time but it'll be here before you know it," and that was said in June.

"I just don't see why I have to keep on auditioning," was my biggest complaint.

"It's not an audition for you, Debrena," Janis told me forcefully. "You're the star of this show. They're just bringing back some dancers for a second look. The director wants them to dance with you so he can see the full picture."

I sighed deeply. "It just seems like I'm the one busting my booty, Janis. It just doesn't seem fair to me."

"I know, Debrena. I appreciate your being patient, and as quiet as it's kept, Walter appreciates it too."

"When am I going to meet this mystery man?"

"Soon, Debrena."

"I'm beginning to think that Walter McCary is a figment of someone's imagination. A media creation like Milli Vanilli."

Janis smiled, on the verge of laughter. "Debrena, I know you didn't go there."

I had to laugh as well. "Somebody has to show me something, Janis. I feel like I'm getting the runaround."

"No runaround, Debrena. I promise you that."

"Will we be in the same place as before?"

"No. They need a bigger room for this. I'm not sure where."

"Look, let me squat here," I said, pointing to the room we were in before. "I want to warm up, go over a few things. Come back to get me when you know where we'll be."

"Just keep the door open, so all I have to do is stick my head in to get you," Janis suggested.

Janis left me alone, and I went into the familiar room. Dominique always stressed the importance of warming up before dancing. She felt it made the difference between a good performance and a mediocre one and I agreed. When I entered the room I came out of my trench coat. My dance costume was a little more revealing than what I was used to wearing, but Janis had picked it out and convinced me that because all eyes would be on me, as principal dancer, I had to represent. I began my isolations and noticed, out of the corner of my eye that I was not alone. Because I didn't want to stare, I continued to work, trying hard to ignore the other person in the room with me.

"I never did get a chance to congratulate you," a voice called from across the room.

I didn't have to look at her to recognize her voice. "Thank you, Tyra," I said, then turned to face her.

She wore a gray crop top with matching shorts. Her simple costume made me feel naked.

"When they called me back, I thought it was because things didn't work out with you," Tyra honestly told me.

"No such luck," I was proud to say, sounding a little harsher than I intended, but she had caught me off guard.

"This is a long way from Dominque's little dance studio," Tyra reminded me. She said it like she didn't think I could hang.

"It's a new day, Tyra. I won't be intimidated by you or anyone else."

"It's not about intimidation, Debrena."

159

"It's sure not about you jumping up and down in joy about my good fortune."

"I was disappointed that I didn't get it. I have to be real about that."

"You can't be happy for me?"

"I'm happy for you, okay?"

"Bullshit!"

"You should know; you're the queen of bullshit, Debrena."

"Tyra, I've always been real with you. You're the one who walked out on me!"

160 "You gave me no choice, Debrena!"

"More bullshit!"

"Debrena, when it comes down on you, it's going to come down so hard!"

"If it does, you won't be around to see it."

"I probably won't, but I just hope the truth doesn't crush you."

"I know who I am, Tyra. Just because I won't go on this gay trip with you, you put me down."

"It's not about putting you down, Debrena. Don't forget how I caught you with Lorrie."

I winced because I couldn't help but think back to that time Tyra let herself into my house with the spare key I had given her and found me in the living room with Lorrie, both of us half naked. I knew I couldn't convince Tyra that we didn't have sex. I had to admit that we did come close, but like Dad always told me, "Coming close doesn't take the prize." I was shocked and embarrassed that day. I hated to be caught like that, especially when I really thought there was some hope that Tyra and I could get back together.

"You came back," I thought out loud, and emotion welled up in me so hard and fast I thought I was about to pass out. I had to ask myself at that moment, whether I wanted Tyra back in my life. "Did you want to get back with me?"

"No, Debrena," Tyra said, bursting my bubble of hope. "I came back to tell you that nobody can hurt you if you'll just be yourself."

Because I misread Tyra so badly, I became angry with myself.

"I am being myself," I snapped at her like a female pit bull.

"Being yourself, huh?" Tyra came back at me. "Like in this video, you'll be the All-American girl? Walter McCary's dream woman?"

"You're just sore because I'm not your dream woman!"

"I had you, Debrena Allen! In every cunt-sucking position! I know what you like and how hard you like it. Just remember that when you have all those people who don't know you at all, all up in your face, telling you what a great woman you are!"

"I'm more woman than you'll ever be!"

"I couldn't agree with you more. You're more than a woman because you're a gay woman."

I moved quickly toward Tyra, and I almost hit her. "Cool it with that gay shit! I told you how I felt about that!"

There was no backing down with Tyra. "Tell that to Lorrie the next time you make love to her."

I wanted to hit Tyra so bad, but I felt that would be playing into her hands. And in spite of my feelings toward Lorrie, I refused to see myself as gay. I wouldn't let Tyra make me own that. I wanted to say something else to her, but that was when I noticed Janis standing in the doorway.

"Ladies, we're ready," Janis told us with a crooked smile on her face.

I moved quickly past her, not even trying to think about how much of the angry conversation between Tyra and me Janis had heard.

Chapter Forty-one

After a grueling afternoon and night of proving that I was worthy of the top spot in the video, I dragged my tired body into the house. Because it was so late, I was surprised to see a light on in the kitchen.

"No, you didn't," I said and smiled when I saw who it was. "You know, Mom. I'm a big girl now. You don't have to wait up for me anymore."

"Maybe I couldn't sleep," Mom said as I came into the brightly lit kitchen.

The time was 1:00 A.M., hours after Mom's usual bedtime. She was in a light robe, sitting at the kitchen table with the family photo album in front of her. "Sit down with me. I was going through these pictures. So many memories."

I had to agree as I sat beside her and looked over the pictures she had pulled out. "Did Dad see these tonight?" I had to ask.

"Not these," Mom told me. "I had to dig real deep for these."

"You need to burn them," I told her as we looked down at the baby picture parents love and children hate. You know the one with your booty naked on a bearskin rug. But in my case it was me naked on a white towel. "I was a dark baby."

"Black and beautiful," Mom let me know.

"I still say burn it." I was firm, but not really angry with Mom. I knew how sentimental she could get.

"I hope I didn't come on too strong with Janis at dinner, Debrena."

"You were concerned. Janis had no problem with that. Janis knows that as a mother, that's your job."

"I just don't want you to think that I don't appreciate the opportunity that Janis is giving you."

"Mom, she knows you mean no harm. You're my mother. You're supposed to be concerned like that."

"I just don't want to be a pain and mess up your chance for a great career."

"It's okay, Mom. I know you want what's best for me."

"And I do. I just want you to have a good time, like you did when you were with Mr. Fred's group."

163

"Wow, you're really going back. I can't live in the past, Mom. I have to move ahead, get on with my life."

"I know that, baby, but I don't want you to get so wrapped up in this video thing that you feel you can't walk away if it doesn't feel right."

That was when I really looked at my mother. "Mom, I'm okay. I'm doing what I love. I'm following my passion."

"I know that, baby. I guess what I'm trying to say is that me and your dad love you for you. Whether dancing onstage or in a music video, it doesn't mean anything to us. We love you, baby. We'll always love you, no matter what."

I had mixed feelings about what she was telling me. "Mom, it seems like you're trying to make a back door for me. Like if the video flops, I can back out without feeling bad, just lick my hurt feelings and come home to your loving arms."

Mom gave me a sad smile. "Is that so bad, baby?"

"I don't need it, Mom," I said, trying hard not to get emotional because all I could see was love in her eyes. "I'm going to be great in the video."

"I know that, baby. But sometimes there are things you just can't control, like when a lawyer has a case. He can know all the case law and present a brilliant closing, but if the judge or someone on the jury had a bad night, well, all his brilliant efforts are for nothing. You see what I mean, baby?"

"I do, but I don't think it applies to me in this," I said. "And even if the video isn't a big hit, Janis has other things lined up for me. I told you about the ad campaigns for Pepsi, FUBU and Dark & Lovely."

"I remember all that but my question then and now is: what do those ad campaigns have to do with your dancing?"

"Mom, it's all exposure."

"I don't like all this exposure," Mom said, then held her arms around herself like she was cold. "I want to see you concentrating on dance, the thing that you love."

"Mom, Janis explained it to me like this: No exposure is bad exposure, especially in the media. I'm not going to let the media catch me wilding out somewhere half-naked and stoned out of my mind. You know me better than that."

"That's what so many people want to see nowadays: young women degrading themselves for some man's cheap thrills."

"You know that's not me, Mom," I said then smiled as I touched her shoulder. "My parents raised me better than that."

"But that's what's popular now, baby. That's what seems to sell."

"Mom, didn't you once tell me, 'Just because it's popular doesn't make it right?' I've never forgotten that. I never leave home without that thought." Mom nodded like I was saying what she wanted to hear. "I would never want to hurt you and Dad. I'd walk away from all this video stuff before I'd do that."

Mom looked at me like she could read the future in my face. "I really didn't stay up because I was waiting for you."

I looked at her, and we both laughed.

"But I am glad that we had this little talk," Mom said as she held out her hands to me.

"Me too," I said as I grabbed her hands. I squeezed them, then leaned forward to kiss her cheek.

When she yawned wide, we both knew it was time for her to go to bed. "Oh my, baby. That was a big one. I have to get some sleep because I know your dad is going to want to get the car on the road first thing tomorrow morning."

"I'm going to miss you two so much," I had to admit.

Mom nodded and then pulled me into her. I wasn't sure but there seemed to be tears in her eyes. I knew I was on the verge of water works. We spent a few more moments looking at the family photo album together. "This is such a great picture," Mom said, and I had to agree; it was so stunning in its simplicity. Two ten-year-old Black girls on the steps of the Frederick Douglass Community Center, Lorrie and me.

Chapter Forty-two

I could always count on the girls at the dance studio to keep me grounded. The new girls, LaToya, Kammie, Erica, Tamara, Shay and LaTasha let me know when I messed up or didn't do something I had promised to do.

"I know I promised and I will," I told LaTasha who looked at me with laser-beam brown eyes as we stood in the locker room.

When LaTasha walked away, dressed in her blue stretch top and matching shorts, she left with my promise to get with her, Shay and Erica after rehearsal to go over the number they would be doing in the summer dance concert, our tribute to the musical legacy of Eddie Kendricks. I hadn't wanted to stay that late but I knew I had to tell her something to get her off my back. I had to admire her persistence; it showed me that she was really serious about her dancing and that was something that was always good to see. It actually lifted my spirits. I had to admit, I was feeling a little down because I had said good-bye to my parents that morning. There were no tears but I couldn't squeeze them hard enough. They promised to come back in August for the summer dance concert. As they pulled away from the house, August seemed so far away.

Out of the corner of my eye, I noticed Lorrie and called out, "Hey, you."

Lorrie turned in the middle of pulling on her shorts. The look on her face told me she wasn't impressed with my gaiety. "What's up, D?" she said so matter of fact that I felt like a stranger.

Her cool attitude really rained on my parade. "I'm working with LaTasha, Shay and Erica after rehearsal today. I'm going to get the key from Dominique and lock up after everybody is gone," I told her, speaking fast to get it all out before she cut me off. "Now that means I'll have to be the first one in tomorrow to open up, but I can do that. I'll just have to set my alarm clock to make sure I get up on time. I wouldn't want everybody to be standing outside tomorrow morning waiting on me."

Lorrie looked at me as if to say, "What does any of that have to do with me?" She obviously didn't know what an "ebony diva" I was. I felt she needed to talk to Janis who thought I was the greatest thing since sliced bread.

"I thought you might want to hang around," I feebly explained. "Help me out with the girls."

167

"Thanks for the invite," Lorrie said and gave me hope for our relationship. Then she said, "But no thanks" and cruelly snatched that hope away.

I turned my back toward her, looking into my locker but seeing nothing, crushed.

"I-I mean, my mother has a doctor's appointment late this afternoon," Lorrie haltingly told me. "I have to take her."

That made me feel a little better, but I couldn't turn to face Lorrie because unshed tears felt like sand behind my eyes.

"I'll see you out on the dance floor," Lorrie said before she left me alone in the locker room.

I sat down heavily on the bench near my locker, the emotional weight even heavier because with all the good things Janis had lined up for me, I should've felt on top of the world. As I sat there I got the strange feeling that no matter what I did, I would never be truly happy. I sat there and looked down at my bare feet. I didn't look up until Angela came into the locker room and called out to me. "Hey, Debrena," she said, a whirlwind of motion as she walked toward me. She held bags from Daffy Dan's clothing store.

"I broke all speed limits getting here from shopping," Angela said as she dropped her bags near her locker. "I have something for you."

I couldn't imagine what she could have for me because since I began hanging out with Janis, Daffy's wasn't upscale enough for me;

I didn't want to see myself as a snob but there was no way that Daffy's could compete with Macy's on Thirty-fourth Street in New York City. Still, it was with some anticipation that I looked up as Angela came toward me.

"I bet you thought you'd never see this again," Angela said as she handed me *The Temptations* videotape she had borrowed.

With disappointment that I couldn't hide, I said, "Thank you, Angela."

"You okay, Debrena?" Angela asked as she sat beside me on the long, wooden bench.

168 *This is ridiculous,* I thought. *If anyone had told me that I'd find myself being comforted by Angela King I would have called them crazy.* On that afternoon, I was the crazy one because I welcomed that comfort.

"Come on now, girl," Angela said. "What's with this long face? You know you got the world by its tail. You're going to be great in that video with Walter McCary. Don't let a little PMS get you down. Don't you know everything will work out okay?"

I sighed deeply, trying hard to get myself under control. "Janis always tells me that."

"It's true," Angela said. "All you have to do is hang in there."

"You're saying that because you don't know what I'm going through behind this darn video," I told Angela. "You're on the outside looking in, and I'll tell you the grass is not always greener on the other side."

"Well, you just let me graze in that green grass and I'll show you how to enjoy it," Angela said, and then laughed out loud.

I had to smile at Angela because she looked so excited and hopeful. This was a side of her that I had never seen, and I was more than appreciative of the glow that she shared with me.

"I guess I'm just a little tired," I said as Angela stood from the bench. "I was up early this morning, saying good-bye to my parents, and couldn't get back to sleep."

"You just need somebody to cheer you up," Angela said as she went back to her locker. She knew she had my full attention as she came out of her clothes. "Somebody exciting, like me, to take your mind off your troubles."

I sat on the bench in full dance gear so there was no real reason for me to remain in the locker room.

"You're traveling with the big dogs now. You should be enjoying all that, Debrena," Angela said as she opened the door to her locker. "I've been checking out your wardrobe, girl. You really rocking that Gucci. I think we're the same size, in some things." That was when Angela opened her blouse. She wore no bra. "Let me raid your closet, see what I like. You know you need to hook a sister up."

I got the impression that Angela didn't want me to say anything, so I didn't. I just watched her. She kicked off her mules, and then opened her skirt and pulled it down. She wore no panties. Suddenly things took an intensely erotic turn. Trying to escape, I stood when Angela turned her booty toward me, then she bent to get something from the bottom of her locker. I had seen Angela naked many times in the shower, dressing and undressing in the locker room, but this time I felt like a peeping Tom. I tried to ignore the desire that stirred in my stomach, but I couldn't take my eyes off her. I knew it was time for me to get out to the dance floor. I quickly made my way to the door.

"Debrena," Angela called out.

When I reluctantly turned to her, I found her still raw naked and looking over a bare shoulder.

"What, Angela?" I asked, boldly looking at her, letting her know that two could play her game.

"It was real nice talking to you."

"Yeah, right," I said, and then hurried out, mad at myself because I fell so easily into her tender trap.

169

Chapter Forty-three

After rehearsal I went to Dominique's office, and even though the door was open I knocked on the wood of the doorframe.

"Come in," Dominique said without even looking up.

"I'm going to need the key," I told her.

She looked up and smiled at me. "We had a real intense rehearsal today," she remarked, and I nodded in agreement. "You girls are still going at it?"

"I promised LaTasha that I would take a look at her, Erica and Shay."

"Those girls are working very hard."

"But they're still a little insecure," I said as Dominique went through a fat ring of keys to give me what I needed. "I'll be in early tomorrow to open up."

"If you want, you can just drop the keys off at my house."

"I don't want to disturb you at home, Dominique."

"No problem for me," Dominique said as she was preparing to leave. "Just make sure you lock the door downstairs. I don't want anyone on the street to wander in here while you are rehearsing."

"I'll be mindful of that," I assured her.

"How's it going?" Dominique asked me.

"Fine," I told her a little too quickly. I really didn't want to talk to her about the video shoot, especially when I really didn't know when we'd begin shooting.

"I'm talking about the girls," Dominique said. "How is it going with them?"

With some relief, I said, "You saw the girls in rehearsal. You said yourself, it was intense."

"What I want to know is if you think the girls will be ready," Dominique explained. "I'm not worried about you or Lorrie or Angela and Marcy. Will the new girls be ready?"

"I really believe they will be."

"You're not just saying this because you think it's what I want to hear?"

"No, Dominique. They want to do well. They want to make you proud."

"Maybe I'm just making too much of this. It's just another summer dance concert."

"It's the summer concert that marks your twenty-fifth anniversary. That's very important."

"I have to admit that it is. Just between you and me, Debrena. This summer concert can make or break this company. It's no big secret that we have lost some of our big corporate sponsors. For the last three years, the Frederick Douglass Community Center has been half full. I never expected a standing room, but a good size house would let our potential sponsors know that we're keeping dance alive and well in Elizabeth. Everybody loves a winner, Debrena."

"I know that, Dominique, but I also know that every dancer here is completely dedicated to this company."

"I guess I can't ask for anything more," Dominique said as she pulled the strap of her black Cole Hann bag over her shoulder. "Have a good rehearsal," she said as she walked past me.

I followed Dominique out of her office and went out to the dance floor.

"Okay, let's take it from the top," I said to LaTasha, Erica and Shay as I walked back into the studio. I was surprised to find Kammie still there and still in her dance clothes. "You don't want to go home?" I asked, knowing she wasn't in the dance routine I had planned to rehearse.

Kammie gave her beauty pageant smile, and said, "I figured you might need some help."

I laughed. "I can handle those three."

Kammie laughed with me. "I know you can, Debrena. I just thought that I could handle the music while you worked them into a puddle of sweat."

I slapped her gently on the back. "Thanks, Kammie. On second thought, maybe I could use your help."

LaTasha, Shay and Erica were in a huddle near the back of the studio. "Come on now, we have work to do," I reminded them.

I worked with them on a segment that combined "He's A Friend" and "Goin' Up In Smoke," songs from the *He's A Friend* album recorded in 1976 and the *Goin' Up In Smoke* album recorded that same year. The two songs were the closest that Kendricks ever came to recording gospel.

It wasn't a complicated routine but because LaTasha, Erica and Shay were dancing together, their movements had to be synchronized and smooth. With Kammie behind the two-way mirror, controlling the music, we did some serious work. There was no letup on my part, and the girls appreciated all that I threw at them.

"Okay," I said after two hours of intense work, "let's try it one more time."

Although I knew they had to be tired, no one complained as they continued to dance for me. LaTasha even looked like she was a masochist who loved punishment.

"You were just like Dominique," LaTasha told me after we had decided to call it a day. "You didn't cut us any slack."

Before I could reply, I noticed Tamara coming into our rehearsal space with LaToya behind her. Because I had failed to lock the downstairs door, they had come in unannounced and Little Erica was pulling up the rear. Suddenly the whole company was there, except for Angela, Marcy and Lorrie.

"You two forget something?" I asked jokingly, but there was a no-nonsense look on Tamara's face. The girl liked to laugh and joke, but when she got serious, she was as serious as a heart attack.

"We need to talk to you, Debrena," LaToya told me.

"I thought you were going to wait until Lorrie was available," Shay said as she stood beside me.

"I called Lorrie," Tamara said, "but all I got was her answering machine."

That was when I became a little concerned. "Is something wrong? Is this an emergency meeting?"

"It's serious," Tamara said. "I couldn't sell a ticket to one of my best friends because of this mess with Angela and Marcy."

"Am I missing something here?" I asked.

"We talked about it before," Shay reminded me. "When we had our little get-together at your house."

I spoke over a lump in my throat. "About Angela and Marcy being gay?"

173

"A good friend of mine, a guy, said he wasn't going to buy a ticket to see a bunch of lesbians dance around onstage," Tamara said. "I'd hate to think about who else feels like that. I'm not going to bust my ass in rehearsal and have nobody come to the concert because they think we're all lesbians."

I felt a headache coming on as the girls formed a circle around me. "What do you want me to do?" I asked Tamara.

"Make them leave the company," Tamara said, and I almost laughed in her face. The summer dance concert was a few weeks away, no time at all to revise the program.

"I don't think that's a good idea," I said.

"Because they're your friends?" Tamara asked, her hands on her hips and her eyes hard.

"Not just that," I began. "You want this summer concert to be a success, and I want the same thing. We can't just go changing things this close to showtime."

"We should take a vote to get them out," LaToya suggested, and Tamara nodded in agreement.

"It's not as simple as that," I told LaToya, but included everybody.

"I don't want to have to go to Dominique," Tamara threatened, and I certainly didn't want to hear that.

"Look," I said, trying hard to hold on to my temper and play diplomat. "This is not something you take to Dominique. We are the Sisters of Soul dance troupe. We're up on that stage, not

Dominique. This is our company; we have to work out things among ourselves. That's the way it's always been."

"Guilt by association, guilt by association," Tamara said, like she was trying to start a riot.

"Look, let me talk to Angela and Marcy," I said.

"About leaving the company?" Tamara asked.

"No. About cooling it with their relationship, to keep it on the down low."

"They shouldn't be officers of this company," LaToya said, and Tamara nodded vigorously in agreement. I got the impression that the two of them had talked long and hard about this situation. All they wanted me to do was rubber-stamp the conclusion to which they had already come. There was no way I was going to let them railroad me into anything. As the senior member of the company, I felt I had to be the voice of reason.

"Like I said, let me speak with them first," I said, feeling like they were all ganging up on me. "Then I'll get back to you."

"And we'll have a big meeting," Tamara said.

I wasn't crazy about the idea of a big meeting. "Look, I'm tired, and it's getting late. I need to get off my feet and relax, but I promise you, first thing Sunday morning I will call Angela and tell her and Marcy how everyone feels."

"We're serious about this, Debrena," LaToya said.

"I know, and I respect that," I told her.

With that said, they all left. That is everybody but Erica, who stood beside me, smiling like the cat who swallowed the canary.

"The show's over," I told her, but she wouldn't even budge. "You want Angela and Marcy out of the company?"

"I don't care about that," Little Erica told me. "I just want to dance."

"Nobody will be dancing if we can't work together," I said.

"You'll talk to Angela and Marcy, Debrena. You'll straighten it out."

I had to smile at Erica. "Thanks for the vote of confidence."

Chapter Forty-four

Sunday is a day of rest for most people but not for me. I spent that morning reaching out to Choice and Janis. I woke Choice out of a sound sleep only to find out that he couldn't spend anytime with me because he was working so hard for NTA. He tried to tell me that most of the work he was doing was in preparation for the calendar he was putting together for the dance company, but I wasn't buying that.

I knew for a fact that he had not yet taken one picture for that project. As far as I was concerned, and I was being a little harsh, he just didn't want to see me. I said, "Bye, Choice," in a real nasty tone before I hung up. Still, I told myself that I would forgive him later, have makeup sex with him and let him treat me to dinner and a movie.

As for Janis, our conversation was more cordial but still frustrating because she couldn't tell me when shooting would start for the video. But she did invite me to another industry party.

To soothe my battered spirit I reached out to Lorrie, and all I got after a few calls was her answering machine. I wanted her to go with me to talk with Angela and Marcy. I kept calling with the same results and even tried to get an attitude, but then I thought about all the times I had ignored her phone messages when I was hanging out with Choice and I wouldn't get back to her. I didn't like it, but I understood that this was payback.

I called and got Angela on the phone. Although it was late on Sunday afternoon, she sounded like she was still in bed. I let her know that I needed to talk to her and Marcy, in person. She seemed happy to have me come over. I took a cab to her place and got there about twenty minutes after we talked. I had to speak into an intercom to get upstairs to her second-floor apartment. I knocked on the door. When the door swung open I let myself into the apartment. I found Angela standing in the living room, wrapped in a long white sheet.

"I thought I had given you enough time to get dressed," I told her as I shut the door behind me.

"I was taking a little nap when you called," Angela said as I walked into the living room. "I had planned on getting up earlier, but I just couldn't get my head off the pillow."

I nodded in understanding as I stood in the middle of her living room. I didn't want to sit because I didn't want to get too comfortable; I wanted to say what I had to say and get out of there. I had put it in my mind that I would not ask either Angela or Marcy to leave the company, but I would ask them to keep their little affair on the down low. I also thought about asking them to resign as officers of the company, but that was only if I had to give Tamara and LaToya more to keep them pacified. No matter which way I went, I wanted to squash this thing fast and move on with the business of presenting a great summer dance concert the following month.

"You ever get like that, Debrena? Have one of those days when you just wanted to lay in bed naked and free?"

I really wanted to get to my business. "Is Marcy here?"

That was when Angela nonchalantly sat in an overstuffed armchair, gathering her sheet around her like a robe. "She'll be right back. I sent her to the store for me, to pick up some female products."

"I need to speak to you and Marcy together," I told Angela. "I thought I made that clear over the phone."

Angela made herself more comfortable in the armchair. She even put a leg over one of the thick arms. It was a sexy pose even though she was fully covered by the white sheet. There was a faraway look in her eyes, like she was looking into the future and seeing something sexy and exciting happening for her. "You know you've become too serious lately. You used to be fun. I'd hate to see you get all stuffy like Lorrie."

I figured that that was the time to stop her in her tracks, let her know that I hadn't come over to talk about sex or Lorrie. "I didn't appreciate that stunt you pulled in the locker room, Angela."

"What stunt?" Angela asked innocently. Her legs were spread wide under the sheet and her left hand stroked a sheet-covered tit, and I could see the outline of a dark nipple. It was obvious that Angela was aroused.

I knew it was time to cut the bull. "Angela, what do you want from me?"

177

That was when she took the two sides of the sheet and opened them, like she was spreading her white wings. Her tight brown body glistened with sweat as she revealed herself to me. I had to ask, "What about Marcy?"

Angela brought a finger to her mouth. "Shush." She ran her other hand down her body, then over the mound of her sex. "I won't tell anybody," she said, sounding like a naughty little girl. With her both hands, she spread herself. "Lick me."

I stood there, trying hard to resist her. Who would know? Who would care? I suddenly had to admit that I really missed the funky magic of being with another woman.

"Come on, Debrena," Angela coaxed, still intimately open to me. The smell of her arousal was thick in the room. "I'm not too proud to beg, Debrena. Especially not for a sweet girl like you, a real music video star. You know I'm the one who really loves you."

That last part stunned me and brought me to a revelation. "You? You wrote that note?"

Angela smiled broadly, her almond-shaped eyes bright. "Who else? I wanted to tell you, but I couldn't find the right time. That was something that I wanted to keep between me and you."

My anger was like a fire burning in my chest. *You don't care about me,* I thought. *You just want to use me.* I had to ask again, "But what about Marcy?"

"Come on, Debrena. This is 1999. Get hip, girlfriend. What's wrong with a little sex between friends?"

"You know Marcy loves you."

"What's love got to do with this?"

"Please cover yourself, Angela." Of course she did nothing to comply with my request, but she did seem to be thinking about what I was saying. "It's wrong, Angela, even if I was down with it. I'm not here for fun and games."

"Just what are you here for?" Angela asked, still refusing to cover herself.

I told her about the conversation I had with the new girls in the company.

178   "And what do you expect me to do?" Angela asked after I was done.

"Just keep it on the down low, Angela," I suggested.

"And if I don't?"

"The girls will vote to kick you and Marcy out of the company."

"What about the summer dance concert?"

"Angela, I don't want it to come to that."

"What's the other option?"

"I thought, to make it all go away, that you and Marcy could resign from your offices."

"You know this shit stinks, Debrena. And I know it's all because of Tamara's homophobic ass. I just need to catch her alone in the shower and rape her sorry ass. I bet she'd be singing a new tune then."

Although I knew that Angela wouldn't do anything to hurt Tamara, the thought of a rape of one girl by another girl made me sick to my stomach.

"They can't just push us out without talking to Dominique."

"Angela, I'm really hoping that this doesn't go any further than this conversation we're having now, and perhaps one or two meetings at the studio with everyone else."

"This don't make no damn sense," Angela said, huffing. "I guess they don't know about Lorrie."

"They don't need to know about Lorrie."

"Or you."

"I'm not gay, Angela."

"Yeah. I know. You're bi-curious."

"Look, we're talking about you and Marcy now. I don't want either of you out of the company, especially so close to the summer dance concert. We've all worked too hard to just throw that all out of the window."

"We can't let anything happen to Dominique's precious summer dance concert," Angela said sarcastically.

"Be real, Angela. We're the ones who would be hurt the most if she has to cancel the concert. Stop trying to be a wise ass and think about that."

"I can't believe they would even think about voting us out."

"If they did, even if it came to that, the vote would have to be unanimous. Lorrie and I would vote for you two to stay."

"I just don't like this," Angela said as she covered herself.

"As soon as Marcy comes through that door, I want to finish talking about this, okay?"

Angela stood and said, "Okay. Let me put on some clothes."

I was relieved to see her moving toward her bedroom for more reasons than one.

Chapter Forty-five

It was another industry party as far as I was concerned, and that was why Janis had to talk me into attending. I let her talk me into it for two reasons: the event was to be spotlighted in an upcoming issue of Jamie Foster Brown's *Sister 2 Sister* magazine and Walter McCary was sure to be there. The event was held in New York City, at the Spy Bar, where Sean "Puffy" Combs held many of his Bad Boy parties. The crowd was wrapped around the block when I stepped out of the limo with Janis. Because Janis was who she was, there was no waiting in line for us. We walked to the front and the velvet rope was lifted. There were so many people in the club that I couldn't see how they could squeeze any more in. I was thinking fire code violation as Janis took my hand and led me through the semi-dark room. At a large round table with a white reserved card on it, we took our seats. As soon as we settled in, a waiter brought over a bottle of Cristal and two long-stemmed glasses.

"To you, Debrena," Janis said as she lifted her glass. "To your success and all the benefits we will share."

I raised my glass in agreement and sipped as a roving photographer suddenly appeared at our table. After he snapped a few shoots, I pushed my glass toward Janis. I knew she would drink what I had left and finish the bottle, and perhaps order another; Janis was always a thirsty girl.

A female deejay from Miami Beach provided the music. She was a Black girl dressed in a multicolored top, a white ruffled skirt and Puma sneakers. Her sets were a mix of old school and new school, but mostly old school. She played tunes that Dad would love like "Super Freak" by Rick James, "Pick Up the Pieces" by Average White Band, "Shaft" by Isaac Hayes, "Word Up" by Cameo, "Forget Me Nots" by Patrice Rushen, "(Every Time I Turn Around) Back in Love Again" by LTD, and "Flashlight" by Parliament.

What really struck me was the number of women dancing together, especially during the fast jams. The superfly brothers seemed content to hold up the walls. The fly sisters, on the other hand, came to party as always. But the thing that ran through my mind was all the bisexual sisters who frequented these see-and-be-seen gatherings. What I mean is that if I were to count all the times sisters at these parties tried to coax me into bed, I would run out of fingers and toes. There were many sisters on the prowl, but not all of them were looking for men.

"I'll be right back," Janis told me before she left our table to mix and mingle among the large, rowdy crowd.

Although I wore a black Dolce & Gabbana bustier with a short black jacket and matching low-rise pants designed by Michael Kors and shoes by Gucci, most of the women, including Janis wore all net tops, lacy shells, flimsy chiffon frocks with carefully placed lace panels. It was a peekaboo paradise for the men, or so it seemed. From my travels with Janis, I came to know the truth.

The bottom line was that so many men were clueless when it came to the true nature of many women's desires. I've laughed out loud many times when I've been at clubs or watched music videos where women were dancing together. I'm sure that sometimes it was innocent fun, out of necessity because the sisters had come to dance and the brothers were too cool to dance with them. And the sisters would dance suggestively, bumping crotches, rubbing bellies and touching gyrating hips. Because I had developed my "gaydar," my ability to spot a woman who was into loving other women, I realized that there were many times when the sisters were shaking their booties, not for the brothers, but for other sisters, and not just for the sisters with whom they were dancing. The brothers were pleased because they thought the sisters were whipping their hips for them, but the joke was on them because for many of the sisters, the dirty dancing was just a prelude to some hot, funky sex.

Just the thought of all that got me aroused. I loved men, but I could not deny the funky magic of two sisters together, exploring each other sexually. I didn't want to send out a message I couldn't follow through on, which was why I was so glad when Janis returned to the table. Because she was not alone, I stood to greet her.

Janis said, "Debrena, I want you to meet Walter McCary."

She didn't have to tell me who he was, I had all his CDs and knew what he looked like.

"Glad to finally meet you," Walter McCary said as he shook my hand.

182

He was taller than I ever imagined, a good six feet three or more with wavy black hair. He was the main man that evening, all eyes on him, dressed in black: a silk shirt, linen pants, wing-tipped shoes, silk socks.

The roving photographer jumped right in, taking several photos of Janis and Walter McCary and me, then several photos of just Walter McCary.

"I'll leave you two alone," Janis said, smiling like she had just hit the lottery. "Walter will tell you all about the video."

I sat down at the table, and Walter McCary sat beside me.

"I want to apologize for the delay," he began, "but there were a lot of people talking about how they wanted it done."

"I thought you had the final say."

"No. It's usually the director; I'm the executive producer, so I had to find a director who shared my vision for the video. We have that now."

Then Walter told me the story of the video for "A Dream." I was to play a high-fashion model and he was to play a high-fashion photographer. It's love at first sight when he sees me on the runway. Our eyes meet as he takes my picture all along the runway. I suddenly disappear. No one knows where I've gone but Walter has the pictures of me. He walks around lovesick as he thinks about me and develops the pictures in his dark room.

At an art gallery opening, the pictures are on display and, although he is commended on these excellent pictures, he is very sad. There is one picture of me that everyone really likes, and Walter gets lost looking into it. In the picture he sees my eyes move and we lock on each other. He accepts my invitation to join me inside the picture and steps into my world.

I had to laugh, amused by the *Twilight Zone* quality of the video.

"Do you think you can handle that?" he asked me, his big smile mirroring my own.

"I know I can," I said. "When do we start?"

"Tomorrow morning at six," Walter said as my mouth dropped. He laughed because he knew he had shocked me. I had waited so long and now it was finally going to happen.

"I'll see you bright and early," he said as he stood to leave.

All I could do was nod.

183

Chapter Forty-six

The location for the video shoot was The Ritz, an abandoned movie theater that had gone out of business when I was a child. It was a good place because of its Broadway-sized stage, which could be extended to accommodate a fashion model runway. When I arrived that morning in a limo Janis had sent to my house, the only people there were the makeup artist, hairstylist and the fashion stylist who were waiting for me in front of the theater. I asked about Janis but no one had heard from her. They let me know that I was in good hands. On the way over I had scanned the script. It was broken down into seven scenes, and I was featured in nearly every one.

I followed the trio up the long lobby with its hard white marble floors to the empty concession stand and up the stairs to the dressing room. There the makeup artist and the hairstylist, two slim Black women, got me ready for the shoot. There were three stools near a long mirror and I was directed to the middle one. The fashion stylist told me to strip, and the makeup artist applied makeup from my head to my toes while the hairstylist worked on my hair. Then the fashion stylist brought out her costumes, which consisted of lace corsets, V-neck teddies, G-strings, leather chokers, patchwork leather boots, fishnet bras with matching panties, Jimmy Cho shoes and borrowed diamond jewelry. I never felt so privileged. Once I tried on most of the outfits, we all realized that there was a big problem: There was no way I could dance in any of them without making the video X-rated. Even walking up and down the runway presented some problems, but if body tape was applied just right I could move without falling out of my outfit.

10:00 A.M.

More than four hundred male and female extras piled into the auditorium and, with "A Dream" blasting from a stack of big black speakers, the shoot actually began. Walter McCary came from the back of the stage but his costume changes were less extreme than mine. As a matter of fact all he wore was a three-piece black linen outfit that consisted of a jacket with matching pants and black sneakers. The only time he would lose the jacket was when he stripped down to a black tank top during the darkroom scene. He popped so many lights from his camera in my face, doing take after take, that I became dizzy. After every skimpy costume change, my body makeup had to be reapplied in certain areas. I changed behind a screen but it didn't stop some guys from sneaking peeks at my body. This childish behavior irritated me, but I didn't say anything about it. I had to walk down the runway in each outfit at least three times. The director wouldn't call "cut" until he got exactly what he wanted.

185

1:00 P.M.

A camera crew had to be taken outside to capture some shots of Walter singing about me as he roamed the streets around the theater. But even with him not there, there was still no rest for weary me. By the loud catcalls of the male extras and some of the females, the director decided on his favorite outfit, which would be the one that I would wear for the rest of the shot. It was a black lace bra with a red flower design, black fishnet pantyhose and thigh-high black leather boots, which I thought were ridiculous to wear in the summer, but the director convinced me that this outfit was every MTV male's fantasy. I also wore rhinestone doggy-shaped earrings, a diamond charm bracelet and a black leather choker. The only saving grace was that between filming I was able to slip into a long blue satin robe. All that open space in the theater made the set a little drafty. The stylist keep telling me how "mad sexy" I looked, but in my heart I felt like a fool and just wanted to leave this glamorous life behind. Janis was still nowhere in sight.

2:30 P.M.

Because the director didn't want me to dance I found myself in the first row of the balcony watching Tyra and the other dancers do their thing on the runway. I can't describe how jealous I was. I wanted to cry and throw up at the same time, then I felt ungrateful. After all, I was the female star of the "A Dream" video. But what got to me was the fact that everybody was having fun. It seemed like it was fun for them and all work for me, especially for the two good-looking girls that the director told to dance with each other. They stuck to the choreography but their close dancing became too hot for words. When the director yelled, "Cut!" someone from the crowd of extras yelled, "Get a room!" Everybody laughed at that, even the director. This video was shaping up to be more than I ever imagined. What had seemed so spontaneous on TV was orchestrated from the beginning. I felt like I was in a plot to fool the public. *Where is Janis?* I asked myself as the director signaled for me to come on down from the balcony.

4:00 P.M.

The art gallery scene was shot in the long lobby with the extras walking around and admiring empty poster-sized gold frames. As the director explained it to me, the photos would actually be moving pictures of me from the morning's shooting. He told me he had used three video cameras and two still cameras to capture all my moves on the runway. This was mind blowing to me because the extras had to act like there was actually something in those big empty frames. Walter McCary appeared in and out, lip-synching his song.

5:00 P.M.

As the extras and crew took a dinner break, the director and Walter watched a video monitor that showed what they had shot so far. Because the catering was done by Amy Ruth's, the food smelled delicious. All I got was a whiff of it and a few bites of red velvet cake because during the break a video disc jockey (VJ) from MTV interviewed me. He was a White guy who blushed red every time he looked at my cleavage. I wanted to change but the VJ begged me not to. He said that my costume was "too hot" to cover with some "old bulky robe." So with his microphone in my face and the cameraman slowly moving around me, I did the interview that would be aired on MTV just before the world premiere of the video. Behind me, the dancers practiced their choreography for the art gallery scene. By that time I'd stop looking for Janis.

187

6:30 P.M.

For the last scene, at the last minute, it was decided that Walter McCary and I would kiss. Because it wasn't in the script, the director and Walter McCary had a meeting with me to discuss this new direction. The director thought it would be "real hot, real sexy" and a "picture-perfect ending to a great shoot." As the director went on to explain, "This kiss has to scream sex!"

Walter McCary looked at me shyly before he said, "What do you say, Debrena? Are you comfortable with this? I wouldn't want to disrespect you in any way."

A sexy kiss, I thought. I felt a little uncomfortable because I had never kissed a White man. Although I wasn't too crazy about the idea, I couldn't see how I could say no. I wanted the video to be successful, and if that would do it then it was something I had to do.

"Why not?" I said to them. "A sexy kiss that screams sex, why not? I'm already half naked." That last part made the director and Walter laugh, moving us all beyond an extremely awkward moment.

8:00 P.M.

I was hungry, cold, tired and I stank. After almost nine hours in the humongous Ritz Theater, the director said the words that I had been dying to hear since six that morning: "That's a wrap!"

Chapter Forty-seven

For some reason that I couldn't understand, Janis had become a stranger to me. After all the intense time we had spent together, she suddenly became unavailable. I tried not to make too much of it, but I had to ask when I called her from the lobby of the dance studio. "Why weren't you at the video shoot?"

"You can blame that on Walter," Janis told me over the phone. "He had me tied up in meetings. In a few weeks we'll be heading back to California. Because he'll be doing some recording, I'll have to book studio time and line up some studio musicians."

I told Janis that I didn't want to hear that. As my manager I felt that she should've been there for me.

"But I also work for Walter," Janis said. "Besides, I heard you did quite all right."

"I made out but it would've been good to have you there in my corner."

"You'll be all right, Debrena."

"Thanks for that vote of confidence," I told her.

"I have to run," Janis said, and I felt like I was being dismissed, like she really didn't want to talk to me.

"Of course, you're a busy woman," I said without trying to hide my sarcasm as I hung up on her.

Although I saw a lot of Choice around the dance studio, we didn't get much time to talk to each other. He was in and out of Dominique's office talking about the calendar project, and I was in double and sometimes triple rehearsals, getting ready for the upcoming summer dance concert. Dominique had reached out to some of the local media—TV, radio, newspapers and cable—but none of them wanted to come around. Even though this was the twenty-fifth anniversary of the company, most of the media saw the annual summer dance concert as old news.

"Tickets sales are awfully slow," I shared with Erica as she stood near me while I did my isolations.

"You know Black people, we don't do anything until the last minute," Erica reminded me as she did her isolations beside me.

Before I could say anything, Choice stuck his head into the doorway and waved for me to come toward him. Erica saw him immediately, and then smiled at me, like I had just let her in on a big, fat secret. Choice's action took me somewhat by surprise because we had decided that we would keep our personal relationship on the down low, especially around the dance studio, where eyes were always looking for some juicy gossip. I didn't want to be in that mix and neither did Choice.

"What's wrong?" I wanted to know, really surprised that he would call me over to him.

Choice smiled as I followed him out into the hallway. "You look beautiful," he told me.

I blushed, but I knew he had more on his mind than my physical beauty. "Thank you, but you could've told me that later this evening." Then I became alarmed. "We are still getting together this evening?"

"No doubt about that," Choice assured me. "What I need to talk to you about is that wrap party with Janis."

"First of all, it's not Janis's party, Choice."

"Count me out, Debrena. I thought about it, I just don't want to be around that phony crowd."

"Because of what Janis did to you three years ago?"

"Not just that. I'm over that, but I just can't stand there acting like I'm having a good time."

"You'll be with me, Choice. Doesn't that count for something?"

"It does, Debrena, but not there. I know Janis. She'll have you all over that ballroom, meeting all the important people." I knew better than to force Choice to do something he didn't want to do. "It's your night to shine, Debrena. I wouldn't want to put a damper on that."

I appreciated his honesty, but I couldn't hide my disappointment. Janis had informed me that all those involved in the production of the "A Dream" video were invited to a big celebration party at the Marriott Hotel in New York City Times Square. I hadn't told Janis but my plan was to invite Choice and have him spend the weekend with me at the hotel. That way we could party downstairs in the ballroom and upstairs in the bedroom. To say I was disappointed was an understatement. I wanted to sink to the floor, cry like a child and beat my fists against the floor.

"I'm beginning to feel a little neglected," I had to admit.

"I'm busy, you're busy," Choice said as if that explained everything. "But we still have tonight."

"Yeah, just give a dog a bone," I said sarcastically. "Okay, I won't catch an attitude."

"I can't hang out with you at the wrap party," Choice told me, "but I can get with you afterward."

"It'll be real late then," I reminded him.

"I'll stay up waiting for your call, in my bed," Choice said, and that sounded real good to me.

"I have a better idea," I said, leaning in to him. "When I get in, I'll call you and you can come over to my house. You know I'll treat you right."

"Breakfast in bed?" Choice asked.

"If you want that."

"I do. But we both have to be at the dance studio, so you don't want to stay out too late."

"How are the photo sessions going?" I asked, even though I didn't want to spend a whole lot of time talking to Choice in the dance studio; I couldn't forget about Erica standing nearby.

"Real good," Choice told me. "Your fellow dancers are very cooperative."

I had to laugh, recalling some of the locker room conversations

I had overheard. "That's because they think you're so cute. Those photo sessions may be work for you, but it gives them an opportunity to get their flirt on."

"Whatever reason, I'm moving right along with this project. I plan to take your picture next, in the studio."

I looked over my shoulder, then said in a whisper, "I have to get back in there."

"Okay. Tonight."

"Your place or mine?"

"My place," Choice said too quickly. "I have a new video."

I had to laugh out loud. "Not another bootleg?"

191

Choice looked like he was in pain, stung by my teasing. He knew how I felt about the poor quality of most bootleg videos. The last one we saw together was *In Too Deep,* and the picture quality was dark and grainy. We got a good sense of the film but it was nothing like watching it on the big screen. The only reason I tolerated it was because we didn't have to get dressed to go out. We even microwaved some buttered popcorn.

"I checked this one out," Choice let me know. "It's not too bad."

I looked at him like he was crazy.

"Really, Debrena. The sound is excellent and the picture is steady, not jumping all up and down like the last one we saw."

"Why don't we just go to a movie theater?" I suggested, not wanting to get into a long, drawn-out conversation.

Choice leaned in close to whisper in my ear. What he said made me giggle, and I playfully punched him on the shoulder for being fresh. But he was right; one of the advantages of watching a bootleg movie at his loft was that we could be naked while we watched it. And if we couldn't keep our hands off each other and had to get it on, we could always rewind.

"I really have to get back in there."

That was when Choice waved at me as he backed his way down the hall. When I got back to Erica, I found her smiling. "What?" I asked.

Erica looked at me like she didn't know what I was talking

about.   Knowing that she wasn't fooling me, she had to laugh. "Nice guy, huh?"

"We have work to do," I reminded her, not wanting to say anything about Choice.

Chapter Forty-eight

That night we watched Choice's bootleg of *The Wood,* a movie about three guys growing up in California that I really wanted to see. It starred that deep-chocolate dream Taye Diggs. I just loved his dark skin and brilliantly white teeth. I didn't swoon over him out of respect for Choice, but I had to admit that after seeing Taye Diggs in *How Stella Got Her Groove Back,* his big-screen debut, I looked forward to each and every movie he planned to make.

The surprising thing about that evening was that although we were half naked, we watched the whole video without touching each other. When Choice stood to rewind the tape, I took a good, long look at him. I still found him sexually appealing but I had to admit that there was a cooling off of my desire. It was not that I didn't want him, but the urgency that I once felt just wasn't there.

I knew one of the reasons was his attitude toward Janis. I agreed that she had done an underhanded thing to him, but I also felt he should've gotten over it, especially after all these years. I got the impression that there was more behind his attitude toward Janis but I could never get him to talk about it. I didn't push it because I just didn't want to argue with him. Still, I couldn't shake the feeling that there was something he wasn't telling me.

I took him into my body that night at his loft, but I felt no need to get buck wild with the sex like we usually did. We had sex like I imagined married couples did: It was still satisfying but nothing to brag about. Choice had become another thing in my life that took more than surface or reflex thinking. I had gotten to the point where I not only wanted to know where all the pieces fit, I had to know why they fit where they did.

Chapter Forty-nine

Janis knew I was less than pleased with her performance as my manager. To try to make things better she sold me on an idea that she thought would make me happy and get the media to talk about my video debut.

It was a hard sell because I was still disappointed that I hadn't danced at all in the video. I tried to explain to Janis time and time again that I signed on to dance, not to be a sex object. So when she suggested that I go to the wrap party as Walter McCary's "date," I really had to think about that.

My first question was: What about Vonda, Walter McCary's supermodel girlfriend? The way Janis explained it to me was that Vonda was on tour, and even if she was in town she would not have attended the wrap party because the attention of the media would shift to them as a couple and that would do nothing for the video. Eventually, Janis convinced me that me being seen on Walter's arm would be good for my career and Vonda would know that it was strictly business, nothing personal.

The wrap party came much too soon for me. It was with great irritation that I took a whole day off from dance rehearsals to get myself ready. My outfit was another Janis Wilson selection and another reason for us to argue.

"Believe me," Janis said for what seemed like the tenth time as we stood in my bedroom, "this is the outfit for you."

"Janis," I complained, sounding like a spoiled child, "I'm showing way too much, in the front and in the back. And the way this dress is made, forget about wearing any underwear."

"Believe me," Janis said again, and I felt like saying, "Cut it with the 'believe me' already, you sound like a broken record."

"This is the last time," I told her as I stood in my bedroom. "The next time I'm dressing just like you."

Janis wore a conservative blue tux that hugged her curves complete with blue silk lapels. "I'm just background, Debrena. You're the star of the show."

"Hurrah for me," I said unenthusiastically. I turned to look at myself in the full-length mirror. The way the red silk dress was cut it rode low on the small of my back. If it were any lower you could've seen the crack of my behind. I felt it was too revealing, but it was appropriate for a female video star. I had to admit that, and that was why I stopped arguing with Janis. Plus, it was getting very late. The wrap party invitation stated that the party was to begin at ten, and we were still in my bedroom way past midnight. I knew I was expected to make a grand entrance with Walter but I felt this was getting ridiculous. Still, according to Janis, we were right on schedule.

195

"I'm a little concerned about the video," I admitted to Janis.

"Why?"

"There were times when I felt I was just flying by the seat of my pants. I could've really used a second opinion. I felt I had no real direction, that I was just going along with everybody else's program, like I was some dumb puppet on a string."

"Sometimes you have to go with the flow in this business, Debrena. You just have to trust the people who are working with you."

"Like the director, the stylist and the makeup artist?"

"They're professionals, Debrena. If you look bad in the video, they look bad. And nobody can afford to look bad, not in this fickle-ass business. We have so many one-hit wonders that it isn't funny. I don't want you to go down like that. Next year, I don't want people saying 'What ever happened to Debrena Allen?' "

I understood what Janis was saying but I felt I also had to think about my parents. "I keep thinking that I exposed too much of myself in that darn video."

"Remember what I said about exposure?"

I quoted Janis word for word: " 'No exposure is bad exposure, especially in the media.' "

Janis smiled at me like I finally got it right. Then I went into telling Janis how I really felt. I was somewhat reluctant to come at her so aggressively but I had to remind her that as my manager she worked for me. I broke it down to her so there would be no confusion about what I expected.

Of course, Janis was not happy about me taking control like that, but I explained that I was the one in the spotlight. Janis was behind the scenes where she belonged. From the look on her face it was obvious that Janis was not the least bit happy with me. I even went as far as telling her that she could be replaced as my manager.

"Do I need to remind you that we have a legal agreement?" Janis said to scare me.

She began talking about her rights as my manager, but I still refused to back down. I think this surprised her, and I waited for her to come at me.

After a tense silence her last words were, "Okay, Debrena, have it your way."

What was scary was the deadness in her eyes and the chilliness in her voice. She stopped pushing but I suddenly got the impression that I needed to watch my back. Janis was not to be played with, and payback was a bitch.

Chapter Fifty

Although I was Walter McCary's "date" I was suppose to meet him at the Marriott. When Janis and I finally got there, it looked like the party was in the brightly lit lobby. The crowd was at least three hundred plus, and they all stood around like they were waiting for something to happen. I knew it wasn't me because as provocatively as I was dressed I got very little attention. Before I could ask Janis, "Where's Walter?" some women began to scream, and the crowd moved to the front of the hotel. Just as suddenly the screams turned to cries of "Walter! Walter!" and I turned to see where he was. I got a quick glimpse of him before he was blocked by an enthusiastic group of photographers and fans.

I was content to stay in the background but Walter had other plans for me. Because he was so tall he was able to look over the bobbing heads of the crowd and gesture to Janis and me. With a gentle push on my lower back, Janis pushed me toward Walter. The crowd parted like the Red Sea mentioned in the Bible and I found myself under the shelter of Walter's right arm. He was dressed in all black: a tux with a silk shirt and a bow tie.

"This is D. Allen, and she is just great in my new video," Walter let everybody know, and I smiled broadly as the photographers took about twenty minutes of pictures.

There were also writers there but none of them wanted to talk to me; all the questions they asked were addressed to Walter. I felt totally unnecessary, like D. Allen was there just to be seen and not heard.

"I think it's time to get this party started," Walter said, then winked at me and escorted me into the grand ballroom with everybody following us. It was like the party couldn't start until he got there.

Inside the ballroom I found myself standing with Janis.

"You're a star," Janis shouted over the music as Walter McCary left my side and disappeared into the crowd. She stood near me with a bottle of champagne in one hand and two glasses in the other. The room was semi-dark and the music from a live deejay was ultra-loud. The rest of the crowd from the lobby quickly filled it to capacity.

"I'm not drinking," I let Janis know, trying to hold on to something with which I was familiar.

198   Janis led me to a table marked reserved. I needed to sit, to get off my feet if nothing else. I wasn't used to wearing stilettos. Janis sat across from me and filled the two glasses.

"Just to celebrate," Janis said. "One drink."

"Janis, are you drunk? I told you no. I don't need that; I'm on a natural high."

There was a quick flash of anger on Janis's face but it went away so quickly that I made myself believe that it wasn't there. I didn't want to make her angry but I just didn't want to have my whole life in her hands. I felt that I had to figure out some things for myself. I wasn't sure where this wild ride was going but I wanted to make sure that after it was over, I respected myself and had no regrets about anything I had done to claim my fame.

Still smiling Janis said, "I think you need to speak to Walter."

"Why?" I wanted to know. "Did he ask to speak to me?"

Instead of answering my question, Janis tilted her head in Walter McCary's direction. He stood across the ballroom, surrounded by a group of well-dressed White men.

"Go," Janis told me. "Your public awaits you."

Because I knew I wasn't that important in comparison to Walter McCary, I reluctantly left the table. As I moved toward Walter I occasionally looked back at Janis. I didn't want to take my eyes off her because I wasn't sure from where she was coming. During my short walk toward Walter and company, I saw Janis leave the table.

"D," Walter called out to me, "I want you to meet some very important people."

I glanced over my shoulder and saw Janis talking to a tall, long-haired, hippie-looking White guy. He looked so out of place among the well-groomed, well-dressed crowd. He looked like the sort of corny White boy who would never be allowed into a hot, upscale club or the grand ballroom of the Marriott. He handed Janis something and she went into her purse. I couldn't make out what was going on. I didn't know if she was reaching for money, a pen, a business card or what. I was distracted because that was when the men surrounding Walter began to introduce themselves.

Their compliments came at me hot and heavy, like proposals from some prospective sugar daddies. They were all old enough, bald enough and white haired enough to be my granddaddy, and the way I was dressed and the way they looked at me made me feel like I was in a lion's den wearing a pork chop jacket. I felt like a gang of dirty old men was truly devouring me.

Just when it got to the point where I was about to run out of the hotel to grab a cab and go home, Janis came to my rescue—or so I thought.

"These men were dying to meet you," Janis let me know, and I found no need to thank her. Thanks to her I was in another fine mess. She was talking to me but I felt her message was for the men. "I propose a toast."

I cut an angry eye at Janis, asking myself, *How many times do I have to tell her, I do not drink?* Behind her was a waiter with drinks on a silver tray. I counted just enough for Walter McCary and the men. Janis was holding a drink for herself and me.

"Seltzer water with a lemon and lime twist," Janis told me as she handed me my drink. What she had for herself was the same dark color as what the men had in their glasses. "To Debrena, a star who will always shine brightly," Janis said as a toast.

We all clinked glasses. I reluctantly drank the strange-tasting water. *Too much lime,* I thought as I let it slide down my throat. All the men, including Walter, smiled at me, like I had done some good deed.

I found it a little strange that Janis was the only one not smiling. As a matter of fact, she looked at me like I had done something wrong. Before I could say anything to her, I was hit by a blinding headache. It hit me so hard and so suddenly that I wanted to go home, but I knew I had to stay.

When I finished my drink, Janis took my empty glass and placed it with hers on the silver tray of a passing waiter.

Walter said something to me but I was in so much pain that I didn't hear him. Still I nodded like I was following his conversation and all the men laughed. I smiled even though I felt like I was sinking in quicksand.

I turned toward Janis and found her halfway across the room. She was speaking to a model-slim, tall Black woman with black hair so short you could see the shape of her skull. The woman was one of those touchy-feely talkers that had to touch your shoulder or your arm when she spoke. Janis stood so close to the woman that their bodies touched. I had no idea who the woman was, but everybody could see that they were really into each other, having a lively conversation that left no room for anyone else.

Chapter Fifty-one

I was in so much pain that what happened next was hard for me to follow. I didn't know if I was dreaming or hallucinating. I was at the table with Janis, and the Black woman with the super-short hair-cut was sitting across from me. I vaguely remember Janis making introductions but I couldn't remember the woman's name or even focus on her appearance. Her round head seemed to be surrounded by a halo of bright light that burned my eyes and made me feel that everything in my stomach was about to come out of my mouth. I think I asked for some ginger ale.

I did ask for some ginger ale because that settled my stomach. I must've felt all right because when the deejay dropped Q Tip's "Vivrant Thing," the woman at the table said, "Go do your thing, girl," and I got up to dance.

I did the routine I had learned at that long-ago audition with Harold. I wasn't dancing long before someone grabbed my arm and a woman's voice said, "Enough. Those suckers don't deserve all that. Let's leave them hungry for more."

Then I was led out of the grand ballroom, and because my head was pounding again I had to close my eyes and hold on to someone. But I had no idea who it was. The only way to keep my head from hurting was to keep my eyes closed. In the elevator it was even worse because the motion of the car made my stomach drop to my feet. My bare feet. I had no idea where my shoes were. I opened my mouth to ask but nothing came out. Or at least nothing anyone could understand. I was helped out of the elevator and led down a long, thickly carpeted hallway.

As I walked down the hallway I got the sense that I was between two women, their bodies pressed against me with sharp, bony angles and soft, pillowlike flesh.

"This is going to be a nice chocolate treat," a woman's voice said as a door opened and I was gently ushered into a hotel room. "We can do a train like the guys do."

"Not this time," another woman's voice said. "I brought her up here for you."

"Is that right? I just think you want to see me do my thing."

202   Then there was loud, head-splitting laughter, and I couldn't, for the life of me, figure out what was so darn funny. How could there be a train in a hotel? And what was this chocolate treat? I opened my eyes to see where I was going. There was so much intense pain that I had to close my eyes again. It was like someone was stabbing my brain with sharp daggers. I opened my eyes once more and noticed the pattern in the thick carpet beneath my feet mesmerized me with its purple and blue and gold and white.

In the room the bed was a white square that glowed in the light and hurt my eyes. Still, the bed was so inviting that all I wanted to do was lie across it and slip into the darkness of sleep. I fell across the bed, flat on my back. Gentle hands with fingers like feathers stroked my hot forehead.

"I'm burning up," was my complaint.

I had to close my eyes because looking at the light hurt so much. Suddenly my forehead became cold as someone placed an ice cube on it. The ice began to melt, and water rolled down the side of my face. I was worried about the bed getting all wet but the coolness was so welcomed, so refreshing. It made me want to search for sleep. Before I could find sleep, featherlike fingers ran over my lips. I stuck out my tongue and licked the fingers, needing the coolness in my mouth. There was a soft, sensual moaning, sounding like a woman drawing up pleasure from somewhere deep inside herself. I had no way of knowing from where the sounds were coming. To look for the woman making those sexy sounds I would've had to open my eyes, and it hurt too much to do that. I didn't want that stabbing pain; I couldn't have that.

Hot hands moved up my neck and then down to the top of my chest. I tried to sit up but firm hands pushed down hard on my shoulders. Then greedy hands pulled open the top of my dress, leaving my breasts bare. I looked down on my torso and with blurred vision I noticed my nipples stood up like dark brown pinpoints, and then there was wetness on my stomach. It was a hot tongue that stroked my stomach and then moved up to my chest. This wet tongue flicked at my nipples, first one and then the other. I became aroused to the point where I began to squirm on the white square of the bed. Then there was a coolness as the bottom of my dress was lifted above my thighs.

I spread wide as gentle fingers ran up and down the inside of my thighs. My legs flapped open like the wings of a bird. Soft fingers ran down my belly, and then up to my slick, wet opening. I rolled my head from side to side. The contact below my waist was intense and intimate. I squirmed, exposed and dripping on the bed, again worrying about the wetness but knowing that there was no way I could hold back. That wicked tongue was all up in me, making my cream come down, making me moan loudly, like some buck-wild woman. My legs trembled and I pushed my bare feet into the bed. I cried out and reached for my climax. My orgasm was like a hard punch in the belly.

Then a woman's voice from far off echoed, "You are one bad bitch." There was more laughter but it seemed to be more than one person laughing. Were they laughing at me? I felt so embarrassed and wanted to get out of there, but I couldn't move. I surrendered to my fate and drifted off into space.

Chapter Fifty-two

Wow, that was a strange dream," I said to myself when I finally sat up in bed the next morning. My head felt like it was stuffed with cotton, and there was a dull ache but nothing like the pain I felt the night before. I looked down at my body and pulled the wrinkled dress together to afford myself some modesty. I was still naked beneath my garment but because I felt that I was alone, I didn't sweat it. But alone *where* was the question.

I got off the bed. Because I was on unsteady feet I fell against the dresser in the room and almost knocked Janis's mini-camcorder to the floor. I was glad that I caught it because I wasn't about to replace it with a new one. Somehow I managed to make my way to the doorway of the bedroom. I found Janis on the phone in her suite. She saw me standing in the doorway and waved at me. Before I could say anything, she turned her back toward me. I stared daggers at her because I wanted to go home, take a shower and get some real sleep.

"I told you that I was going to call you," Janis said, speaking into the phone. "You did your thing, I'll give you that. I couldn't do two things at the same time. No, I was okay where I was. I had a front-row seat. Come by later, we'll watch it together."

When Janis finally turned toward me, I really thought she was ending her phone conversation.

"You are terrible, girl." Janis went on, more animated than ever. "I thought you were going to climb in there and come out the other end. I do admire your technique."

I cleared my throat loudly.

"You are just nasty, a nasty girl," Janis said into the phone, and then laughed loudly. "No, no more. I really, really have to go." After Janis hung up, she said, "Good morning."

"What's so good about it?" I asked, recalling how fast my evening went downhill after Janis handed me a drink. "You tricked me. It wasn't just water, was it?" Janis just gave me a crooked smile. "Why, Janis?"

"I thought you needed to loosen up a bit."

"I want out of here," I told her, disgusted with the way she had deceived me. "I'm going to need some clothes. Can you loan me a shirt, some jeans and some slides?"

205

Janis looked at me like she was sizing me up for some special activity. "I don't think any of my clothes will fit you like a fashion model."

"I'm not looking for a perfect fit, Janis. At least I won't be half naked."

When I said *naked* Janis looked at me strangely, like I had accused her of something. Then she made herself busy, gathering clothes from her oversized suitcase. As she moved around her suite, I took a good look at her. Without her makeup and no ghetto-fabulous outfits, she looked like a plain Jane to me.

"You know you were wrong, Janis," I said. "What if I were allergic to that stuff?" Then I really got mad. "You got me drunk, Janis. I think I have a darn hangover. I can't be sure because I've never had one."

Janis found that hysterically funny. "You had a great time at the party, believe me."

"I can't believe you got me in this mess," I told her. Then because I felt I was about to pass out, I sank into a nearby chair. "I have to sit."

"You'll be all right," Janis said as I looked up at her, noticing her self-satisfied smirk.

I opened my mouth to say something, but my dream came back to haunt me. I uttered in horror as I recalled the soft touch and the smell of a fruity perfume. I shuddered because its meaning was so obvious. It was all that I associated with the funky magic of two women making love. It made me want to get away from her but I didn't trust myself to make any sudden movements; I didn't want my head to hurt, and I didn't want to fall off my feet. The thought of what I had seen made me sick to my stomach.

"Do you have to use the bathroom?" Janis asked and I shook my head. I just couldn't shake the image of a woman between my widespread legs; a long, brown woman stretched out naked before me, burrowing into me. "Just give me a few seconds. Let me clear my head." But this image wouldn't fade; it was like a stain on my brain.

206

"Whatever you need to do, Debrena," Janis said, that darn smirk still on her face.

"I had a crazy dream," I reluctantly shared with her.

"What made it so crazy?" Janis wanted to know.

"A real strange dream about the party," I told her, promising myself that I wouldn't tell her anything else. Everything else was so weird and embarrassing, especially the part with Janis between my thighs.

"Oh yeah. What was so strange about the party?" Janis asked with some concern in her voice.

"That's the crazy thing," I had to admit. "I don't really remember much after I met those men with Walter McCary."

"Very important men," Janis reminded me.

"Dirty old men," I had to say, remembering them vividly. "They undressed me with their eyes and then tongued me down with their dirty minds. Janis, that is not my idea of a good time."

"Debrena, you're going to have to face the fact that you're beautiful and you have a dynamite body."

"Janis!" I said too loudly, making my head hurt. "I want to be known for more than my body. I have a brain, you know."

"No one doubts that, Debrena."

"They will if every time they see me, I'm shaking my booty. And speaking of booty, in my dream, I got up to dance at the party. Then I reluctantly asked, "Janis, did I dance at the party?"

Janis seemed distracted when she said, "A little."

I had to know. "Did I embarrass myself?"

Still distracted, Janis said, "What do you mean?"

"Was I acting all crazy? You know, dancing all wild?"

"Debrena, you had a good time." Then she sighed, like she had had enough of me. "And like most people who don't drink, you put your head down on the table and fell asleep."

"What about your friend?"

Janis seemed shocked by my question. "What friend?"

"I don't know. Maybe it was part of my dream. I could have sworn you introduced me to this woman with real short hair."

Janis looked at me, and then shook her head. "Girl, you were dreaming your ass off."

Not wanting to seem really crazy I got off that track. "How did I get up here to your room?"

"I brought you up here."

Suddenly I flashed on myself walking down the hall between two women. "By yourself?"

"What?"

"Did you get me up here by yourself?"

"What difference does it make?" Janis snapped.

"It makes a big difference to me, Janis. I don't know those people. They don't know me, not really. They saw me at that party; they'll probably see me in the video. I don't want anybody thinking that's all I'm about. That might not mean anything to you but it means a heck of a lot to me."

"Debrena, you just make too much out of nothing," was all she could say.

"I want to go home," I said firmly.

"Debrena—"

I cut her off. "Now, Janis! Get me a ride or I start walking!"

She laughed at me. "How far do you think you'll get in that dress?"

"The dress you picked out," I reminded her, and I wasn't smiling. I noticed a nasty undertone in Janis's voice, and I didn't like it at all. I knew I was in no shape to fight her, but at that moment, I really wanted to get ghetto, show her that I was not a pushover.

"Janis, get me out of here before I say something we'll both regret."

Janis looked at me like she saw something she had never seen before, something that could hurt her if I choose to let it. "I'll get you home," she told me, like she really didn't want to help me. It was like she enjoyed seeing me in that wrinkled red dress with no shoes. Like she could handle me better that way.

"I'm going to need some clothes," I reminded her.

Janis moved around the room like she couldn't get me out of there fast enough.

Chapter Fifty-three

When I finally got home it was late in the afternoon, and the only thing I wanted to do was take a hot shower and crawl into my bed. But because I couldn't sleep, after my shower, I went through the messages on my answering machine. Of course there were several from Choice. I knew I had disappointed him but I was in no shape to spend the kind of time he wanted. Of course I couldn't tell him why I didn't come home. All I could imagine him saying was "I told you to be careful around Janis," and I really didn't want to hear anything like that from Choice.

Janis had done me dirty but I blamed myself more than I blamed her. I had let myself get too relaxed around her, and I had suffered the consequences. Of course Janis wanted me to see her actions as positive; she was just trying to "loosen me up." I didn't completely believe her, but what could I do?

After a little more tossing and turning, I gave up the thought of getting any sleep. I went to the phone, dialed and got Choice on the third ring.

"What happened to you?" was his first question.

"I didn't leave my house until after one," I told him. "It was so late after the party that I crashed at the Marriott."

I was convinced that he hadn't heard a word I said. Choice had his own agenda: He wanted to make me suffer for standing him up. Because I knew Choice, I let him go off on me, knowing he wouldn't bitch for long and then we could go on to more pleasant topics. "You should've called," Choice scolded me. "I didn't know what to think."

"I can take care of myself," I said. I was getting a little tired of people looking at me like I was some kind of pushover. Sometimes a lot of people take kindness for weakness. I knew that pretty soon I was going to have to put some people in check.

"I didn't say you couldn't take care of yourself," Choice snapped.

"Wait a darn minute now," I said as I sat up in my bed, ready to do some serious battle. "I'm grown, Choice. I don't have to answer to you or anybody else."

"I know that. I just wanted to see you last night. Then when I didn't see you at rehearsal, I didn't know what to think."

"I don't want you to worry about me. I didn't make rehearsal because I just wasn't feeling up to it. I tried to dance when I wasn't one hundred percent and I stank. I'm not going to put myself through that humiliation again, Choice. I'm not going to fake the funk like that. I'm really sorry we couldn't get together. Even if we had gotten together, the way I felt, I wouldn't have been a lot of fun."

"We could've cuddled."

I laughed out loud at that one. "Choice, the only time you cuddle is after we get down."

He had to laugh along with me, knowing he was stone-cold busted. "Can't a brother change, Debrena?"

"Yes, but not overnight. Besides you know how these industry parties run."

"Yes, I do. About four more hours than they need to," Choice said as if the thought made him want to smack somebody. "That's why I can't hang out like that. I'm ready to go home, and they just seem to go on and on. "

To change the subject I said, "Did you take any photos today?"

"I had a great session with Kammie and LaTasha."

"I'm sure they enjoyed that," I told him with a mischievous smile in my voice.

"I don't know about all that. But Kammie was very good, showing me a lot of great moves."

"Did she tell you that she was a beauty contest winner?"

Choice laughed. "I think she mentioned that a time or two."

I found myself laughing along with him.

"You're next," Choice informed me.

"Okay. I'm ready for my closeup, Mr. Photographer."

After talking another hour with Choice, I was so relaxed that I drifted off to sleep. I had to admire the man. He put me to sleep without having sex with me. Anyone who did that, just with a soothing voice and lively conversation, had to get props. Although I was no longer head over heels excited by Choice, he was still someone I wanted to remain in my life. With him, things were simple, more black and white.

211

Chapter Fifty-four

A few days later Janis came to say good-bye. Although we had a good conversation sitting in my living room, she could tell that I was distracted. I didn't want to tell her what was really on my mind because it was something to do with Dominique and the dance company. In my mind, Janis had gotten so beyond the dance studio that she couldn't be bothered with the trials and tribulations of Dominique St. Claire.

"You all right?" Janis asked. I got the impression she was asking about more than my general health. I didn't want to tell her but she asked and seemed sincere.

"You know the summer dance concert is in two weeks," I reluctantly told her.

"Are you ready?"

"More than ready. I'm really looking forward to it."

"So that can't be the problem."

"Yes and no."

"You're confusing me, Debrena."

"This is a big year for Dominique, a major celebration. Tickets sales are going very slow."

"You want me to buy a ticket?" Janis asked and smiled.

"It's a little more than that. I was thinking that maybe you could help Dominique."

"Me? How?"

"Well, this may be a little far out, but it's something I've been thinking about."

"Something that involves me?"

"Moreso, Walter McCary," I confessed.

Janis gave me a puzzled look, which was what I expected. "I don't even know if he does things like what I'm about to suggest."

"What is it, Debrena?" Janis pushed, showing her impatience.

"The dance concert is a tribute to Eddie Kendricks, but I once read somewhere that Walter was a big Motown fan and that he admired Kendricks's unique vocal style."

"I don't know, Debrena. You're not saying it but I get the sense that Walter will be doing this for free."

"Just to help with ticket sales. I wouldn't expect him to do a concert, just a song or even a guest appearance. Sort of like a salute from one artist to another. I mean I haven't even talked to Dominique about this. I know it's asking a lot, but if there's a way to guarantee the success of this summer's concert, well, I'm willing to do anything."

"It wouldn't be you doing it, Debrena. It would be Walter, and I would be the one to approach him about this."

"You know him better than me."

Janis shook her head, and then said, "I'll have to think about this. I can't make any guarantees. As you know, there are no guarantees in this business, but I'll see what I can do."

"I know it's a crazy idea," I said as Janis stood to leave.

"Not so crazy. It shows that you're thinking ahead, and that's always good. But if I do get Walter to do this you're going to owe me big time."

I paused before I said, "I really believe Walter's appearance will be good for the company." We looked at each other, and I felt like I was signing another contract, this one written in blood.

"Come on, walk me to my limo."

I stood beside Janis, and we walked outside.

"Well, at least you got the video behind you," Janis reminded me as she leaned against the long white limo. "Now we can move on to bigger and better things. Speaking of moving on, there's something else you need to think about."

I looked into her eyes because her tone captured my complete attention.

213

"You can't be all you can be in this part of the world," Janis began. "Elizabeth, New Jersey, is nowhere, Debrena. The only reason it's a dot on the map is because it's close to New York City. If you really want to make an impact and reach your full potential, you're going to have to think seriously about moving to L.A."

My heart dropped to my stomach. I know it wasn't cool but I couldn't hide the fear and uncertainty on my face.

Of course Janis noticed it. "Don't get me wrong, I like Dominique. I have a lot of respect for her, but I see you doing more than that. I'm not asking you to move tomorrow, but I'm serious about taking you to the top. I just hope you're as serious as I am. I've worked with many talented girls, but I had no problem with kicking them to the curb when they became slackers."

"I'm not a slacker," I said, angry that she would even suggest something like that about me. Everyone who knew me knew I hated slackers.

Because Janis didn't want to offend me further, she said, "Walter was impressed with you."

Despite my irritation, that made me smile. "What did he say?"

"Walter said you were a real trouper. He said you did everything the director asked you to do and never once complained. You didn't go off, you didn't play the diva. You hung in there and got the job done. That means a lot in this business."

"I want to be successful, Janis. Massively successful."

"I believe you do, and I'm here to help you with that, to make sure that happens for you. If this is what you really want, you have to have tunnel vision. Nothing else can be more important than your success. You tell me you want this, and I'm going to hold you to that. Remember, we have a contract."

"I know. I signed it," I said and felt a measure of discomfort because I still hadn't gotten a copy from Janis. "When will you be back?"

"The editor will be editing the video in L.A.," Janis told me, "so I'll be around for that. Then I'll be on some promotional junkets with Walter. The video for 'A Dream' should be ready for MTV in two weeks. I'll be back here for that. You just keep yourself busy and focused."

"I will," I promised as Janis got into the limo. When she got inside, I couldn't see her because the windows were tinted. I figured she would tell the driver to pull off. I waved good-bye. I was really surprised when the window came down. Janis smiled at me, and then said, "Speaking of focus, give Choice a big, sloppy kiss for me."

Before I could say anything, the window was up and the limo was moving down my street.

I shook my head in wonder. Janis had stunned me because I never expected her to say anything about Choice. Kiss my man for her? Was she trying to be funny? Or tell me not to let Choice take up too much of my valuable time? I had no way to be sure of what she really meant. Besides that, I had a lot of work to do on the summer dance concert. I didn't have any time to play detective.

215

Chapter Fifty-five

I didn't stop reaching out to Lorrie. Although it was obvious that she didn't want to talk to me on the phone, there was no way she could avoid me at the dance studio. After rehearsal, I slid up to her before she could make her way to the locker room. "Hello, stranger," I said, trying hard to keep things light.

Lorrie looked at me like I had cursed at her. "What do you want, D?"

"Can't we talk?" I asked and immediately thought, *I sound like a wimp.* "I want things between us to be the way they used to be."

"D, there is no way to go back in time," Lorrie told me, looking hard into my eyes. "I accept that, I think you should too."

"I have no problem accepting that," I said, my voice cracking with sudden emotion. I felt like I was going to break down in front of her.

"I think you do, " Lorrie told me, then looked around, like she was checking to make sure no one was listening to her. "I'm doing you a favor."

"By staying away from me?" I asked, not believing that Lorrie thought that would help me.

"Yes, because you're a confused girl. You have these people fooled because they don't know you. They don't care enough to know you; they have their own selfish agenda. I know you, D, and I'm telling you, you better check yourself."

I became paranoid. "What have you heard about me?"

"I'm not spying on you, D. But with all this sudden fame through the music video and hanging out with all those fancy people that Janis introduced you to, you look miserable, girl."

"What do you suggest I do?" I asked, putting up my defenses.

"You see, that's why I don't want to talk to you."

"Because I ask questions?" I asked angrily.

"No, because you want somebody to tell you what to do. You want a director for your life. It doesn't happen like that, D. You have to be the director, the cast, the crew and the guy who does the lights and the music. I could tell you what to do, but if it doesn't work out you'll have somebody to blame. I'm not about to play that game with you."

"So you'd rather see me fall flat on my face?"

"Of course not, I want to see you happy."

"How happy can I be if you don't think enough of me to help me?"

Lorrie shook her head. "You haven't heard anything I've said, have you? That's why I don't talk to you, D. You're just not ready to hear me."

"Well, if you'd just answer one of my darn phone calls," I said, a little more forcefully than I intended, but Lorrie was just adding to my frustration, my confusion about my life.

Lorrie tried to walk away from me, but I moved to block her exit.

"D, I have to go," Lorrie told me with sadness in her voice.

I didn't want her feeling sorry for me. "Look, we need to go over our dance routine," I said, pulling up any excuse to make Lorrie stay with me.

Lorrie looked at me like she was about to give in, then said, "There's always tomorrow."

As Lorrie walked away I wanted to say, "Not for me, not for me like this."

Just the night before I felt like I was losing my mind. I just couldn't get that dream about some woman licking between my thighs out of my mind. And although Choice called me on the regular, I just couldn't get with him. I knew he couldn't help me because when I really wanted to talk, all he wanted was my body hot and wet beneath him. I let Lorrie go because I didn't feel comfortable telling

217

her about Janis and, of course, there was no way I could ever tell Choice.

As I heard my fellow dancers coming out of the locker room, I stepped back into the studio. I didn't want anyone to see me in this wild, desperate state of confusion. I didn't move as I listened to the sounds of bodies moving through the building on their way to the outside world. The silence of the studio was weird, like that sudden stillness after a major rainstorm. I looked around the studio as if I could find something to make me feel complete. I felt so shattered, so torn, that I knew I had to do something. That was when I turned to the one thing that had always comforted me, my dance.

I walked across the bare wood floor and opened the door that looked like a part of the mirrored wall. Behind the door was the stereo system that Dominique used when we rehearsed with her. It was a large room behind a two-way mirror, where Dominique would watch us. I removed the George Clinton CD from the system and put in Eddie Kendricks. I cued it to "Can I?" the song to which I was to dance solo. I came out of the room and left the door open. The music came on as I spun out onto the dance floor. And when I began to dance, nothing else mattered.

When Kendricks went into the fast section of the song, my favorite part, I became one with the music, letting it cover me like a blanket and a nice, cool breeze, all at the same time. The movement made me happy, so happy for as long as Kendricks sang his six-minute, twelve-second soul classic. When the song ended, I found myself breathing heavily, and there were tears on my cheeks.

"Bravo," a voice called out, and I suddenly realized that I had not even bothered to lock the door that opened onto the street. Dominique always said that anyone could just walk in, but I'm sure she meant someone none of us knew.

"How long have you been standing there?" I asked Choice.

He gave me a great smile as he held up his camera. "Long enough to get some great shots of you."

"I don't think I want those shots in the calendar," I said, feeling too wide open, too vulnerable. I walked across the room to grab my towel.

"It would save me a whole lot of work if I could use them," Choice said. "Of course I'll need to have you sign a release."

"I'm afraid that I might've revealed too much," I confessed. "If I had known you were there, I would have posed."

"That's exactly what I don't want. You're beautiful in your dance, in your world, in your own little paradise."

That's when I told him a lot more than I intended. "No paradise for me, Choice. I'm in hell now, hell on earth," I said, and that was when Choice moved toward me. "I don't want you to touch me," I told him, trying desperately to hold on to myself. "I'll sign your release if you'll go, leave me alone, for right now."

219

I knew that Choice didn't like that deal, but I saw how he looked at me when he talked about the shots he had just taken. Like any artist, he lived for that perfect picture, and observing Choice, I'm sure he thought he had captured that in the dance studio. Without a word, Choice bent to pick up the camera bag at his feet. He pulled out a model release form. I knew when I signed it there would be nothing more for us to say to each other, that we had had our time together and now it was over. It made me sad. Suddenly I found myself in his arms. He kissed me deeply, trying so hard to hold on to what we had. But the most surprising thing for me was that I hungrily kissed him back. *Not here,* I told myself. *Anyplace but here.*

I did nothing to move away from him. If anything I held him even closer. I even closed my eyes to block out any physical structure that would remind me where I was that afternoon. But inside, I knew I wasn't being fair to Choice or myself. I had to make a very hard decision. I pushed away from him, and there was a struggle, but because I had finally made up my mind to take charge of my life, do the right thing, there was no way that Choice could seduce me. I pushed him away as I opened my eyes.

Looking beyond Choice's broad shoulder, I saw Lorrie in the doorway. The look on her face was pure heartbreaking. Our eyes met, and the deep sadness in Lorrie's made me want to turn away from her, but I knew that this was not the time to duck and dodge my feelings for her and the repercussions of what she had caught me doing.

In the stunned silence, Lorrie turned and ran. I pushed Choice to the side and ran after her. He cried out in surprise because with his back to the door, he didn't know that Lorrie had been there. He grabbed at me, but I easily shook him off; there was nothing that would've kept me from going after Lorrie. Because she had such a head start on me, I didn't catch up with her until she was in the street, next to her car and fumbling for her keys.

"Lorrie, please," I called out to her. "We have to talk."

Lorrie looked at me like a wild woman. "What is there to talk about, D?" She tried so hard to calm herself down; her struggle touched my heart. "D, you owe me nothing. You live your life the way you want to, okay!" Tears filled her eyes, the hurt and pain so heartbreaking written on her face. "You owe me nothing, you hear? Not even honesty!"

"I love you, Lorrie," I said as tears came to my eyes and slid down my face. I knew right then and there, I was speaking from the depths of my heart and soul.

"You don't love me or anybody like me," Lorrie snapped. "You love that in there. What that man can give you. I'm some kind of freak to you, something to play with."

"Did you hear what I said, Lorrie?"

"You can't love me, D. If you loved me, you'd be like me. We both know you'd die before you admit to that."

I wanted to tell Lorrie that she was wrong. I was still too shaky inside myself. I knew that I loved her with all my heart and soul. I just didn't know what to say to stop her from getting into her car. All I could do was stand there with my lips trembling as Lorrie drove off, leaving me so all alone.

If I weren't barefoot and dressed in my dance clothes, I wouldn't have gone back into the dance studio.

"I'm sorry," Choice said as soon as he saw me. "I, uh, went downstairs, saw who you were talking to. I didn't mean for Lorrie to see us like that. I'm sorry."

"Not as sorry as I am," I said as I shut the door to the room that held all the sound equipment.

"I can talk to Lorrie," Choice said, and I looked at him like he

220

was crazy. "I figured she ran out because she was embarrassed," he said. "I know I'm not supposed to be up here like this. I can talk to her, let her know that it was just a kiss, that we weren't going to take it any further than that."

I just kept staring at him, not knowing what to say. "Right, you came to take my picture and things just got out of hand?"

Choice nodded like that lie settled everything. *I am so darn sick of lying,* I thought.

"I'll see you later," Choice said, although as far as I was concerned, that was totally out of the question. Choice left me alone because we both knew I needed to be. Things had gotten out of hand because I had let them get out of hand, and I had to own up to that. In order to be truly happy I had to take charge of my life. I wanted to do that. I had to do that.

Chapter Fifty-six

The night of the world premiere of the "A Dream" video I was very nervous. So much so that I seriously thought about canceling the viewing party that Erica had suggested take place at my house. Even as the Sister of Soul dancers filed in, loud with good spirits, I thought about sending everyone home, getting into some ratty old pj's and watching the video in the dark. I knew I had done a lot of good work on the video but lately I had been reading horror stories about good videos gone bad in the editing process. I had spoken to Janis over the phone, and she assured me that the video looked great and everyone on the West Coast really enjoyed it. Still, I didn't know what to expect, and I didn't want to be embarrassed so publicly. But with my fellow dancers so excited, it was hard not to get caught up in the energy and goodwill of their happiness for me.

"My dog gon' be a video star," Erica said as she sat beside me on the couch.

Shay, LaToya and LaTasha decided to sit on the floor, resting on pillows they pulled from the couch. Angela and Marcy, although invited, decided not to come to my house, but they promised me that they would watch the video at Angela's apartment. As for Lorrie, she told Erica that she would watch it at home with her mother. Of course, Mom and Dad were camped out in front of their TV set in Florida. Because Dominique was so busy with promotion and costuming for the summer concert, I had no idea where she would be or if she would even bother to tune in. I found it hard to imagine her at home watching MTV.

Even before the video came on, I decided that I hated seeing myself on screen, especially after watching the interview that I did on the set of the video shoot. After the music video for Naughty By Nature's "Jamboree," the "A Dream" video made its debut. Erica led the applause when it came on and the credits were plastered across a pale blue sky. *Walter McCary. A Dream.* Then the camera came down and the next scene was a fashion show with me coming down the runaway. The applause was even louder when the girls saw me.

"Who's that hot sister?" Shay said as the first scene unfolded: Me coming down the runway, cutting so fast that all my outfits were displayed in a matter of seconds. Walter McCary was taking my picture as his singing voice filled the background. The extras in the video enthusiastically applauded my entrance as the dancers performed behind me.

Tamara wasn't the only one who gasped when I disappeared behind a puff of smoke. "Where did you go?" she asked, her eyes glued to the TV screen.

"To Paradise," I jokingly told her. Then I thought, *so far, so good* and began to relax a little. Erica glanced at me looking at the video so hard that I turned toward her and said, "I'm on the screen, Erica."

That seemed to snap her out of her infatuation with me. "I know that, Debrena, but you're here and on the screen, that's blowing my mind."

By saying something like that Erica made me nervous all over again. *I hate seeing myself on screen,* I told myself again as Walter McCary walked around singing as a ghostlike image of me haunted his every waking moment. In the video, the headline read: SUPER MODEL DISAPPEARS!

"That's you, girl," LaTasha said, stating the obvious as Little Erica grabbed and squeezed my hand. "You look just like a supermodel." As Erica held my hand, I didn't know whose palm was wetter. We all watched as Walter McCary crumpled the newspaper and then threw it in a nearby garbage can. He really acted upset; he was a great actor and a great singer.

"He's cute," Erica had to say, and Kammie told her to hush.

223

"I want to hear this," Kammie let her know.

"How many times have you heard this song on the radio?" Little Erica asked. "It's a hit; they play it on all the stations."

"This is different," Kammie said.

So they wouldn't get into a full-fledged argument, I gently placed a finger on Erica's soft lips. She laughed at my gesture, but she did stop talking for a little while.

"That's a walking man," LaTasha observed as she watched the shot of Walter McCary walking the streets at night. *That has to be L.A.,* I thought because when we finished the shoot it was not dark at all. What impressed me the most was the art gallery scene, with the photos of me being shot from the opening runway. There was wild applause from all the girls when Walter McCary was drawn into the picture with me.

"I know that's right," Shay said as Walter McCary took me in his arms. "You know that White boy want all that brown sugar."

"Please, Shay," I said, blushing like crazy. I really did hate seeing myself on screen, especially the way I was dressed. When Walter McCary actually kissed me, Shay laughed out loud and rolled over the floor, shouting, "You go, girl!"

"Shay is so ignorant sometimes," Tamara said, a big smile on her face.

"That was not my idea," I said, but that didn't keep them from clapping loudly at that particular scene. The video ended in a freeze of me with Walter McCary, in his arms like we would be lovers in paradise forever.

Shay jumped up and came over to me on the couch. "That was da bomb," she said and hugged me around my neck. She was the first to congratulate me, but the others followed her lead. They gave me so much love that I almost cried.

Kammie did cry as she said, "Debrena, you looked so beautiful in that video. I am so proud of you, girl."

"I just wished you had done more dancing," Erica said, and I didn't have the heart to remind her that I didn't do any dancing in that music video.

"It was still good," Kammie said.

"That White girl did enough dancing for everybody," LaTasha said. In her hands was an empty bowl that once held some yummy microwaved popcorn. "Do you know her, Debrena? Although we didn't see a whole lot of her she was really good."

I didn't want to speak Tyra's name but it was obvious that LaTasha didn't want to let it go. "I'm talking about that redhead girl."

"That's Tyra Woodstock," I told her and prayed that no one would ask me anything else about her.

"Tyra Woodstock," Kammie repeated. "Is that her real name?"

Let it go already, I thought, but I said, "As far as I know, it is." 225

"And what's this thing with this D. Allen?" Kammie asked.

"That's Debrena's stage name," Erica explained before I could say anything. I wanted to tell her that I wasn't onstage, like in a Broadway show, I was in a video.

"I like Debrena Allen," Kammie told me. "It's sorta like Debbie Allen. You see, people remember a name like that."

That was when I recalled Janis's discussion about brand names. But could D. Allen stand up there beside Madonna, Diana, Aretha, Whitney, Teena Marie? I realized that I was thinking in terms of singers, but I didn't know enough famous models, except for Naomi Campbell, Beverly Johnson, Tyra Banks, Beverly Peele and Iman. They were all household names and I couldn't see D. Allen in that group. And I didn't think that I was putting myself down; I felt I was being realistic. One music video appearance didn't make me a household name.

"When you gon' do another video?" Erica asked.

"Girl, I'm not trying to do a whole lot of videos, at least not like that," I told her, but my message was for everybody. "The next one I do—if there is a next one—I will be dancing."

Then the phone began to ring. First it was Mom and Dad; they thought I was "just so beautiful" in the video. Angela and Marcy called and said they liked all the costume changes and some of the dancing. The girls in my house asked me more about the making of the video well into the night. It got so late, and they had gotten so comfortable, that I playfully said, "You don't have to go home but you got to get out of here. I have to get some sleep. You know, rehearsal tomorrow?"

They laughed at that but they did begin to file out, kissing and hugging me before they disappeared into the night.

What should have been a great evening ended somewhat bitter-sweet for me because Lorrie hadn't bothered to call. I had to wonder what was up with that.

Chapter Fifty-seven

The next morning at the dance studio I was on cloud nine. The girls kept coming up to me in the locker room, telling me how much they loved the video. As they came over to me in twos and threes, I glanced over at Lorrie. As she was changing into her dance clothes I tried to catch her eyes, but she always slid away from me. It was only when I stared at her that she acknowledged my presence.

"I watched the video," Lorrie told me. "You didn't get to do any dancing."

I giggled, so happy that we were actually having a conversation. "Tell me about it."

"But you did look good, D. My mother said your makeup was great."

I giggled again. "I almost didn't recognize myself," I had to admit. "I never wore that much makeup."

"They probably had to put on a lot of makeup for the cameras."

"They used three cameras."

"You did well."

"I really tried to do my best."

"Well, you got what you wanted? How does it feel?"

"It feels good, real good. And it's so good to have friends to share it with."

I wanted to say more but it was obvious that Lorrie wanted to get out to the dance floor. "I'll see you out there," I said, a little disappointed that we couldn't continue talking.

Even though Angela and Marcy called the night before, they

came over and again expressed how they felt about the video.

The only sour note was when Tamara came over to me. She made sure that we were alone in the locker room before she spoke. "I still want us to have that big meeting about Angela and Marcy," she told me.

"Tamara, isn't it enough that they're keeping their relationship on the down low?"

"I still believe they should lose their offices."

"Tamara, isn't that a little harsh?"

"Debrena, I'm not just speaking for myself."

"Why don't we pick this up after the summer dance concert?"

"This is no small thing for me, Debrena. I don't want Angela and Marcy to think they got away with something."

"I understand, Tamara. But believe me, after the concert would be the best time to deal with it."

Tamara looked at me like she thought I just didn't get it. But instead of continuing to argue her case, she walked away from me. I emitted a deep, long sigh; I was so relieved. As the sweat trickled down from my armpits, I felt like I had just dodged a fatal bullet. But my ordeal for that day was far from over. I walked into the dance studio a little later than I intended and found my sister dancers going through their isolations. I felt like I had warmed up in the locker room because I was still sweating.

"Come on, Debrena," Dominique snapped at me. "We've got work to do."

I was so much into myself that I hadn't noticed her when I stepped into the studio. Without saying a word, I joined the troupe and fell into place. That was when Dominique disappeared into the small room behind the two-way mirror and began the music.

"The finale," Dominique's voice came out to us from powerful hidden speakers, then Kendricks's voice washed over us.

Before we began, as a result of a meeting we had the day before, we all knew that this rehearsal would be brief. The tickets for the summer concert had been printed, and this was the first day of box office sales downstairs. Still, our rehearsal was intense, with Dominique coming from behind the two-way mirror to make what she called "minor adjustments." That was what she usually did, but what disturbed me that day was that she had nothing to say to me. I knew I was far from perfect. It was like she was purposely avoiding any personal contact with me.

I'm getting paranoid, like Tamara, I thought as we went into the last half hour of our rehearsal. Kammie and Erica had already left to shower, change into some street clothes and to try and sell tickets from the box office. I wished I could've gone with them because I felt Dominique's disapproving eyes on me. My first mind told me to leave well enough alone, but then I got a little angry. Here I was the lady of the hour, and Dominique just wouldn't give me my due. I know that sounds a little messed up, conceited maybe, but I had just had a major video debut on MTV, and I felt I deserved some props.

229

After rehearsal I found Dominique in her office with the door wide open. Even though she knew I was there, she still tried to ignore me, but I wouldn't go away. I stood there until she said, "Can I help you, Debrena? Do you want to borrow the key for a late rehearsal?"

"No, Dominique, I was just wondering, did you see the video last night?"

That got her complete attention. She looked at me with her hands on her round hips. "I saw it."

I stood there, expecting her to go on. She didn't, as a matter of fact, she suddenly became real busy in her office. I wouldn't leave that doorway. When Dominique stopped her busy work, she looked at me. "What do you want me to say about it?"

I felt that was a strange question. "Did you like it?"

"I'm still thinking about that, Debrena."

"What's to think about?"

"I'm thinking I put you in a very bad position."

"It was a great opportunity."

"That's what I thought when Janis first called me: A great opportunity for two of my girls."

"You don't feel that way now?"

"Truthfully, I don't know how I feel," Dominique told me, pain all over her face. "No, that's not entirely true. I feel angry, I feel used. I feel used by Janis. I feel that she took advantage of my selfish desire to promote this company."

"Exposure is so important," I said, sounding like Janis.

Dominique turned her anger on me. "Not that kind of exposure, Debrena. I'm even more disappointed that you can't see it. But you're young. I thought Janis would look after you, but she's young too."

I wanted to say something to defend Janis, but I said nothing because I felt that Dominique would really get angry if I did. "I did the best I could," I said lamely.

"It wouldn't have been so bad if they had just exploited your dancing, Debrena. I probably would've made peace with that, but, it seems to me, that that video was all about exploiting your body."

I blushed, embarrassed for myself and the company.

"Forgive me for being so harsh, Debrena. But I can't ignore what I see. I saw about five minutes of cheap thrills for young boys and dirty old men. How does that help you? How does that help this company? Advance ticket sales are at an all-time low, and I don't know what to do about it. I have to face the painful fact that the Dominique St. Claire Dance Studio is old news in this town."

Before I could say anything, there was a loud noise in the hall outside the office. Then there was the sound of running and girlish screams. We both turned toward the door to find Erica in the open doorway.

"You have to see this?" Erica said, and I thought the worse.

"What's going on?" Dominique asked, her voice like that of a parent whose child had just run out into traffic. She was concerned and protective at the same time.

Erica just shook her head. "You have to see this."

Chapter Fifty-eight

I followed Dominique out of her office. We couldn't keep up with an overly excited Erica who ran as fast as her short legs would carry her. At the top of the stairs, Dominique stopped abruptly, and I almost ran into her. The scene outside the lobby was unbelievable. All I could think of was fire code violation. I had never seen so many people crowded outside the dance studio.

I noticed Janis and Walter McCary in the crowd, followed by a group of White guys in MTV T-shirts with cameras on their shoulders. Janis managed to look up at me and Dominique standing at the top of the staircase as the crowd was yelling out, "Walter! Walter!"

The strong lights came on from the cameras, and that was when Walter McCary began his impromptu press conference. "We are here at the Dominique St. Claire Dance Studio to announce that I will be making a guest appearance during their upcoming summer concert," Walter began, and the crowd noise became so loud that he had to raise his hands to quiet them. "Being a big fan of the late, great Eddie Kendricks I am honored to have been asked to perform a couple of the songs that he made famous. This is not a major concert, just an opportunity for me to give something back to the community."

The lights from the cameras went out and Walter's security held the crowd back as Janis led him into the middle of the lobby along with the MTV camera crew. Dominique and I walked down to join Walter and Janis. Erica was right behind us mumbling something about how unbelievable all this was. I looked over at Dominique, and all she could do was shake her head in wonder.

LaTasha came up from behind us. "Dominique, the phone in your office is ringing off the hook."

Distracted, Dominique said, "LaTasha, take a message."

"That's what I've been doing," LaTasha said as she held up a stack of pink message slips. "But as soon as I hang up, another call comes in."

"From who, LaTasha?" Dominique asked.

"The New York Times, The Daily Journal, Newark Star Ledger, City News," LaTasha read from the slips. "They want to talk to you about the company and the summer dance concert with Walter McCary."

232

Janis smiled, then said, "Dominique, the newspapers will be here soon. I think we need to go upstairs to your office to discuss Walter's guest appearance."

"When Janis told me about the tribute to Kendricks," Walter cut in, "I just had to be involved in some kind of way. When Janis suggested a mini-concert, I thought that would be the best way for me to get involved."

"I thank you for thinking of us," Dominique said, sounding like a shy girl. Then she turned to LaTasha with a little more control of the situation. "I'll get back to everyone who called," Dominique said. "In the meantime, we can go to my office."

As Janis and Walter walked up the stairs ahead of us, the MTV crew remained in the lobby.

Dominique held back so she could talk to me. "It's obvious that a lot of people from your generation like Walter McCary very much. As to the video, I can't even begin to understand the public's taste. What I think is vulgar, they think is art. What I'm trying to say is: I don't know everything."

"You know you don't like the video," I had to remind her, and I wasn't too happy about that.

"Does it really matter what I like to them downstairs?" Dominique looked at me like an overly protective mother hen. "What do I know," she said as she gently touched my cheek, and I knew it wasn't a question. It was more like an apology. That was when I glanced down and saw a camera crew from E!, a new entertainment television company, come through the doors.

Chapter Fifty-nine

For someone on top of the world, you look absolutely miserable," Janis said as I stepped into her suite at the Plaza hotel. As I moved past her I couldn't help but notice her outfit: a black ribbed tank top, five slide bracelets on her right wrist, a camouflage miniskirt and snakeskin sandals. She looked cute.

"I didn't come in here to bring you down," I stated as I found a comfortable chair near the window, "but you did call and say you wanted to see me."

"Just to share some great news with you, Debrena," Janis said.

"More videos?" I asked, I had to admit that I wasn't very happy about that prospect. All it meant to me was getting into something else I had no control over. In the past few days I have seen so many half-naked photos of me from the video that I couldn't blush anymore. I was to the point where I wanted to throw darts at all of those pictures.

"Not right now," Janis said and looked at me strangely, like she just couldn't see how I had anything to worry about. She saw me on top of the world. What she didn't see was how far I had to fall when I fell off. "What I wanted to tell you was that the video has been picked up by BET, VH-1 and The Box."

I know she expected me to be happy, but all I could think about was the million more eyes that would see me on all those other video outlets. All I could do was sigh heavily.

"I don't get you, Debrena," Janis said. "Anyone else would be jumping up and down with joy."

"I'm jumping up and down inside," I deadpanned.

"You ungrateful bitch!" Janis said with such heat that I thought she was going to jump on me and beat me down.

"Now that's not necessary, Janis," I said. She looked at me like she really thought she could kick my butt.

"You just can't be satisfied," Janis said.

"You don't understand me, Janis."

"I don't think you understand yourself, Debrena."

"Sometimes I don't," I admitted, trying hard to lighten the situation, "but I do know when I feel uncomfortable. I understand how that makes me feel. Whenever anyone tries something new they feel uncomfortable. It's natural, it's human.

"I have to go with my first gut feelings, Janis. When I don't do that I screw myself up."

"Why can't you just trust me?" Janis wanted to know.

"I do trust you, Janis. You've brought me a long way. But you weren't on the set of the video. The things they asked me to wear—"

Janis cut me off. "You looked damn good in them!"

"Maybe I did, but that's not me. Believe it or not, I'm a lot more modest than that."

Janis turned away from me like I was just being ridiculous.

"The next thing you know, the photographers will be asking me to pose in wet T-shirts and little bikini bottoms."

"What's wrong with that? A shot like that would definitely make the cover of *XXL* magazine."

"I'm sure it would, but would I be able to live it down? I don't like the idea of people thinking I'm loose like that."

"I told you before, Debrena, you have a dynamite body."

"And I told you that I didn't want to be known for one thing." As I grabbed my bag tighter, I said, "This is crazy. You just don't understand. Just count me out of your big money-making schemes. I just want to dance." Then I walked toward the front door.

I only stopped because Janis grabbed my upper arm so hard I winced in pain. "What are you doing?"

"Trying to keep an ungrateful bitch from fucking up the best thing she ever had," Janis said. I couldn't ignore the smell of liquor on her breath. I was doubly alarmed because it was so early in the day.

"Janis," I said. "Janis, you need to let me go."

"I'll let you go when you start talking sense."

"Janis, let me go now or we'll both be sorry!"

Only because she wanted to avoid a catfight, Janis let go of my flesh. My upper arm burned so hot with pain that I wanted to rub it, but I didn't want her to know that she had hurt me in any way.

"I thought you were different," Janis told me.

"Obviously," was my reply.

"I thought you wanted to do something, something big. I thought you wanted more than what you could get at Dominique's little dance studio."

Janis talked like she thought Dominique's dance studio was some small-time operation. I never thought that the Dominique St. Claire Dance Studio was the Alvin Ailey Dance Theater but I got the impression that our "little dance studio" was well respected by New York professionals. I had seen "Summer Sizzler," the annual student dance concert from the Ailey company, and I felt that we measured up well alongside them, now Janis was making me feel uncomfortable, like I had put my bet on the wrong horse.

"What I want is something you can't give me," I told Janis, knowing that she would never understand me. "Something I can't expect to get from you or anyone else."

"What is that, Debrena?" Janis asked with hands on her hips, like she was taunting me.

"Self-respect!" I said loudly. "Do you know what that is?"

Janis laughed in my face. "I'll give you self-respect."

"You can't."

"I can. I have. You're no Goody Two-shoes."

"What are you talking about?"

"I'm talking about your other side, girl. The side you only allow to come out at night."

"Don't play with me, Janis. I'm not in the mood."

"All right, let's keep it real. No more games. Do you know why everybody loves that video?"

"Because of those scandalous outfits they talked me into wearing?"

"Maybe in small-town Jersey, but in the better circles, where the real action is, they see that video as a breakthrough, and one I plan to capitalize on. It's not just about you, girl."

"Walter McCary's people?"

"I can't believe how small-minded you are. In that video you are the all-American girl, Debrena. And because you're dark skinned it gives it a whole new flavor. That's what the big boys are looking at. That image is money in the bank for you. And me, too, Debrena. You think I'm about to blow that? You think I'm going to let you fuck this up?"

Janis smiled broadly, like she knew something I didn't. "I've been around in this industry for a long time, Debrena. You're hot right now and everybody is calling me about you. And that's the way it should be."

"Because you're my manager?"

"You bet your sweet ass! I got a call from the William Morris Agency asking me if you had representation. I told them that I had it locked. They hated to hear that shit, but they'll call back. They want you. And not just them."

"What if I don't want to be wanted like that?"

"When are you going to realize that it's not about you, Debrena?"

"It's all about my all-American girl image."

"And how I can exploit that," Janis reminded me.

"I don't want to be exploited."

"It's too late for that."

"I have to live with myself, Janis."

"My heart bleeds for you, Debrena. But it's out of your hands. We are going to get paid."

"By destroying my self-respect?"

"Get real, Debrena. If you just shut the fuck up and do what I tell you, we'll be rich!"

"But what if I don't want to go along with this?"

"Then you'll be out, but I'll still be rich."

"How do you figure that?"

"I own the personality 'D. Allen'; I own that brand name.

Nobody gives a fuck about you. It's all about D. Allen. I'll make my money as your manager because you'll go where I tell you and do what you're paid to do. I'll get my cut, and if you don't want yours, I'll take that too. You see, it's win-win for me because I don't get all sentimental about some self-respect bullshit."

"I have to look in the mirror every day, Janis."

"You keep on looking while I'm on my way to the bank, salting away all the revenues I got from your modeling and video contracts. And when it's all over, I'll be sitting pretty in my Malibu beach house, and you'll have your self-respect and your little spot in Dominique's dance company."

"You know I could just walk away from all this fame and fortune bullshit you're giving me."

That was when Janis got all up in my face. "No, you can't. Why? Because you want self-respect, even if it's based on a lie."

My face got real hot, and I began to sweat. I knew that the moment I had always dreaded had arrived. "What lie?"

"You're a fucking lesbian." Any protest I had stuck in my throat. "Oh no, not the all-American girl next door," Janis said sarcastically. "You eat pussy and you like it, Debrena! All I have to do is go to Tyra Woodstock for all the details. She wants success, Debrena. And she's more than willing to do whatever it takes."

"You would blackmail me with that?"

"This is business, Debrena. I don't give a good goddamn about what you do in bed, and you shouldn't either, but you do because you want everybody to like you, respect you. How many of your fans would respect you if they knew how you really were? I have to hand it to you, that was brilliant what you did with Choice. Surely a girl with a fine-ass like Choice couldn't be gay. How did you get Choice to be a front for you? Maybe he's another one who doesn't know the real deal. Does he know? Do your parents know? Does Dominique know? Do the girls in the company know? Does anybody know who Debrena Allen really is? Do you know?"

Because I was so blown away, so confused and on the verge of tears, I knew I had to get away from Janis. I pushed past her on the way out of her suite. She laughed loudly behind me but I refused to look back. She had the goods on me, and I thought she would tell everybody in an all-out effort to destroy me. I felt like a puppet on a string, a dumb-ass puppet on a string. Right then and there I felt that I needed to go to someone who had some understanding of me.

But because of the condition I was in I thought it was best for me to go home.

238

Chapter Sixty

I had been crying for the past two days and letting the answering machine take all my calls because I felt that Janis had my neck in a noose and that I could do nothing to keep her from tightening it.

I didn't cry at rehearsals or where anyone could see me, but at home in the midnight hour, in my bed I let the tears flow freely. I just didn't know what to do. I got through rehearsals and didn't bring any undue attention to myself, but I didn't extend any invitations for company, and as soon as rehearsal was over, I got out of the studio and to the bus stop.

When I got off the bus I found myself not too far from Choice's loft. I wore a cute outfit to cheer myself up more than anything else. If I had dressed like I felt, I would've worn a gray oversized sweat suit that wasn't fashionable or flattering.

Choice didn't seem real happy to see me. Of course that was understandable. But after the way I had spent the past two days thinking about Janis, Choice was the only one who I could think to come to. He had seen me at my best and at my worst, and I felt that he was someone who could still be called a friend.

"I know I should've called first," I said as I stood on his doorstep. I smiled at Choice but he didn't seem like he wanted to join me. I wore tinted glasses, rose-colored shades, to hide my eyes. "Can I come in? I feel a little overexposed outside. I don't want everybody knowing my business."

"No, we can't have that," Choice said sarcastically, and, if I really knew where I stood with him I would've snapped. But that afternoon

I had come begging for his goodwill, and I couldn't afford to be overly sensitive.

"It's amazing what they can do with those camcorders nowadays," Choice said, talking like he was having a double conversation, with himself and me. It made me feel a little uncomfortable because I had no idea where he was going with his ramblings. "Yeah, you can set your camcorder up on a dresser in a hotel room and record yourself doing your thing."

"Choice, what are you talking about?" I asked.

"I think you know what I'm talking about," Choice said, a flash of anger in his eyes. "What do you want, Debrena?"

"I thought we could talk," I said lamely.

We walked upstairs to his loft. Being with Choice on that afternoon made me feel uncomfortable, like I was talking to a stranger, definitely not someone with whom I had shared my body. I had never seen Choice look so serious, and that scared me. I walked into his loft and found a seat near the big picture window. He had some new photos up, shots of some of the members of the SOS troupe.

I tried not to stop and stare, and I definitely didn't ask about what happened to the shots he took of me. Why did I come? I had asked myself that too many times, and the only answer with which I came up was that I needed Choice to appreciate me as a woman. I just couldn't accept what Janis had labeled me, even though I knew I loved Lorrie and didn't love Choice. I wanted to look into Choice's eyes and have him see me as a desirable young woman. It was crazy, I know, especially after the way I had dismissed him at the studio.

Choice stood in the middle of the room, looking at everything around the room but me. And then he began speaking, talking like he was looking deep inside of himself. "I came to the East Coast because Carrie Nelson invited me," Choice began. "She said that NTA was looking for a young man like me. She said she and Dany could take me to the top. Every artist likes to hear that. She said that she would never make me do anything that I didn't feel comfortable with. I always held her to that."

I wanted to say something but I didn't know what to say.

"The only time we ran into any trouble was on the last shoot I put together before I began working on the calendar for your dance group. I owe Carrie and Dany a lot, for setting me up in this loft, managing my career on the East Coast. After my last assignment for them, I owed them even more. They lost a major account because I walked off the set. I was supposed to shoot two White high-fashion models. I don't like doing that sort of thing; it's not as creative as I'd like to be but it pays the bills. Carrie asked me to do it, and I didn't see how I could say no."

I sat on the edge of my seat, wanting Choice to get to the point of his story.

"The models were beautiful, international runway stars," Choice said and tried to smile but couldn't. "I know so many photographers who would kill to be in my place, on that set, with those two models. Because they had so much experience on the runway and in print media, I didn't have to do any coaching. All I had to do was point and shoot. They even had ideas about how they should look in the pictures. Some European theme they thought would be real hot in the international fashion magazines. They would look good and I would look good. Unfortunately, when I saw what they were up to, I couldn't go along with the program. The shoot began to get real hot with them paying more attention to each other than their fashions. They began groping each other and caressing each other and kissing each other. I guess they figured that like any hot-blooded young man I'd really enjoy the show. Instead I went off. I called them sick, perverted fucks and got the hell out of there, leaving them half naked with their mouths open. Of course, word got back to NTA. Carrie tried to be understanding but the client was just not pleased. Carrie suffered a big loss, and I wouldn't have been surprised if she sent me back to Cali."

That was when I noticed all the sweat on Choice's face. He looked like a man who had just run a marathon.

"I don't understand that freaky scene, Debrena," Choice told me directly. "Never could, never will. I'm no prude but women on women just don't make my day. Dany said I overreacted. I couldn't argue with her, but she didn't know my history."

"You were drawn into something like that before?" I asked.

241

His eyes were scary, and I looked at the door, thinking about making a fast exit.

"I think maybe I just didn't ask the right questions, Debrena. You asked me about Janis. I didn't tell you the whole story. I told you about that first encounter. I didn't tell you about the second."

There was another girl, according to Choice. Another good-looking girl who Janis was managing. And this time he went to Janis's place, for dinner. It was supposed to be just him and Janis. But then a model came in after Choice and Janis had a few drinks. Janis's plan was to have a threesome with Choice being the man in the middle. Because he felt so manipulated, he even thought about joining them until they were all naked in the bedroom, and Choice realized that the women were in to each other a lot more than they were in to him.

"I got out of there," Choice told me, "but you would've thought that I would have seen the signs at the photo shoot with you."

"With me?" I asked, stunned and surprised. I had no idea that I fitted into his scenario.

"You asked me if I ever went to bed with Janis," Choice said, the anger making his face tight. "I should've asked if you ever went to bed with her."

"What? What kind of question is that?" I didn't mean to be loud, but I was.

"Don't play me for a fool, Debrena! I'm not judging you, I just can't appreciate your lesbian lifestyle."

"Lesbian lifestyle?" I asked, standing from my chair, ready to defend myself from all Choice's false accusations.

Choice sadly shook his head, like I needed him to feel sorry for me. "I should've known at the studio. I saw you in the front of the building with Lorrie. You were crying and she was crying, but at that time I didn't put two and two together."

Then I got very, very scared. "Two and two together. What are you talking about?"

After a deep sigh, Choice said, "It's obvious that you and Lorrie are lovers."

242

I almost fell off my feet when he accused me of that. "That's just not true, Choice."

Choice shook his head like a man in the grips of some intense turmoil. "I can't compete with your female lovers, Debrena. I won't even try. That's your scene, and you're welcomed to it. Your little secret is safe with me, but I can't compete with that woman-to-woman thing."

That was when Choice walked over to his entertainment center. "I can't prove a thing about Lorrie or even Janis for that matter," Choice said as he pushed a videotape into the VCR. "But I think this says it all."

243

The video began and I watched my dream unfold before my eyes. Even though Janis had a camcorder, she never took any video of me, and when she tried I would always make a silly face to mess up the shot. I didn't want Janis documenting any part of my life. Unfortunately, Janis had caught me totally off guard. I watched in horror the videotape that was taken in the bedroom of Janis's suite. She had caught me good, in a drugged state with her almost bald-headed friend stretched out butt naked between my widespread thighs.

"Turn it off! Turn it off!" I told Choice when I had seen enough.

I quickly walked over to the VCR ejected the tape and ran out of there.

Chapter Sixty-one

Janis said she would show me the power she had over me but I had no idea that it would be in the form of character assassination. Now that I knew with what I was battling, I was more than ready to go to war. I knocked on the door to Janis's suite so hard that I thought it would come off its hinges. When she finally opened the door, she stood in the doorway, wrapped in a short cream-colored silk robe, her hair still wet from the shower. On her face was a look of smug satisfaction as if she just knew that she had me where she wanted me. I pushed past her and into the room. She slammed the door behind me.

"You don't want to fuck with me, Debrena," Janis warned as she tightened the sash of her robe. "Just like I showed Choice who you really are, I can send copies of that tape to Dominique, to your parents, to the media."

"How could you have done that to me, Janis? You know how I felt about Choice. Why, Janis? Why?"

"I just want you to know that *I'm* the one in charge, not you."

"You don't scare me," I told Janis although I was trembling on the spot. I just hoped that she thought it was because of my righteous anger. I didn't want everybody to know about me like that. I felt I could explain to Dominique, maybe even my parents, but when I thought about my SOS sister dancers and the media, all I wanted to do was dig a hole and jump right into it. "You set me up, Janis!"

"You seemed to be enjoying yourself. You even came," Janis let me know, and I couldn't say I didn't because I hadn't seen the whole tape. I yanked it out of the machine before I reached my climax. But if my "dream" was accurate, I had cum, shaking wildly upon the bed.

"I was raped, Janis! You drugged me and had your friend took advantage of me!" I said, sticking to what I knew, holding on to my righteous anger.

"Who's to say that you and me wouldn't have gotten together eventually?" Janis said nonchalantly. "When the big bucks roll in, who's to say you wouldn't be so grateful that you let me take you to bed?"

"Janis, that would've been a completely different thing," I told her, speaking rationally when all I wanted to do was pull her hair out. "And I choose my lovers. I don't let anybody push up on me like that. What you did was crazy. You made me think that I was losing my mind."

245

"Get real, Debrena. I'm the best thing that ever happened to you."

"Girl, you are sick. Or drunk."

That was when she really got mad at me. "You are an ungrateful, spoiled brat! I can even pull the plug on Walter's appearance at Dominique's little dance concert if I wanted to."

All I could do was shake my head and wonder how low Janis would go to hurt me.

"That's no excuse for what you did to me! You stupid, drunk bitch!" I shouted and moved toward her.

And that was when Janis hit me. She smacked me so hard that my rose-colored glasses flew off my face. Because I was a physically fit dancer, I could always run like the wind, but it was not the time for running. Janis Wilson had pushed me up against a wall, and it was time for me to come out swinging.

We fought like cats and dogs all over Janis's suite until I pinned her to the floor. I straddled Janis's torso and wrapped my hands around her neck. It was difficult for Janis to breathe, and I realized that I could kill her. I didn't want to do that. I just wanted Janis to stop exploiting me. When I stood, Janis was still on the floor, gasping for air and her robe was wide open.

"You are pathetic," I told Janis.

Then I went to the door, opened it and slammed it behind me.

Chapter Sixty-two

Back at the house, after dealing with Janis, I threw my body across the bed and cried myself to sleep. The next day, my thought was to take a cab to and from the dance studio, get in as much dancing as I could and disappear before anybody had a chance to talk to me. But as I dressed, then called a cab, something dawned on me. I realized that I did not have to carry this burden all by myself. If I was willing to admit that I had a problem, I could get some real help.

I had stood up to Janis, but I had to admit that she still had the upper hand. After that adrenaline rush of standing up to Janis I soon fell back into my overwhelming anxiety. There was no way that I wanted everyone to know about how I expressed my sexuality. I felt like I was living in a goldfish bowl and nothing was off limits to inquiring minds and prying eyes.

The cabdriver had to only blow his horn once to get me out of my house and into his car, but when I got to the dance studio, I realized that dancing was the last thing on my mind. I even went into the locker room and sat on the bench near my locker. There was a lot of activity around me, and I acknowledged all those who acknowledged me, but I made no move to get out of my street clothes. I just sat on that bench, and before I knew it, the locker room had emptied and I was still there. I was what my mom would call a bump on a log. Because I didn't want to be that I got on my feet and found myself at the doorway of the dance studio. They were all in there: LaTasha, LaToya, Tamara, Kammie, Erica, Shay, Angela, Marcy and Lorrie. They were just doing their isolations, but it was obvious that they were ready to go to work.

I recalled a day not too long ago when I attempted to dance when I knew I wasn't ready. I made myself look like a fool, but even worse than that, I made my sister dancers look bad. There was no way I would allow myself to do that again. They deserved more than that from me.

I stepped back from the doorway and then found myself walking down the hall. *Talking to Dominique St. Claire will be like talking to my mom,* I thought as I stood in front of her office. Dominique was in there and she looked up when she saw me. I stepped into her office, and said, "You mind if I close the door?"

247

Chapter Sixty-three

It was two days after my talk with Dominique that she was able to get Janis and me into the same room. It was on a Friday afternoon, after hours, and in Dominique's office. Janis couldn't even look me in the eyes when she came in. I felt real strange, like we had been called down to the principal's office in school because we had been caught fighting. I knew that was far from the case, but I still felt like I was facing a punishment, like being expelled from school, only to return after one of my parents had visited the guidance counselor, and together, they had gotten me back on track.

Although Janis and I sat on chairs, Dominique chose to perch on her desk. I found that a little strange because there was an empty chair between Janis and me. But that was Dominique's habit, to sit on her desk when she held court in her office. There was a large manila envelope on the lap of her sharply creased black tailored slacks. She also wore a blue silk blouse.

"I want to thank you both for coming," Dominique began, her manner all business. "I feel responsible for a lot of this because I did recommend Debrena and Lorrie. Although your company could only use one dancer, Janis, I was glad that they decided to use Debrena. Once the video was produced and shown on cable, I figured that was that, but I learned from Debrena that there are some other things that need to be straightened out." Dominique looked from me to Janis, like she was making sure that she had our complete attention. Because of the respect Janis and I had for Dominique she deserved our full attention.

I thought that Janis was going to say something, but she didn't. She just looked up at Dominique, then down at her well-manicured fingers.

"Janis, I suggested that you bring a lawyer to this meeting," Dominique reminded her. "You told me that you felt that your contract with Debrena was solid and that you knew exactly what you were doing."

"She signed the contract, Dominique," Janis said as if she was ready at that moment to end the meeting. "That's the only thing I need to know. I gave Debrena a big break, and she thanks me by shouting me down in my hotel room. Now she thinks she's going to walk away from me without paying a price? I think not."

249

Janis's little speech made me blush because I had never read the contract and when Dominique asked to read it I told her that I didn't even have a copy. I knew that although I hadn't read the contract, I was obligated under law to abide by all the conditions in it even though I had foolishly signed it without letting a qualified person look it over.

"I'm sure you are aware that Debrena never read the contract and only signed because she saw you as a friend," Dominique said, trying to make Janis see reason.

"That would wash if Debrena hadn't jumped in my face," Janis told Dominique, "but when she did that I felt no friendship from her. As a matter of fact, I thought she was going to do me some bodily harm."

"Is that why you hit her?" Dominique asked.

"Yes. I was afraid. As it was, she caused me a lot of embarrassment and pain. My robe fell off when we tussled, and I have some black and blue bruises on my body. She should be glad that I'm not filing assault and battery charges."

"You know that Debrena is not even twenty-three years old, Janis."

"For God's sake, Dominique! Debrena is not a child! She knew what she was getting into when she signed the contract. She was glad to sign it. Why she thinks she can just walk away from it is beyond me. That's why I don't need a lawyer. All I'm looking for is my twenty percent, which I am entitled to."

I was surprised it was twenty percent, the highest possible rate. Most contracts started at fifteen percent. I was screwed and everybody knew it.

"After you faxed the contract," Dominique said, which I was truly surprised to hear, "I read it. I'm no lawyer but I don't think that Debrena should've signed it."

"Like you said, you're not a lawyer," was Janis's reply, a smirk on her face. I wanted to choke her, but I remembered what she said about assault and battery.

250

"But I do have a friend," Dominique said.

That was when Mom walked into the room. She was dressed in her lawyer's dark suit and carried a slim brown briefcase. She took the chair between Janis and me. I couldn't take my eyes off her I was so amazed. She went into her briefcase and took out a copy of the contract I had signed with Janis.

"Debrena, give me a dollar," Mom said and I reached into my purse for my wallet. I gave her the money. "You have just retained me as your lawyer."

Janis looked at Mom, and then looked at Dominique like they were engaged in some conspiracy to bring her down.

"The contract with your manager is the most important decision you will ever make in your career," Mom told me. "Many artists choose family and friends to serve in this capacity and it seldom works out. In my thirty years as an entertainment lawyer I've seen many bad deals, false promises, poor negotiations and unfulfilled dreams. Because the lifespan of most careers in the entertainment industry is not long, the artist must be protected at all times."

Mom spoke directly to Janis. "I know you had a genuine belief in Debrena's talent as an artist. You worked very hard on her behalf." That's when Mom put on her reading glasses. "I see you have put a serious value on your time. Twenty percent is extremely high, but I understand how you feel that you deserve that, and Debrena signed the contract so she must have agreed."

I didn't want to tell Mom I never read the contract; I didn't want her to see me as a complete idiot.

"Still, as Debrena's legal counsel, I see some problems," Mom went on as Janis squirmed in her seat. "According to this contract, you as the manager of record have stated that you will receive twenty percent of Debrena's gross income. This is not ethical; especially when we look at the fact that this is before expenses. Expenses which you list as clothing, spa visits, meals and hotel lodgings."

Janis screwed me good, my mind screamed, but I was too ignorant of the contract to say anything that would justify my anger. My mom's dissection of Janis's contract was so on target that it took my breath away. I saw that Janis was never a friend to me, and it hurt so darn bad.

251

"Management fees, to be fair, should be based on net profits and all monies should be paid only after a full and complete accounting," Mom went on.

"That can be adjusted," Janis told Mom, but it was obvious that she still felt she was in the right.

"It will be," Mom assured her, "but the contract buster as far as I am concerned is found here at the end. Dominique, will you give my client and Janis a copy of the contract in question?"

Dominique pulled out copies for Janis and me from the manila envelope on her lap. I took mine and turned to the last page. Needless to say, Janis did the same. The only person who didn't have their nose in the contract was Dominique; she was too busy watching the drama of my ignorance unfold before her.

"Under entertainment law," Mom continued, "all contracts must have a starting date and an end date when the aforementioned contract expires. Because this contract does not have that, under law, this contract signed by Debrena Allison Allen and Janis Harmony Wilson is null and void."

Of course, Janis was speechless. With subtlety and grace, an iron fist wrapped in a velvet glove, Mom delivered a knockout blow. I emitted a sigh of relief but I knew my ordeal was far from over. There was the matter of the videotape, and I didn't see how Janis wouldn't use that against me, to embarrass me if nothing else.

"One more thing," Dominique said. "Sandra, I know you have to catch a plane, so I don't want to hold you, but I'd like a few minutes alone with the girls."

Mom nodded, indicating that she understood, and then made her exit.

That was when Dominique got up to close the door, indicating that what she had to say was of top secret importance. "Janis," Dominique began, "I'm sure you really enjoy your position with Walter McCary. It's gotten you to the point where you hobnob with the stars in Hollywood on a regular basis. I'd say that's super for a Jersey girl. Still, I know your heart is in artist management. You're in a good position to realize all your dreams, but you know, one wrong move could destroy your perfect world.

"To make a long story short, this woman I know managed rap acts. She started sleeping around with males and females and making all kinds of promises to upcoming artists. She had the best of both worlds, all her male and female lovers, until some label executives found out. And you know how labels get when they feel they might catch a bad rep or lose money behind someone's stupidity.

"We all know there's a lot of sex going on in the entertainment industry, but no one wants their noses rubbed in it. Especially when it can be documented on videotape. All parties would be embarrassed but the one who made the tape would be the one who would be blackballed in the industry; no one would want to take a chance on that person. No one would want to touch that person. Do I make myself clear, Janis?"

Although Janis looked like she was ready to explode due to her anger and frustration, she nodded.

"I'm so glad that you were able to make this meeting," Dominique said to Janis. "I know your schedule can be hectic at times."

Suddenly Janis stood and walked out of the office.

"I can't thank you enough," I said to Dominique as I stood, "especially for not telling Mom about the tape."

"It was good that you told me everything, Debrena. I hate to go into meetings like this only to get blindsided and slapped silly by something I don't know."

"I feel so stupid."

"You're young. It comes with the territory. "

I wanted to say more but I didn't know what to say.

"Your mom has to catch a plane," Dominique reminded me.

"Okay. And thanks again," I said and then left to face my mother.

Chapter Sixty-four

I stood outside of the dance studio with Mom as we waited for a taxicab to take her to Newark International Airport. I stood as close to her as I could. "Mom, I can't thank you enough for coming to my rescue. I mean, you and Dominique."

Mom smiled at me. "Well, I don't know why Dominique was being so helpful, but I got paid big bucks."

I had to laugh when Mom pulled out the dollar I had given her in Dominique's office. She waved it in my face and I grabbed at it.

"I earned this," Mom said as she kept the dollar away from me and put it in her briefcase. "I came out of retirement for this."

I couldn't help it, tears filled my eyes.

"Baby, baby," Mom said in her most soothing voice. "It's okay now. I don't think Janis will come back with anything else. What she did was greedy and selfish. A lot of people think they know the law, that's why people say, 'A person who represents himself in a court of law has a fool for a client.'"

"I heard that," I said as I wiped my eyes. I thought I was doing a pretty good job, but it was Mom who saved the day with a fistful of tissues. "Still, I can't thank you enough."

"That's behind us now, baby. Now I want you to concentrate on your dancing."

"That's all it should've been about in the first place," I had to admit.

"Live and learn, baby. Live and learn. I'll call you when I get home. Even if I don't get you, I'll leave a message on your machine."

"After all this, I need to come down to visit you and Dad."

"After the summer dance concert, you know you're more than welcomed."

I held the balled-up tissue in my hand, nodding.

"One more thing I wanted to say to you, baby." Of course Mom had my complete attention. "Your dad has been invited to a jazz festival in Paris."

"Good for Dad."

"We think so. But there's a little problem."

"Dad loves performing in Paris."

"Very true. But this time he wants me to go with him."

255

"You're going, right?"

"Only with your permission."

"My permission?"

"If we go together, we won't be back in time for the summer dance concert. We'll miss you dancing."

"Mom, look, I want you to go with Dad."

"But we've never missed a summer dance concert."

"Well, you'll miss this one. I want you two to go together and have a wonderful time."

Mom smiled and looked like a schoolgirl. "It'll be like a second honeymoon for us. No, more like a first honeymoon. We were so poor when we married that all we could afford was a weekend in Asbury Park." We both had to smile at that.

"Go, Mom. I insist that you go. I'll be all right."

"I told your dad you would be. You'll be with your young man."

I definitely didn't want to think about Choice. "Mom, there's something you need to know about Choice. We're not as close as I led you and Dad to believe. We dated, had some good times, but Choice is not my soul mate. What we had was good but it wasn't meant to last."

"No hard feelings between you two?"

"No, Mom. At least not on my part, and I think that now that Choice has gotten to really know me, I don't think I'm his cup of tea."

"It's so good to have someone you love who loves you back."

"I know, Mom. That's why I don't feel so bad about Choice. I know there's somebody out there for me. I just have to muster up the courage to go after them."

"Or let them come to you."

"Whichever way, we'll be together and in love."

"And I'll be so happy for you. No matter whom it is."

I didn't think Mom would agree with who I had in mind, but I didn't want to have that discussion with her at that time. If ever. Still, I knew eventually I would have to discuss my sexual orientation with Mom and Dad. I became weepy when the cab pulled up to the curb before us.

256

"You take care, baby," Mom said, then pulled me into her arms. She gave me the motherly hug that I needed so much. "As soon as we get back from Paris, I want to have a big family dinner."

"Me too," I said, my face buried in her bosom. "I love you. I love you so much," I said. The cabdriver came out and opened the back door. I grabbed Mom's briefcase and carried it to the cab. I put it on the backseat and Mom sat beside it. That was when the cabdriver slammed the door shut. When the cab pulled off, Mom turned around in the backseat to wave at me. I waved back with tears in my eyes.

I thought about just walking to the bus stop, but I had some unfinished business with Dominique. Because I wanted to break my habit of procrastination, I felt now was the time to do it.

Chapter Sixty-five

Did your mother get off on her way all right?" Dominique asked as I stood in the doorway of her office.

"No problem," I said, standing awkwardly in the doorway.

Dominique gave me her full attention. "You don't have to thank me again."

"That story?" I had to ask. "Was it true?"

Dominique smiled. "It could be."

"I destroyed my copy of the tape," I told her, feeling stupid all over again. "I don't know if Janis has any other copies."

"It doesn't matter if she does," Dominique assured me. "Janis has found her niche, out there in Hollywood, or as some would say 'Hollyweird.' She won't do anything to jeopardize that."

I emitted a sigh of relief because what Dominique said made a lot of sense.

"But there's something you need to consider, Debrena."

I gave her my full attention.

"In this business, gossip doesn't have to be proven to cause harm. I don't know about you, but when I feel I'm being attacked, I strike the first blow. I do that because if I'm hit first, I may not be able to recover enough to defend myself; I might be wiped out. We have a closed shop here at the dance studio, but the girls hear things from outside all the time. And if they hear it enough, they come to me. Especially someone like Tamara. If there is anything anyone else needs to know about you, it would sound a lot better coming directly from you. That way there's no confusion. You understand what I'm saying?"

I nodded in agreement.

"I'm not asking you to do anything," Dominique said, cutting me off because it was obvious that I was suffering. "All I'm saying is that you have to do some deep thinking about how you want folks to see you."

Coming clean like that was like standing naked onstage before a packed house. I just didn't think I was ready for that. "I understand what you're saying, Dominique."

As far as I was concerned, this summer was all about finding me. It was an exciting and scary journey. Every time I thought I found myself, I would turn a corner and become lost again. It was a frustrating puzzle, and I knew I had to figure it out by myself.

"Thank you," I told Dominique, then I finally left the dance studio.

258

Chapter Sixty-six

I sat in the middle of my bed, yoga style, listening to the radio in my room and knowing that I was in for another sleepless night. Spread out before me were three family picture albums, but the photo that really captured my attention was the one of Lorrie and me on the steps of the Frederick Douglass Community Center when we were ten years old. *Two little divas,* I said to myself as I looked down at the photo. There was nothing fancy about the photo, just a simple shot from an amateur photographer, Mom. I longed to get back to that simpler time because now I found my life so complicated that I thought seriously about giving up, walking away from everything.

Who would really care if I stopped dancing? I asked myself, and I knew the answer was simple but complex. I would miss it because it was such a part of me. I wouldn't go so far as to say that I couldn't live without dance, but I knew that I was only fooling myself if I thought I could be happy without that form of self-expression. As I let all this run through my mind, Monica's summer song came on the radio.

I had heard it before, but I had not really listened to it closely. The song, "First Night," seemed like just another tune from the young R&B artist, but that night, it spoke to me in a very profound way. And this was so surprising to me. It began with Monica singing about being out with a guy and having strong sexual feelings, even though it was their first date. She wanted to "get down" but was worried about how he would feel about her if she gave in to her strong desire.

I smiled as she sang about wanting to kiss and wanting to touch. Then Monica got to the real deal: it wasn't so much about the guy; it was really about what society would think. I could really relate to what Monica was singing about. It was like the first time I went to Choice's loft. I knew what I wanted to do with him sexually but I was almost paralyzed by that age-old question: What would he think about me after we had made love? Would he think I was too fast? Would he think that I always got down on the first night?

I could really relate to that struggle in Monica's sweet song, but I knew that playing it safe could never be the solution. Not for someone like me who just wanted to live her life openly and honestly. This thought was heavy on my mind as Monica finished her song. Her choice was not to get down on that first night. I could see from where she was coming but I was just not that type of girl. I would not have been true to myself if I had done that.

When the song ended, I felt sad but somehow energized, full of hope and purpose. I knew all my problems had not been solved in the course of that four-minute song but I had realized that people had power over me if I gave it to them. Right then and there I decided to take my power and make my life what I wanted it to be. Before I drifted off to sleep, I promised myself to take care of some unfinished business.

Chapter Sixty-seven

Debrena," *Erica* called out to me when she saw me standing alone in the locker room the next day. "Where have you been?"

I had spoken to Dominique that morning. I told her that I was going to miss rehearsal, but what I didn't tell her was that I had planned to meet with my dance mates after theirs.

"Debrena," Tamara called out to me as soon as she walked into the locker room. "What's going on?"

"I need to talk," I told Tamara and saw concern and confusion on her face. "I need to talk with all of you."

"I know what it's about," Tamara said, whispering so that only I could hear her. "And I agree, Debrena. It's time we got to the bottom of this thing with Angela and Marcy. I told Kammie we would have a big meeting."

I tried hard to smile at Tamara but found it much too painful. "Not now, Tamara."

"I know," Tamara said, looking over her shoulder, then back at me. "But this is so much better. To get it out like this." It was obvious that Tamara misunderstood my reason for wanting to talk to everyone. In her small mind it had to be about old business. I knew I had to disappoint her. Before I could even begin to explain myself, Marcy and Angela came into the locker room.

"Hey, guys," Tamara called out to LaTasha, Kammie and Shay who came in behind Angela and Marcy. "Debrena, wants to have a meeting."

Of course everybody was excited about the prospect of a meeting, except Angela and Marcy because the way that Tamara looked at them, they were given the impression that the meeting was about them.

"Everybody is here but Lorrie," Kammie said, and I felt a lump in my throat. But I knew that what I had to say was important for Lorrie as well as everyone else. Lorrie walked in casually and froze when she saw me. I guess the look on my face let her know that I wasn't there for some casual conversation.

"Debrena, wants to have a meeting," Tamara told Lorrie.

With a thick towel wrapped around her neck, Lorrie sat on the long bench in front of her locker.

"I don't want to hold you long," I began. "You just probably had a tough rehearsal and want to get into the showers. I wasn't here this morning because I had a lot on my mind; I knew I couldn't concentrate on dance." I took a deep breath, then jumped in. "This summer has been the best, and the worst. I've experienced crazy highs and scary lows; I've cried and I've laughed. A few nights ago I convinced myself that I didn't have a future, that the new millennium just wasn't for me."

I looked over at Lorrie for the strength to go on; her smile was just what I needed.

"I'm going to be all right. I know that now. No matter what happens here today, I'm going to be all right. I have too many people who love me not to be all right. And all I have to do is open my arms to receive that love. But no one can love you if you don't love yourself." I almost lost it right then and there because the words seemed to be clogged in my throat. "I learned that the hard way. I was so busy hiding who I was. But then, with the help of a true friend, I found myself, but I still couldn't fully accept that."

Lorrie kept on smiling at me, and I kept on drawing strength from that. "What I'm trying to say is that I'm not going to fight with myself anymore. I'm not going to hide who I am. And if you love me, truly love me, and not just for my dancing or the fact that I appeared in a music video, you'll accept me the way I have accepted myself."

Kammie looked at me like she was saying, "Hurry up already," but I knew I had to say it in my own time, in my own way.

"I know many of you think I'm here to talk about Angela and Marcy. But I'm going to have to disappoint you with that." Angela smirked and looked around the room, glad to have the spotlight off her and Marcy I supposed. "Well, this meeting is not about that. What Angela and Marcy do behind closed doors, as consenting adults, is their business. I still love them; they're my sister dancers. I just ask them to forgive me for my hypocrisy."

"What is this about?" Tamara asked, obviously angry that I wasn't talking about dealing with Angela and Marcy.

"Let her speak," LaTasha said, curious as to where I was going.

263

"Because what they do behind closed doors, in their bed, is what I do," I went on, and there were gasps from many of the girls. "Now you can call me bisexual, lesbian, freak, whatever. It doesn't matter because I've called myself all of those names, and they are nothing to me but labels." Shay and Erica stood with their mouths wide open.

"But I know some of you have problems with the way some people express their sexuality. I-I had a problem with it too. But now I realize that there are much more important things. And it's not as important as to what you call me; all that matters is what I answer to. You can call me what you like, but in the real world, I am Debrena Allison Allen."

Then I stood in the stunned silence and waited for the world to explode around me.

Tamara broke the silence by muttering something about "this gay shit," then she was out of the locker room and out of my sight. Then Kammie followed her. And that was it until Lorrie walked off into the showers. The noise of everyone else getting ready to follow her lead filled the locker room. Because there was nothing more for me to say, and because there was no one who wanted to say anything to me, I walked out of the locker room.

That was when Angela called out to me. I turned to face her with unshed tears feeling like sand in my eyes. She came to me looking sheepish, like she had done something wrong and needed my forgiveness.

"What you said," Angela began, then stopped. "You came out like that and you didn't have to." She stopped again and took a deep breath before continuing. "What I mean is that I was really touched by what you said."

I wanted to say, "Thank you, Angela," but I couldn't trust my voice. I felt if I said anything I'd cry or mumble incoherently. The best thing I could do was put my hand on Angela's shoulder and nod.

"And I want to apologize for the way I came on to you," Angela managed to say.

I tried to smile as I nodded again and said, "It's okay," removing my hand from Angela's shoulder but continuing to look into her eyes.

Angela blinked and then her eyes became wide. She stood before me making no move to wipe the tears that ran down her face. We hugged briefly, then Angela walked back toward the locker room.

And I walked out of the dance studio alone.

Chapter Sixty-eight

After what had gone down at the dance studio, there was nowhere for me to go but home. I felt so fatigued, like I had emptied myself out and all that was left of me was the shell that I parked on my living room couch. The phone rang a few times as I sat there, but I made no move to answer it. It was almost four in the afternoon, and there was really no one I wanted to talk to. I ignored the phone and sat with my arms wrapped around me, holding myself like I was the only person who could love me unconditionally. I thought that there was nobody I could trust with my heart, but I had to let that thought go because there was someone. I just didn't know how to reach out to her. I stood from the couch and took off my fanny pack. I let it fall to the floor as I thought about a nice, long, hot shower. I took off my jacket and then I thought of slipping into my bed to call it a night. But for some reason I couldn't move toward my bedroom; my scattered thoughts held me in one place. I couldn't move, and I couldn't stop holding myself.

When the knock came, it inspired me to move.

I opened the door and found Lorrie standing there. Lorrie was my mirror image, dressed in a short black jacket, a dark red tube top, skintight jeans and Lucite sandals. But her eyes were scary, wide and wild, like she had run all the way to my doorstep.

I was struck speechless by her breathtaking beauty. Her square face was bold and clean, and I couldn't take my eyes off the exquisiteness of her high cheekbones, almond-shaped eyes and full lips. She was a light-skinned woman who could not only turn heads but she could stop traffic. As I looked at her, I realized that she was at the pinnacle of her youthfulness. She would never be this beautiful, this radiant. And because I realized this, it took nothing away from Lorrie Cunningham because I knew in my heart that Lorrie would always be attractive. It had taken years for her to get to this and I, for one, was more than proud of her. Her natural beauty was presented before me with no self-consciousness, no fear. I had never seen her like this, this woman looking at me so boldly, like she was on a mission. I could see the determination in the firm set of her mouth. She wasn't smiling because there wasn't anything funny. She was as serious as cancer, and I knew I had better pay attention to all that she had come to tell me.

266

"I did call first," Lorrie let me know as she stepped inside.

"It doesn't matter now," I told Lorrie as I closed the door behind her.

"You really said a mouthful at the dance studio," she said.

"I don't even remember what I said, Lorrie. All I know is that I spoke from my heart. Deep inside my heart."

"I could feel that, D. I could really feel that."

"I'm so glad you were there."

"I was always there, D."

"But I thought you were mad at me, I thought you hated me because of how you caught me with Choice."

"I could never hate you, D. As for Choice, I know that was something you had to do."

"You know that's over?"

"I don't think it ever started. You never convinced me that you loved him."

"I tried to convince myself that I did."

"When you have to work that hard, it can't be right."

"Is this right? What's between me and you?"

"As far as I'm concerned, it was always right. From that almost kiss when we were ten years old."

"We have to move beyond that, Lorrie. See if it's right for us."

"I'm willing to take that step."

"What if it doesn't work out?"

"What choice do we have, D? What choice do we have? We do this now, or I'm going spend the rest of my life on your doorstep, waiting on you to take me in your arms and kiss me."

And I wanted to kiss her, but thinking about last time when we were interrupted, I knew there was something I needed to do. I walked over to the front door, determined to do it right. I triple-locked the door before I turned back to her.

Then Lorrie pressed tight against me, almost suffocating me with her body heat and musty scent. And I knew that whatever Lorrie had come for was exactly what she was going to get. And no one, least of all me, was going to stop her. She slammed her crotch into mine and ran her hands up and down my hips. There was urgency and intensity in her stroking that set my hips on fire. I was so caught up in Lorrie's assault that all I could do was moan and throw my crotch into her, which was exactly what she silently demanded. To make the contact even more intense, Lorrie moved her hands behind me. She grabbed my booty with both her hands, squeezing my cheeks and stroking me. All I could do was moan because Lorrie was stone cold running the show. She was hungry for me.

I gasped in surprise as this super-aggressive Lorrie stripped me of my tube top. We kissed hard as I held her tightly.

267

Chapter Sixty-nine

I reluctantly pulled away from the sweet honey of Lorrie's mouth and the warm comfort of her arms. Lorrie pushed my tube top down and ran her hands up to my breasts. She found my nipples hard. She caressed them and tweaked them and then pushed my tube top all the way down, leaving my breasts completely exposed. Fully accepting what was happening to me, I put my hands under my breasts and offered them to Lorrie like they were a special gift. I watched in fascination as Lorrie stuck her long, pink tongue out and licked her lips. Then she held my arms down as she bent her head to attack my super-aroused nipples. "Lorrie, baby," I moaned as she gently sucked my nipples, teasing them with her wicked tongue. I wanted to do something but I knew, somewhere deep inside me, that that wasn't allowed.

She talked to my body in a sexy language that set me on fire. "Can you feel what I'm saying?" I imagined Lorrie saying. "Open up. Open up, D. Let me get inside you, deep inside you. Let me show you how real my love is. Let the funky magic happen between us." Her intensity rocked me, made me tremble. I tried to pull away but she wouldn't let me. She held me in place with one hand on my booty and her other hand running all up and down between my breasts.

I've got to fight you! my mind screamed. *I've got to fight you, baby, because you're taking me someplace I've never been.* That was when Lorrie pushed her hands into my jeans. She had one in the front and one in the back. The pleasure was almost painful as she stroked my front and back. I had on a thong but that was no defense against Lorrie's probing fingers. I found myself pushing my tube top, my jeans and my thong down. Then Lorrie knelt in front of me and pushed everything down to my sandals. When I kicked off my sandals, I let Lorrie help me step out of my clothing. Suddenly I wanted to run to my bedroom and lock myself in because I found it hard to deal with this new aggressive Lorrie.

No more, no more, Lorrie! my mind screamed but Lorrie just continued to attack my body, until she wore me down and made me a puddle of quivering flesh at her feet. She had come to me with a need of such intensity that it swept us up in a passion that was mind blowing. We both breathed hard and heavy in my living room.

269

I looked down at the hand that Lorrie ran up and down my hot belly. Although Lorrie was fully clothed and not talking to me, I instinctively knew what she wanted me to do, and she stepped back to let me do it. I trembled as I ran my hands up and down my hot, bare thighs. She could've done it for me—her hands had been there—but we both knew, without speaking, that it would mean more if I did it. I thought about sitting on the couch, but I knew, somehow, that would break the connection between us. I didn't want to stop our intense flow. I just knew I couldn't start all over again, and I wanted to reach the highest heights with Lorrie who stood fully clothed with me naked in front of her. Her eyes were on me, willing me to do it, to open myself completely to her. I smiled at Lorrie, letting her know that I was hip to her game, but also letting her know I still had some game of my own.

I slowly turned and only stopped when I had my back toward her. For a few moments, I let her take in the full view: my short hair; my tight shoulders; my long back; my high, round booty; my long dancer's legs; my smooth, bare feet. With me standing like that, Lorrie couldn't resist the urge to stroke my sweat-soaked back and the high rise of my booty. Then Lorrie stepped back to let me do what I needed to do. I reached behind and spread my butt checks. For Lorrie. For me. I grunted loudly when Lorrie got on her knees behind me and stuck her tongue inside me. She licked me good between my cheeks, so thoroughly back there, that I almost came like that. But I knew that wasn't the way Lorrie wanted to finish this.

When Lorrie finished tonguing me down, I turned to face her. Lorrie stood and pressed herself into me. We kissed, and I could taste my funky self in Lorrie's mouth. It didn't matter because I had decided to go wherever Lorrie wanted to take me. When Lorrie sank to her knees, I reached down with both hands to spread myself open for her. Her tongue was wicked inside me, and it wasn't long before I shivered, screamed and came as my legs gave out.

"The bedroom now," I told her with tears in my eyes.

Lorrie nodded.

I reached out to her with both my hands. Helping her up, I then held her face between my hands and kissed her hard on the mouth, tasting her and sucking her tongue, and then sucking her lips. We had done so much but I knew she wanted more.

"I want your dick," Lorrie told me, referring to my dildo. "I want your dick in me."

Chapter Seventy

The rawness of the request made me tingle. I nodded, knowing that whatever Lorrie wanted that afternoon was what she was going to get. I left the living room and walked down the hall to my bedroom. Inside, I looked at myself in the full-length mirror. I tried to see myself as Lorrie saw me but I knew I did not have that much love for myself. The love I saw in Lorrie's eyes was without judgment, unconditional. And I couldn't help but wonder if I deserved that kind of love from anyone. I bent down to dig inside my bottom dresser drawer. When I stood, the dildo and harness were in my hands. As I strapped it on, Lorrie came into my bedroom. She was naked, as I knew she would be. Without a word, Lorrie climbed up onto my bed. Then she lay there with her hands covering her breasts, her hard, brown nipples peeking through her slender fingers, her thighs spread wide, her feet together.

"Fuck me, D," Lorrie said as I put my knee up on the bed, both hands around my dildo. I got between Lorrie's thighs and aimed my dick at her. The pink inside her was shiny and wet as I pushed it into her. She brought her hands down between her thighs so she could rub her clit while I moved in and out of her. My eyes locked on hers. "Ohhhhhh, D," she cried out as I humped her. "You gonna make me cum, you gonna make me cum," she said, saying it like it was a wish she wanted to come true.

And she came loudly, convulsively, her arms and legs flapping out of control. But that was the way she wanted it; she wanted to give me her all and all. For Lorrie there was no Choice or Tyra or anyone else. All Lorrie could see was us, together, forever. I sat back on my heels after I pulled out of Lorrie's most receptive hole. "I want what you want, Lorrie," I told her as I took off my harness. That was when I put my hands behind her thighs and pushed up so that her full bottom was turned up to me.

"You don't have to do that, D."

"I want to, Lorrie. I want to do this. Just let me do this. After all you've done for me. I can't give you enough."

Because we were on the same vibe, I didn't have to say anything else. Lorrie drew her knees back to her breasts, and I bent my head to her bottom. "Ohhhhh, D," Lorrie moaned loudly as I licked and sucked, then let my tongue travel down. Her breathing was heavy in the room as I worked her with my lips and tongue. When I got to the deepest part of her, Lorrie began moaning and groaning and calling my name. I held her open and sucked up all the juices flowing from her. Then I lay atop her and rubbed myself against her. We came together with me holding Lorrie's trembling body like it was my only hope.

"You're the one," Lorrie whispered into my ear. "The only one. I couldn't get with Angela because I wanted you. I've always wanted you."

I reluctantly slid off Lorrie's hot, sweet body and rested beside her.

"I love you, D," Lorrie told me, turning to fold her body into mine.

"I know, Lorrie. I think I've always known that. But I was never ready to deal with that. Until now. Until I learned to accept myself."

"Why now, D?" Lorrie wanted to know as the tears ran down her face. "Because of the way I came at you?"

I tenderly touched Lorrie's face, attempting to wipe away her tears, her pain. "You had to come at me like that, Lorrie. Shock some sense into me. Make me open to you like that."

"If you don't want me, I don't know what I'll do," Lorrie confessed. "I can't go back to anything I knew before."

"I know."

"What about you and Choice?"

272

"Choice is not ready for me, Lorrie. He thinks I'm a freak like you." I smiled, letting Lorrie know that I was making a joke, but also letting her know that we deserved each other and that we were going to be together, forever. There was joy in Lorrie's smile, a joy that dried her tears, but there was still more for me to say. "This is not just about sex," I said.

Lorrie looked at me with wide eyes, silently begging me to go on, to let her know from where I was truly coming, what I had in my heart.

"More than sex," I assured her. "More than sex could ever be. This is love."

273

Lorrie touched my lips and I sucked her finger. There were tears in my eyes when I said, as I held her body to my body, her mind to my mind, her spirit to my spirit, "Lorrie, I-I love you."

Chapter Seventy-one

The stage was bare except for a huge blowup of a photo from the Motown archives: a closeup of Eddie Kendricks bent over a microphone he held between his hands. He wore a goatee, and his eyes were closed as he sang into the microphone. He was painfully thin. And below the photo was a quote from Kendricks that read: "Nobody gives this (talent) to you, nobody says, 'Come on, I'm gonna make you a star.' You have to have something. I'd like to think I had it." Then it was: Eddie Kendricks. Born 12-7-1939; died 10-5-1992.

The show began when the curtain lifted to reveal DJ T-Moon onstage, standing behind a long table with two turntables on it. From where I stood backstage, it looked like a sea of people out there, loud and rowdy. But DJ T-Moon got them quiet with some fancy scratching. Then Dominique came from the wings, dressed in a red leotard and a long black skirt.

Across the stage from me, LaTasha and Shay were doing their isolations.

"We welcome you to this very special concert," Dominique began, speaking into the silver mike that DJ T-Moon handed her. "This concert marks the twenty-fifth anniversary of the Dominique St. Claire Dance Studio and features the SOS dance troupe." There was loud and rowdy applause at this.

"The Sisters of Soul are anxious to perform for you," Dominique went on. "They have worked hard all summer, and I know you will enjoy them very much. We thank you for coming out."

There were more applause. "This program is dedicated to the proposition that the Motown sound will never die; you can hear a lot of this music sampled in many of the rap songs that you listen to today." More applause and wolf whistles. "We call this program for the summer of '99, 'Keep on Truckin' and 'Boogie Down: A Tribute to the Music of Eddie Kendricks.' As you all know we have a very special guest performing, Mr. Walter McCary."

Then the applause was so loud that Dominique had to stop speaking. There was no way she could talk over all that enthusiasm. She had to raise her hands to get the crowd to calm down. "I guess there is nothing more to say. Enjoy the program and come back next year."

We were finally here. This was what we had worked so hard for and to think I was going to give this up for Janis. Everyone was there; even Tamara and Kammie, who decided that this would be their last performance with the SOS dance troupe. They had told Dominique that they wanted to look for a new home. I was just glad they decided to take this opportunity to perform in the show. I knew I would miss them both, but they had to know that their feelings toward me would not change the reality of who I was.

When Dominique disappeared into the wings, I looked over at Lorrie, and she nodded at me. Half of the company was on one side of the stage and the other half was on the other. When DJ T-Moon dropped "Keep On Truckin'," it was time for us to meet in the middle of the stage. I couldn't help but look at Tamara and Kammie and wonder if I'd ever see them again.

Before I knew it, we were halfway through the show. Then I was out there alone, dancing to one of my favorite songs, "Can I?" As I danced I couldn't help but think about Choice in the studio when Lorrie walked in on us. That wasn't the way I wanted him to find out about Lorrie and me, but I was glad that it didn't get real ugly. I was no longer confused about my feelings for Lorrie, but I didn't want Choice to feel bad, especially when all he did was try to love me. In the back of my mind, I thought about how we met in Stella's Diner, how handsome and strong he looked, and how I wanted to love him but couldn't because I wouldn't have been true to myself.

And in the end, I would end up hurting him anyway, more than I did and more than I had to. As Tyra once told me, I was more than a woman because I was gay.

I ended my solo turn to a wave of applause, and suddenly couldn't move. From the wings, Dominique motioned for me to take a bow. I was a little confused because my solo was not the end of the show, but the crowd just wouldn't let me go. They wouldn't stop clapping and when they stood from their chairs, I knew that they wouldn't let me go unless I took a bow. I took a bow, and then ran offstage to the comfort of my dance mates.

Dominique winked at me as she passed by on her way to the microphone. She was on the way to bring our special guest star to the stage. Because of what had happened with Janis I thought we had blown it with Walter but he proved to be a man of his word. Dominque convinced me that Janis had not told him what really happened between us. As Dominique had explained it to me, Janis would not say anything because she had too much to lose. Whatever had happened did nothing to keep Walter from gracing the stage at the Frederick Douglass Community Center.

A chill went up my spine when Dominique said, "At this time it gives me great pleasure to bring to the stage a very exciting performer and a dear friend of our dance company, Mr. Walter McCary."

The crowd went wild like I knew they would, and then Walter took the stage. Needless to say the rest of the performance added up to a massive success!

Chapter Seventy-two

Debrena!" *Erica* called out to me in a voice that seemed bigger than she was. I ran out of the kitchen because the way that girl called my name was between a scream and a shout.

"What is wrong with you, girl?" I asked as I came into the living room. "Hollering like somebody's killing you in here." Lorrie was right behind me. We had been talking in the kitchen, and the shouting had gotten us out of there real fast.

"Look!" Erica said as she pointed to the TV screen.

It was a headshot of me taken from the "A Dream" video.

Shay, LaTasha and LaToya were in my living room with Erica. "Right after Naughty By Nature's video, this came on," Shay told me.

Suddenly Kurt Loder, an MTV VJ appeared on the screen, with my picture a backdrop to his reporting: "Will lightning strike again! Walter McCary's latest video featured another model-slash-dancer from New Jersey."

That was when Tyra's headshot appeared behind Kurt Loder's head.

"I saw that video," LaTasha blurted.

Of course she was talking about the video for "Now I See Me," Walter McCary's followup to the one I had appeared in. Because I hadn't done any more work with Janis, my video got a little more airplay but soon died a natural death in the weeks after its premiere.

"She goes by the name of Tyra," Kurt Loder continued, "no last name, and is featured in the video for the latest single from Walter McCary's platinum-plus best-selling CD. After the success of the 'A

Dream' video, it seems that McCary has a knack for finding beautiful talent in New Jersey. First it was the African-American beauty, D. Allen, and now it's the natural redhead, Tyra. No last name."

Then there was a live shot of Tyra, dressed like a diva in a peach-colored chiffon mini-dress covered in gold and red beads, rhinestones and studs, showing well-toned arms and long legs. On her feet were gold stilettos with wide crisscrossed straps in the front. She was accessorized with platinum and diamond earrings, bracelets and rings.

"Looking good," Shay said.

278   We all had to agree, but what really knocked us out was Janis standing in the background.

Still smiling, Tyra gushed, "None of this would have been possible without my manager, Janis Wilson."

We all laughed at that because this close inner circle knew the real deal about Janis. Not Tamara or Kammie, who never came back. Just those who I knew would be with me forever as the Sisters of Soul.

I couldn't help but grab Lorrie's hand because she had given me the extra courage I needed to explain everything to Erica, Shay, LaTasha and LaToya. She squeezed my hand, and I laughed out loud, so happy that I was no longer a part of the media madness that Tyra and Janis seemed to be enjoying. I had tried to reach out to Tyra, to warn her about Janis, but she didn't return any of my calls. Lorrie told me that Tyra had to learn the hard way. Reluctantly, I had to agree. There was only so much that I could do. Summer had come to an end and I found myself in good shape, real good shape.

"Kurt Loder here for MTV News. Stay tuned for more."

AT MIDNIGHT

Choice Fowler's Story
By

Terry B.

Coming Winter 2004

Chapter One

They were two among the fifty in my loft located in Elizabeth, New Jersey. They were whispering, but because I was listening so hard, I heard every word, breathed in every inflection and absorbed every secret meaning. The couple was at an invitation-only event, displaying photos by me, Choice Fowler. A man and woman talked like they were at home alone. They were well groomed and expensively dressed like all the others floating around them. Everyone was expected to not just admire the photos but to dig deep into their fat pockets and buy something at this summer showcase. According to Carrie Nelson, the founder and CEO of the Nelson Talent Agency, I was "the next big thing in Black photography, the Black man rising."

It was eleven o'clock, still early in the day as the couple stood with their backs toward me, not even realizing I was breathing down their necks, listening to their conversation as "Love Don't Love Nobody" by The Spinners played softly in the background.

"She seems to be in another place," the woman whispered, her voice baby-skin soft and silky smooth.

"Like she's dancing, but it's more than that," the man said in a hard baritone with a touch of bass. "More like sex."

The woman put her hand up to her mouth and giggled as she moved closer to the man. "You can't have sex on the dance floor."

"Why not?"

"I know you have to be joking because what you're saying, what you're suggesting is just too crazy," the woman said. "We've done some wild things."

"But not that," the man said, cutting the woman off. "Not yet."

The woman giggled again and moved even closer to the man. "You need to see somebody, somebody professional. You must be some kind of sex addict."

The man moved in closer to the picture. "She seems to be at peace."

That shot was a gift from the gods. It wasn't planned but it was perfect, nothing I could get from a model posing for me. I had come upon her dancing alone in the studio. I wasn't supposed to be there, but I was glad I was. I called the photo *Dancer's Paradise*. It was a picture of Debrena Allen, a featured dancer with the Dominique St. Claire Dance Studio, and a former lover.

I knew any thought of us getting back together was crazy. Yet I had fantasized that somehow, someway, we'd get back together. That by some miracle, things would work out for us. A way to make whole the love that fell apart so abruptly. Of course there was no way things could have worked out when I discovered that Debrena was into sex with women. I hated that scene; I just couldn't understand what that was about. I once read somewhere that the most popular male fantasy was sex with two women at the same time. What was the biggest sexual fantasy for women? I couldn't find any research in that area, but I had known women on both the West Coast and East Coast who swung like that. Maybe I'm a little strange but watching two women together or sharing a bed with two women is not a turn-on for me, especially if I had some respect and love for one of the women involved.

My mental wandering came to an abrupt halt when a hand rested on my shoulder.

"You have to mix and mingle, brother man," Curtis Walker said as he stood beside me, dressed in a white linen suit. His custom-made shirt was two-tone, blue and black, and he wore a bowtie around the stiff collar. On his feet were silk socks and ridiculously expensive Stacey Adams shoes. He was a pretty-boy fashion plate. I had tried hard not to like him but he was funny and he worked hard at NTA. Curtis was a talent scout for Carrie and Dany Nelson, founders of NTA.

"You're doing enough mixing and mingling for both of us," I

said, noticing that he had a glass of wine in one hand and a plate of cheese cubes and whole-wheat crackers in the other. I didn't expect him to spend too much time with me because he was working the room.

"It's my job," Curtis reminded me, "the job I do for NTA."

"And I can't thank you enough," I replied sarcastically, knowing that Curtis would not take it personally.

"You'll thank me and Carrie and Dany when this show ends and the big bucks start rolling in," Curtis said, his eyes all over the room. "Good for you, a lot of people like to look at beautifully shot photographs."

283

"There are a lot of voyeurs in here," I observed, lowering my voice as not to offend anyone who might be thinking about buying some of my art. I also couldn't help but notice that the sexy whisperers seemed rooted to the space in front of Debrena's photo.

"I like to watch," Curtis admitted, and of course it was no surprise to me. From our many drunken conversations he let me know that watching two women together was at the top of his sexual fantasy wish list.

"Sometimes watching is a lot safer than getting involved," I said, and then hoped that Curtis didn't take my confession any further. Although many say that confession was good for the soul, I didn't want to go there with Curtis. It was the summer of 2000, a year past the summer I met Debrena, and I had to admit that I was still trying to get over her. Love is a bitch, and then you get dumped. I put that in the same category with that popular saying, shit happens.

"It seems like that photo is going to bring in some big bucks," Curtis said, and I had no doubt which one he was talking about. "And to think, you didn't want to include that in your show."

I couldn't explain to Curtis, Carrie, or Dany why I didn't want to exhibit the photo, *Dancer's Paradise;* they all loved it. My thinking was that by exhibiting it, I was labeling myself as a lovesick fool. I didn't want to go out like that. I had to admit that love had done me dirty that past summer, but no one liked to be ass out in public. I had loved and I had lost. I didn't want to dwell on that. All the classic R&B songs that I loved to listen to talked about that. What they didn't tell you was how long the hurt would last. Nor how hard it would make a man cry. And because I felt so uncomfortable with that revelation, there was no way I could mix and mingle; I didn't want to expose myself in any way.

How could I move on in the summer of 2000 when my mind, body, and spirit had been crushed in the summer of 1999? Still, I felt that the healing was about to begin in this very public place because I had to admit to myself, a fact that assured me many sleepless nights and restless days: I was madly in love with Debrena Allen.

284

How I would get her back was something that had been on my mind. Moreso than the current showcase or the other projects that NTA had lined up for me. For me, that summer of 2000 was about getting back with Debrena Allen at all costs. No one had to tell me that it wouldn't be easy.

Chapter Two

I felt a little shabby standing next to Curtis. He in his fancy clothes, and me in my white burgundy-trimmed tracksuit, trying hard to feel the stirring emotions in Earth, Wind and Fire's "After the Love Has Gone," now playing in the background.

"Are those your formal sweats?" Curtis asked me, trying hard to be more hip than insulting. I knew I wasn't a fancy dresser but he didn't have to rub it in.

"Like I always tell you, Curtis," I replied. "It's not about me being a fashion plate, it's about the models. Besides, you've seen my work; I'm all over the floor. A fancy suit wouldn't stand a chance with me."

"Do you even own a suit?" Curtis had to ask, always curious about my wardrobe.

"One black suit," I had to admit. "A dark suit for funerals and weddings."

Curtis laughed as I looked around the loft, I figured that would end the talk about my wardrobe-or should I say lack of wardrobe.

"I got to take you shopping," Curtis told me as he also looked around the loft. To make Miss Carrie happy if nothing else."

"Don't do me any favors," I deadpanned.

Curtis laughed again. "I'm doing it more for me, brother man. I'm about to make some serious moves, and I need Miss Carrie on my side. With your sweats you make me look bad. With your track suits, muscle shirts, khakis and leather running shoes, you look like a professional athlete relaxing around his million-dollar home."

"What's wrong with that?" I had to ask, really liking that part about relaxing around a million-dollar home. "I'm neat and clean and well covered."

"You're not a jock, brother man," Curtis said in a harsh whisper. "You're an artist. I'll give you that, but you also need to be a businessman."

"And dress like you?" I had to ask, digging into his ego.

Curtis smiled like he thought he was smarter than me. "I'm about art and business, and that's not a bad combination. You should take a lesson."

"I got to be me, Curtis."

Curtis shook his head. "You're almost helpless."

"You saying I have nothing going for myself?"

"I can't say that. You're a bad man with that camera, a wizard in the darkroom. Can't nobody touch you behind that. You can walk up to any honey on the street and talk her into posing naked for you."

"And you're impressed with that." It wasn't a question because I knew Curtis Walker that well. He called my nude studies "nekkid pictures" and loved to hang out in the loft to check out who I had "talked out of their panties."

"Hey, man, call me shallow," Curtis admitted with no shame, "but I got to wine and dine a honey before she even thinks about taking her clothes off."

"I always tell you, Curtis. It's all about art."

Of course he didn't believe me. "A naked woman is a naked woman, whether she is in a museum or in *Black Tail* magazine," Curtis said with proud ignorance.

Because I knew that Curtis would never see the difference between art and exploitation I let our conversation die a natural death.

Dany Nelson came over to Curtis and me with a worried look on her face. But I wasn't too concerned because she always wore that look. When it came to business-and selling my work was her business-she was a no-nonsense woman. That afternoon she was the voice of gloom and doom.

"Things couldn't be worse," Dany said instead of hello.

"You got to get big ballers up in this piece," Curtis told Dany. "Some shot callers. These people are here for show. They're here to see and be seen. They'd break all of the Ten Commandments before they'd break a dollar bill."

"Not so loud," Dany whispered. "We still have a few more hours."

"You are the eternal optimist," Curtis told Dany, and I had to step back and look at them. They were both beautiful, expensively dressed. Especially Dany, with her dark, summer-weight coatdress and stacked heels. At five-nine, and what looked to be a size six, she had sharp features that made her stand out in any crowd. If Dany had any flaws, it had to be her black-rimmed, oversized eyeglasses. Curtis was always telling her that she needed to wear contact lenses.

287

"This is business," Dany told Curtis. "I know my business. I just wish Choice would help me more."

I felt a little offended by that. "I'm here, Dany. I'm minding the store."

"You have to mingle, Choice. They know your work, but they don't know you. Nobody knows you."

"You want me to work the room like I'm running for some type of office? I can't do that. I'm not comfortable with that."

Dany's dark eyes cut me from behind her eyeglasses. "I don't know why I bust my ass for you," she said, still whispering but forcefully.

"Because I'm cute?" I asked, trying hard to lighten the mood.

Dany did smile. "You're cute all right, but you'd be cuter if you'd help me sell some of your work."

"I'll do what I can," I told her, knowing that meant a lot less than what Dany hoped for.

"You know it would help if you'd let me sell *Dancer's Paradise*. There's a lot of interest in that photo."

"We had this discussion," I reminded her. "I told you and Curtis that I didn't even want that shot in this show. You not only didn't want to hear me, you even put that shot on the cover of the invitations you sent out.

"It worked," Dany quickly added. "This is not a bad crowd."

"Just a cheap crowd," Curtis had to add.

Dany looked at Curtis like she wanted to punch his lights out. "Like I said, we still have some time left."

I knew Dany wanted me to give in and offer to let her sell the photo of Debrena, but I knew there was no way I could. It was more than my being sentimental; I just couldn't deal with the idea of anyone having that image of such a beautiful dancer hanging on their wall. It made no artistic sense, no monetary sense, for me to think like that, but I was like a dog with a meaty bone-I just couldn't let go.

288

"Well, it was nice talking to you guys," Dany said, "but I got to jump back into the arena. You will come out of this with some money, Choice Fowler. You will get paid, and so will NTA. We've got too much invested in you to leave you to your own devices."

I knew that Dany was saying all that to make me feel valued as an NTA artist, but all it did was put more pressure on me. "I want to help," I blurted out over Luther Vandross' "There's Nothing Better Than Love" before Dany left to continue her mixing and mingling. And because I got her attention, she stood still before me. "I'll move around a little, let these people know who I am."

Dany put her hands together in the prayer position. "Thank you, Choice Fowler, the magnificent."

"I can do without the sarcasm," I told her, but I was smiling and so was she, and that meant everything was all good. "You know I have to leave for L.A. by the end of this week," I reminded Dany.

"I know. That's why I rushed to put this together."

"Let's do this then, and let's get that other thing together. I talked to your mother, and she really wants that to happen."

Dany knew that I was referring to needing a makeup artist to begin the *Urban Vibe* magazine shoot.

"I know that, Choice," Dany said, somewhat defensively. "I know what kind of team you need to start that project."

"I just want to do the best job for NTA. I have my stylist, I have my hair person, but I can't really make it happen without a makeup artist."

"I know that, Choice," Dany said with her eyes darting around the room, like she was afraid everyone would leave without buying something. "I plan to have someone for you to look at before you leave for your vacation."

And with that said, Dany disappeared into the crowd.

Chapter Three

Lorrie

That afternoon there were too many people in one place. But the way Debrena's home was set up, the foyer was wide and opened into an even wider living room. Even with all the furniture pushed back against the walls, it was a little tight. But with a nice breeze coming in through the large windows it was not stuffy.

Angela King and Marcy Chase stood before Reverend Jackie Brown, looking absolutely beautiful. They both had their hair done at a local beauty salon. As for their clothes: Marcy wore a white mini-dress with lacey panels and ankle-tie sandals. On her fingers were white crocheted fingerless gloves. Angela wore a black man's style tuxedo with black lapels and a pinched waist. On her feet were black patent leather pumps.

They stood before Reverend Brown as she raised her hands, her long black robe completely covering her petite frame. "Good afternoon, everyone," she said, silver rings sparkling on each of her fingers, smiling so broadly it became contagious; we all smiled along with her. "And it is a good afternoon and a great pleasure to welcome you all to witness and celebrate such a wonderful occasion. On this wonderful day, we celebrate the love between Angela King and Marcy Chase."

I looked around for Debrena and found her standing near the entrance to the kitchen. She looked extra special in a green embroidered tank top and a rust-colored miniskirt.

"At this time I have two questions for those gathered here today, and hopefully you will answer in the affirmative—you will say, 'we will,' " Reverend Brown went on.

I felt queasiness in the pit of my stomach because I hated all forms of audience participation. I hated when performers asked concertgoers to sing along or wave their hands in the air, or yell, or scream like idiots. I hated that because I felt like I was doing their work for them; I had come to be entertained, not to be a part of the performance.

The two questions Reverend Brown asked were, "Will you support Angela and Marcy as a loving couple and growing individuals?" and "Will you support them in their trials and tribulations, rejoice in their happiness and lovingly remind them of the vows they will make to each other on this great afternoon?"

291

Everyone present said "we will" to both questions.

Then there was the exchange of vows. Under the direction of Reverend Brown, Angela was the first to say: "I, Angela King, take you, Marcy Chase, as my partner for life." Marcy repeated the words, and then they exchanged rainbow rings. After that, two gay men sang two songs a cappella, Anita Baker's "Giving You the Best That I Got" and Luther Vandross' "Here And Now."

The commitment ceremony wrapped up with Angela and Marcy lighting candles, another symbol of their union. After they kissed and had Reverend Brown's final blessing, they led everyone out of the house and onto the sundeck.

I hung back because I didn't want to get smashed by the crowd, and I also wanted to say something to Debrena. I found her deep in the kitchen alone. But what shocked me was that she was standing with her face in her hands, weeping so hard that her shoulders shook. I was so shocked because I had never known Debrena to be so emotional, and I had known her since we were both ten years old.

"D," I tentatively called out, "you all right?"

Instead of answering me, she walked forward and hugged me so tightly that I found it hard to breathe. Even though it hurt I held on to her.

"I didn't want anyone to see me like this," Debrena had to admit, wiping her face with her hands and smudging her makeup in the process.

"I understand," I said, although I didn't completely. I looked around the kitchen and found some napkins. I handed them to Debrena and she used them to dry her face.

"I don't want you to think I'm a softie," Debrena told me around a crooked smile. "It's just that I can't believe how strong their love is. I feel like Angela is ready to do anything to make Marcy happy."

I was stunned again when the tears began to flow. I handed Debrena another wad of napkins.

"This is getting ridiculous," Debrena said, trying to make light of her emotional breakdown. "But Angela is so there for Marcy. When Marcy approached me about using my house for their commitment ceremony I thought it was about Marcy wanting this. But Angela is there, Lorrie. Angela is so there for Marcy."

I thought that Debrena would break down again, but somehow she was able to keep herself together. "Would you be willing to go all out for me like that?"

"Yes," I said without hesitation.

Debrena looked at me like she just couldn't believe me, like there had to be some kind of test before I could truthfully answer her question. It made me think of that night a few months ago when Angela and Marcy were hanging out with Debrena and me in Debrena's house. I still couldn't believe what Marcy did. I could never be sure if it happened because we all had been drinking rum and Coke, or if it was something that Marcy needed to do to prove her love for Angela.

We were playing Truth or Dare, like Madonna had done in her movie *Truth or Dare,* and Angela dared Marcy to walk around the block in her underwear. That dare was so outrageous that it ended the game; there was just no way anyone would do that. It was evening, but there was still a lot of light outside.

Marcy did it.

We all gathered on the front porch as Marcy came out of the house, barefoot and in her thong panties and an almost nothing bra. There were neighbors on their porches and there were cars on the street blowing their horns, but there was no turning back for Marcy.

She disappeared around the block, and it had to be a good ten minutes before we saw half-naked Marcy again.

Her face was tight as she walked toward us, like a soldier on a mission. Angela stepped off the porch and met Marcy in the middle of the block. They embraced, and then kissed. When they stepped up onto the porch it was Angela who was in tears, mumbling something about how she couldn't believe that Marcy would do something like that; put herself out there like that.

"How far would you go for me?" Debrena asked me as we stood in her kitchen.

"Whatever you want me to do I would do it," I told her without hesitation.

I wanted to prove my commitment, my devotion, my love to Debrena. I wanted her to test me like Angela tested Marcy.

Naomi's Blues

By

Terry B.

Coming Spring 2005

One

NAOMI

I couldn't believe what I was hearing. I sat up in bed, my heart pounding hard from the excitement of knowing that my brother had finally come home. My eyes stung like someone had tossed sand in them, but I wasn't asleep. I really couldn't sleep that night.

I kicked off the covers and stepped out of my bed. At the partially opened door of my bedroom I could hear the voices from the kitchen drifting up to my room. As hard as I tried, I couldn't make out what was being said until I stepped into the second-floor hallway. I sat on the top of the steps in my long pink T-shirt, my bare feet resting on carpeted stairs.

I hadn't seen my brother, Amir Moore, in more than two years, and on this fall night, I was listening to his voice drift up from the kitchen. Two years ago, Mother had put him out after they had a violent argument. She felt with his musical talent, he should be doing more with his life, maybe something like teaching at a college or recording his own music instead of going from band to band, traveling all over the place. Mother wanted Amir to settle down and be the man she knew he could be. Of course, Amir had to resist her, make his own way. Anything else would be like being controlled by a woman, and there was no way that my brother would submit to that.

"Ain't nobody gonna control my life but me." He once said with a forty ounce in one hand and a cigarette in the other, standing up there in the attic that Mother had let him take over and convert into his room.

Mother told Amir, "You got to straighten up and fly right," and Amir didn't want to hear any of that. All he wanted to know was what would have happened if he didn't do what she told him.

"I don't even want to talk about that," Mother said, standing up to him like they were enemies in the street about to square off.

"You don't control me," Amir had to say.

"That may be, but I do control this house," was Mother's comeback.

Now I would have stayed silent right there, but not Amir. He had to push it to the next level.

Mother laid out his options after he told her what a man he was. Under her roof he had to obey her rules. In other words, it was her way or the highway.

297

Amir was never one to take an ultimatum lightly. Even though he didn't have as Mother would say, "A pot to piss in or a window to throw it out of," Amir wouldn't let Mother have the last word. He was convinced that he was a man and had every right to live his life the way he pleased. Of course, Mother disagreed, of course, they continued to argue and of course, Amir lost.

Jamming his meager possessions in his green duffel bag, Amir left in the middle of the night two years ago, and now I was hearing his voice in the house, in Mother's kitchen.

"It's good to see you," I heard Mother say. There was pain but also joy in her voice.

"It's good to see you," Amir told Mother, a new humbleness in his voice. "How's the little princess?"

My brother started calling me that when I was five, when I found that his name meant prince and my name, Naomi, meant nothing special at all. He told me that if he was the prince then I was the princess and Mother was the queen and Father was the king. Him saying it like that made me feel so good. I never asked anybody else to call me Princess; that was Amir's name for me. No one, not even Mother or Father when he was alive, called me Princess. I just didn't think it would feel right coming from anyone else.

My brother always called me that. It made me laugh. It made me feel so special. It made me feel like I was worthy of admiration by a handsome Black man—a man like my brother who was tall, dark and fine. He attracted many women, all slim and beautiful. I couldn't count the times in the past two years when young women would come up to me on the street and ask about Amir.

"He's living in New York City," I would tell them with pride.

"New York City," I remember one brown girl saying, savoring the possibilities in her mind like a sweet mint. "You tell Amir I was asking about him. Tell him I know he's knockin' 'em dead in the city, but we could use some of that brown sugar in Jersey."

I would tell his female admirers that I'd pass on the messages, but I never did because I could never remember their names, and I knew that my chances of seeing Amir were slim to none.

"You know Naomi really misses you," Mother told him. "She asks about you all the time. She wanted to write you a letter, tell you that she's in her last year in high school. But you never write, you never call."

"I know. I know. But I've never been a letter writer and I didn't want to call unless I could tell you how good I was doing, how I was making something of myself."

"You don't have to impress your family, Amir. That's something you men don't seem to understand. You want to be a hero every time you walk through that door. It was never about that."

"You were always pushing for me to make something of myself. You had a fit when I dropped out of William Patterson."

"I just wanted you to get your degree in music. You started that program; I just couldn't understand why you didn't finish."

"I told you a million times, Mother. I went into that college thinking that I wanted to teach. When I decided that I didn't want to do that, I didn't see any reason to keep on going."

"So you'd rather hang out on the road, playing your music?"

"It's not hanging out if I'm playing good music and making people happy."

I know that Mother didn't like to hear her son talk like that. It was almost as if he was a boy who never grew up. Mother had nothing against happiness but she felt that working a good job and making a good living were the most important things.

"So, are you back?" Mother wanted to know, filling in the silence that Amir had left.

My brother took time to loudly clear his throat. "There's nothing I can do in New York that I can't do here. I'm writing more music now; I'd like to go into the studio."

"You're going to drop New York, just like that?"

"Ain't nothing but bad things on the road. I get in too much trouble out there. Here I can do the studio thing while I get my music together. I want to record some of my tunes."

"Does this mean you're ready to settle down? Are you ready to give me some grandchildren?"

299

Amir laughed loudly at that. "You know me better than that. But I did meet a nice girl. Sharon Simmons. You would've liked her."

"What happened with that?"

"Same thing that happens with all my ladies, Mother. Sharon Simmons wanted to settle down. What do I know about commitment? It sounds like I'm in a coffin and someone is nailing the lid down."

"It's not always like that. It wasn't like that with your father and me."

"I remember that, but I'm not like my father."

"He did the music and he took care of his family very well."

"A high school music teacher. I just can't see myself like that."

"You could do it for a little while."

"Life is too short, Mother."

"You have time, Amir. You're still a young man."

Amir laughed, but it wasn't a happy sound. It was one that said, I tried to duck but you caught me, and now I have to pay the price. "Mother, you know I hit twenty-eight last month."

"I know. I even bought you a card. I just didn't know where to send it. Last letter I sent came back 'return to sender.' "

"I've been all over New York City, Brooklyn mostly. Nothing to write home about."

"We still wanted to hear from you. If you got killed there, shot down in the streets, I wouldn't know where to pick up the body."

"I wasn't living a good life, Mother. I wasn't doing anything to make you proud."

"I still need to know, Amir. I'm your mother. I have no options when it comes to my children. You're my concern and you're a part of me. There's emptiness in my soul when I don't know where my children are, and you've been gone for two years."

"I know. I know. Two years that went like one long night, and not a good night, Mother. Not a good night at all."

"What are you going to do now?"

Amir told her that he would stay and help out, and I couldn't have been happier. I tiptoed back into my room so I could put on some clothes. I knew after Amir finished talking to Mother he would come upstairs, on his way to his attic room. I knew he wouldn't be expecting to see me, probably thinking I would be sound asleep at this late hour. I planned to surprise him once he got settled in his room. I pulled on a pair of jeans up under my T-shirt and slipped into some sneakers. I wanted to welcome him home and I couldn't wait until the morning; I was too excited for that.

I didn't want to crowd him, be a pest of a little sister, so I waited in the dark, in my bedroom. Mother came up first; I knew it was her because I peeked through my partially opened bedroom door. I watched her as she walked down the hall to her bedroom. Because it was so late I knew she would fall asleep once she climbed into her bed. She had on her nightclothes and her hair tied in her scarf, and I knew she would sleep like the dead. That was good because Amir and I could sit up half the night talking, catching up and being close like we used to be.

I waited for him to come upstairs. My thought was to let him walk past my bedroom like Mother did and then catch him going up into the attic. But after waiting for what seemed like a good twenty minutes, I changed my plan. I figured I'd just wait for him at the top of the stairs. I slipped out of my room and made my way to the staircase. The light was still on in the kitchen, but it was so quiet down there, like no one was in there.

With my heart pounding hard in my chest, I made my way downstairs. Amir wasn't down there, but the front door was slightly cracked, as if he was so much in a hurry to leave that he couldn't bother to close it properly. I didn't have to tell him that Mother hated that kind of carelessness. I know why he did it like that: He wanted to be able to slip back in after his little walk around the block, something he did on those nights when he couldn't sleep.

I often wondered if Mother ever had any trouble sleeping, if she never told me anything about it.

When I slipped out of the house I left the door unlocked because I didn't want to go back upstairs to get my house key. I wanted to catch up to my brother; I wanted to welcome him home. Before I realized it I found myself running. I wanted to get around the block as soon as I could. Just knowing I would find Amir walking the streets of East Orange, New Jersey, made me excited. Darkness was so thick around me I felt like I was in a narrow tunnel, then I saw him, his back toward me, but I knew his walk.

I was just about to call out to him when the car came around the corner, motor loud, gansta rap music blasting and tires screeching. Then shots rang out and cracked the dark night with pinpoints of flashing lights. The shots got even louder, each bullet hitting my brother and making him dance—a death dance that made his body wave like a sheet in the wind. The impact of the bullets spun him around, and I could see all the pain on his face. Thick dark blood dripped from his bug eyes and pencil-thin lips as the bullets hit his chest and blew up his torso.

I covered my mouth so that my screams wouldn't escape into the night.

It was all a dream. In my bed I could hardly breathe but I didn't want to scream and wake Mother. My shoulders rocked with unshed tears, and perspiration covered my whole body, making my sleep shirt feel like a wool overcoat on my body. I kicked the covers off and pulled my tee off at the same time. Then I lay back in my bed, my naked body clammy and sticky, disgusting. I needed a shower in the worse way, but I couldn't move. The stink from my body rose up to my nose and made me nauseous. It was the sweat of fear and it stank so badly because it came from so deep inside me. What I feared most, what I tried so hard to suppress was the fear of what would happen to Amir in the streets—whether it was the streets of New York City or the streets of New Jersey made no difference. The way I saw it in every dream I had about Amir was him not making it, of him dying in the streets because of the life he lead, that musician's life, always being on the road.

Knowing there was no way I was going back to sleep, I used my tee like a towel to dry my body, then threw it on the floor. My little white clock on my nightstand read 3:20 A.M. *Mother, do you know where your son is?* I thought.

Two

AMIR

I awoke from a bad dream and came down hard from my cocaine high. There was the banging on the dressing room door. My plan had been to chill in the dressing room of the nightclub until it was time to hit the stage. I had copped some blow earlier that Friday evening and found myself with no privacy to do my thing. Almost at the end of a fifteen-city tour with The Trevor Thompson Jazz Band, I figured I deserved a reward for staying straight for so long. I had done tons of weed and gallons of alcohol with fans, groupies and band members, but I hadn't powdered my nose in a long while. Especially not after that time in Chi-Town when I caught a nosebleed that just wouldn't stop. There was so much blood that I thought I had busted a vessel and needed emergency surgery. By tilting my head and putting an ice pack to the back of my neck I managed to stop the flow. I have to admit that little incident shook me, making me think it was time for me to stay away from blow for a little while. After Chi-Town it was five other cities and now we were in the Big Apple, not far from my hometown in New Jerusalem (New Jersey)— I'm talking about Ill-Town, which some squares continue to call East Orange.

Can't a brother celebrate a little bit? I asked myself as I tried to chill in the pitch-black darkness of the dressing room. I didn't know how long I had been out but there was no doubt that my good time had come to an end. I tossed and turned on the beat-up black leather couch as the banging on the dressing room door continued. At that point, I wasn't ignoring the inconsiderate intruder. I was just trying to pull myself together so I could get off the couch and walk over to the locked door. The door pounder began to call my name— "Amir! Amir!"—like I didn't know who I was.

I cursed under my breath because when I turned to get off the couch, I fell onto the stone-cold floor of the basement dressing room, hard. The only thing that cushioned my fall was the thick material of the hundred percent wool suit I wore.

"Amir! Amir!"

The door pounder almost made me hate my own name. Hate it because in that voice was pity and impatience. The voice was saying, "Amir Moore, get your raggedy butt up and open this door so I can see how much you abused yourself this time."

Of course I didn't want to hear anything like that—no freakin' way did I want to hear anything like that. What I wanted to hear was "Amir, my man, you can chill all you want. I was just checking on you, making sure that everything was okay. Man, you know this band of Trevor's wouldn't be anything without you on the keyboards. Man, you got that touch, baby. That magic touch. You a keyboard genius, Amir. You the man, my brother."

"Amir, it's Rabbit."

I knew it was Christopher Cooley, whom we all called Rabbit because of his two prominent front teeth. He was a funky drummer who got me the gig with The Trevor Thompson Jazz Band. I owed Rabbit big time and in many subtle and no-so-subtle ways, he wouldn't let me forget that. I knew that the least I could do was answer his knock, but I had hurt my shoulder when I fell and my long legs just didn't want to act right. Somehow, I managed to drag myself to the door. Using the knob as a crutch, I pulled myself up and hit the light switch nearby. I groaned in serious pain as the sudden bright light entered my eyes and stabbed my brain. Suddenly, my stomach ached and I felt like I had to vomit, which was strange because I couldn't remember the last time I ate anything.

"Hold on, Rabbit, hold on," I said as I held on to the door knob with both hands and pressed my hot face against the coolness of the plywood.

"I got to get in there," Rabbit said with an urgency that made me feel like a criminal for not letting him in on his first knock. He sounded like a man on a mission to rescue me from the enemy that was myself.

When I finally opened the door, Rabbit stared into my eyes so intently that I had to turn away from him. I didn't want him staring, looking deeply into my soul.

"What's going on, Amir?" Rabbit demanded, like he was the daddy and I was his child.

I grunted and shook my head, letting him know there was no way that I was playing that game. I was nobody's child, nobody's punk. "You better be glad I let you in," I told him, my voice a harsh whisper as I stood on shaky legs. I needed to sit down but I didn't want to put myself lower than Rabbit. My six-two was the only advantage I had on his five-eleven frame on that September night in the basement of that New York City nightclub. If I sat he would tower over me and make me feel small, like a child, a boy, a punk. And I just couldn't have that. I felt that I had to fake Rabbit out, to make him think I was in total control.

305

"I know it's not time to go on," I said, even though I had no idea what time it was. I wore no watch and the moon-faced clock in the dressing room was only there for decoration.

Rabbit stood there and looked me up and down from my raggedy mini-Afro to my crooked tie, rumpled suit and scuffed shoes. I knew I wasn't ready for the cover of *GQ*, but I had at least shaved that day. "You got some time," Rabbit said, sounding disappointed that he couldn't hit me with that criticism. I made all my gigs and performed well onstage so I felt what I did off the bandstand was my business.

"You get a chance to look at the new arrangement?" Rabbit asked, like he was just making conversation or waiting for me to become completely sober. I was almost there because all that pounding on the door had brought me down hard.

"I don't like it but I got it," I said as I tapped my forehead with my index finger.

"You were always a quick study," Rabbit said like this was some credit he didn't want to give me. Learning to read music was something I was forced to do at home. If I was to pursue music, my father insisted I take lessons. He also insisted that I study the trumpet, his instrument of choice, but that instrument never really appealed to me. This controversy was the source of one of our many ongoing arguments. The only way I could get him to leave me alone was if I showed him that I was serious about playing the keys. I was more than serious; by the age of ten I was composing my own instrumentals and arranging a little something for the Baptist church my mother begged us all to attend.

"They should let me do some arranging," I told Rabbit, and he looked at me like I was crazy.

"Wait awhile," Rabbit said. "I mean, like how long have you been with this band?"

I smirked, and then said, "Three months and ten cities."

"Yeah, well, I'd say give it some time."

I looked at Rabbit and he backed up a little. There was no way he could miss my angry eyes. "Rabbit, man, don't play with me. I know Trevor Thompson is the only one who does any arranging for this group."

"Well, it is The Trevor Thompson Jazz Band."

"And that's another thing," I had to say although I knew Rabbit would see me biting the hand that fed me. "A jazz band? This is not a jazz band. What we play is top forty instrumentals. Real jazz is McCoy Tyner, Oscar Peterson, Gail Allen and sometimes Herbie Hancock."

"Trevor plays the music that the people in these clubs like to listen to."

"Great, but it's not jazz, Rabbit. No way is this stuff jazz."

"You're making good money playing with Trevor," Rabbit said, looking like I had hurt his feelings.

"Rabbit, you know I can't do that groupie thing," I said firmly. "I'm a man just like Trevor. I think I have some talent; he thinks he has some talent. You respect me; I'll respect you, but don't go thinking you the shit because the band is named after you. I've had my own groups."

"In high school, Amir."

"I know it was in high school, but what I'm saying is that I can be a leader."

"Yeah, well, sometimes to be a good leader, you have to be a good follower."

"Man, you trippin'. I can't follow behind some bullshit."

"Is that what you're playing with Trevor?"

"Look, I know he's your boy and everything but this arrangement is straight up garbage. Where's the complexity? Where's the challenge?"

"Be fair, Amir. You've seen the crowds Trevor has attracted on this tour."

307

"Most of the time when he's playing, the crowd is talking. Some guy is out there trying to get his mack on or a group of shorties talking about who's cute and who's not on the bandstand. All I want to do is play some good music, some real jazz, Rabbit."

"I thought you were happy to get this gig."

"I was in the beginning, but then this bullshit, everybody bowing down to Trevor like he the new Miles Davis or the new John Coltrane."

"Miles wasn't afraid to do some commercial stuff."

"Yeah, but that was after he established himself as a jazz giant. The way Trevor is going he ain't even gonna be a jazz midget." I stopped because I had to laugh at that; I could be really funny when I wanted to be.

"Well, Amir, I'm sorry you're not happy with the band."

"It's not about being happy, Rabbit. I got to pay some dues like everybody else. I know that. It's just that sometime—"

Before I could finish my thought someone knocked on the door.

"Yeah," Rabbit yelled out in acknowledgment, "we're in here, me and Amir."

"Showtime!" the man from behind the door called out.

"Amir, we got to get out of here," Rabbit said as he walked to the door. When he opened the door he realized that I was still standing in the middle of the room. "Amir, we got to go, man."

I waved my hand at him. "Go on, Rabbit. I'll catch you on the bandstand."

Rabbit looked at me like he was afraid I was going to jump ship that night, leaving him to tell Trevor Thompson that he was the last person to see me before I just up and walked out of the club. I had already made up my mind to stay with Trevor's group until the end of the tour. Not because I liked what I was playing but because the music community was too small and I couldn't afford to get a reputation for being unreliable.

I turned away from Rabbit and looked into the mirror in the dressing room. When Rabbit saw me smoothing down my lapels, he left me alone. I tried to put a smile on my face as I straightened my tie. I couldn't do that so I settled for what I considered a sexy smirk. It was just too hard for me to fake it. I shook my head at the unfairness of my life and said, "Showtime."